MOLLY MOON

and the
Morphing Mystery

Georgia Byng

MACMILLAN CHILDREN'S BOOKS

As always, a forever grateful thank-you to my agent Caradoc King,
who believed in me and Molly so early on.
And to Sarah Dudman, the best editor in the world!

First published 2010 by Macmillan Children's Books
a division of Macmillan Publishers Limited
20 New Wharf Road, London N1 9RR
Basingstoke and Oxford
Associated companies throughout the world
www.panmacmillan.com

ISBN 978-0-230-74801-9

1 3 5 7 9 8 6 4 2

A CIP catalogue record for this book is available from
the British Library.

Typeset by Ellipsis Books Limited, Glasgow
Printed and bound in the UK by CPI Mackays, Chatham ME5 8TD

and the
Morphing Mystery

Georgia Byng made her debut as a talented new children's author with *Molly Moon's Incredible Book of Hypnotism*. This exciting and funny adventure starring Molly Moon, an orphan who discovers a hidden talent for hypnotism, was a runaway success. It was published in thirty-six languages and forty countries, and won the Salford, the Stockton and the Sheffield Children's Book Awards. Its sequels, *Molly Moon Stops the World*, *Molly Moon's Hypnotic Time-Travel Adventure* and *Molly Moon, Micky Minus and the Mind Machine*, have firmly established Molly as a favourite with readers all around the globe.

Georgia Byng grew up in a large, noisy family in a house in Hampshire. She now lives in London with the artist Marc Quinn and her three children. Georgia loves to travel, whether it's flying off to India to research ideas for a new book or whizzing around London in her little electric car.

For Christopher, with lots of love

Chapter One

It was a winter afternoon. Briersville Park was sodden and glistening. Rain pelted down, hitting the vegetable garden path with a vengeance, smacking its green algae surface so that each drop split into a hundred smaller drops that bounced up again. Two frogs hid under the outstretched leg of a stone cupid in the centre of a pond and the orange fish there dived to its murky bottom for shelter.

Water dripped down AH2's dark face. His black, snug, weatherproof trousers and jacket were covered in mud, since he'd just spent fifteen minutes crawling through three llama fields towards this grand house. Now he pulled his balaclava back behind his ears so that he could better hear. Children's voices, whoops and shouts, and the sound of barking were coming from the other side of a high wall.

There was a heavy door set in the brickwork, but he didn't dare use that. Instead, taking a furtive look about to check he wasn't watched, he put his hands on the leafless branches of an old apple tree that was fastened to the wall. With the ease of a trained soldier, he climbed up to its crest.

There she was. He was certain. The alien girl who went by the name Molly Moon was playing at the edge of a swimming pool with two boys who AH2 guessed were the same age as the Moon girl – about eleven years old. One was the black boy AH2 recognized from an advert that he and Molly Moon had starred in. Beside him was another boy who looked like he was the alien girl's twin. He had similar light brown curly hair and the same potato-shaped nose and identical strong but closely set green eyes. Was this boy an alien too?

AH2 twitched. Then he got a shock.

All of a sudden a large, grey object that he had presumed was a sunken, blow-up dinghy emerged from the pool. It was an elephant and it squirted a few gallons of water at the children, drenching them further and making the small black pug that was with them bark. The children laughed and shouted at the elephant before it tipped its body back towards the deep end for another swim.

AH2 shook his head in nonplussed amazement, then returned to his task. Quickly, he unzipped his front jacket pocket and pulled out a small loaded rifle, resting it on the top of the wall. He peered through its sights. Molly Moon's head and shoulders came into view. Her wet hair fell to one side, exposing a fairly wide expanse of her neck. AH2 gritted his teeth. If only Molly Moon would stop jumping up and down and if only that look-alike boy would get out of the way. AH2 waited patiently until Molly Moon's neck was aligned in the red target circle of his rifle's sights again. He waited for the elephant. His aim was to use the animal as a distraction and to shoot at the same moment as the elephant hosed the children down.

The elephant rose up from the water and fired. At the same time, AH2 pulled the trigger. His dart hit first; the water hit Molly Moon a split second later. Everyone screeched, and in the commotion of the moment Molly Moon's yelp was lost. She reached up and cupped her neck.

'Ow, Amrit!' she complained. 'That water had a stone in it!'

'Bingo!' AH2 murmured. He dropped silently from the garden wall and ran towards the llama fields. Running swiftly and darting behind the animal-shaped bushes there wherever possible, he made his way to the far woods beyond to where his black car was parked. Slipping into the front seat he took his bala-clava and his jacket off and reached for the brown package on the passenger seat.

Drying his hands, he unpacked the red radio-like box inside it and pulled out its aerial. Switching the device on, he pointed it in the direction of Briersville Park, to its gardens and its swimming pool. The machine bleeped reassuringly.

'Got you, alien Moon girl,' AH2 said with a satisfied smack of his lips. He picked up his phone and tapped in a message to his superior, AH1.

'MISSION ACCOMPLISHED.'

Chapter Two

Molly and Micky Moon were sitting in an emerald-green sports car, speeding up the motorway under a heavy grey sky. Molly felt like some sort of pet animal, as she was stuffed in the cramped space behind the two front seats. Her twin brother, Micky, was in the passenger seat, and their new tutor, Miss Hunroe, sat at the wheel.

Miss Hunroe was very glamorous-looking and not at all like Molly thought a tutor should be. Her hair was peroxide blonde and kinked so that it almost formed stairs down the side of her head. Her hazel eyes, which Molly could see in the rear-view mirror, watching any approaching cars that might be trying to overtake her, were large and long-lashed. And her pale skin had a clean translucent beauty. Her cheeks were tinged a pretty, wholesome pink. Her clothes were very un-teacherly too.

She wore a smart cream suit with a silk shirt underneath and on one of her red-nailed fingers she wore a heavy gold ring with an emerald embedded in it.

She steered the car with her left hand. Her right hand meanwhile held a gold coin. As she drove, she flipped it along her fingers so that it turned like a rolling wheel in between her knuckles. Every time another car obstructed the fast lane, she would flip the gold coin, saying, 'Heads!' or, 'Tails!' She'd catch the coin on the back of her right hand. If she won the toss, she'd flash her lights and drive really close to the car in front until the vehicle moved over and let her pass. Then she'd speed off – well over a hundred miles an hour, until the offending car was a long way behind.

Molly gripped the back of Micky's chair. Miss Hunroe's driving, along with her rose-scented perfume, was making Molly feel sick. She hoped she wouldn't be. That would really spoil the day, she thought, if she was sick all over the leather seats of Miss Hunroe's car.

'Interesting way of driving,' Micky commented drily, looking up from his crossword puzzle book as yet again Miss Hunroe flipped her coin and started to flash at the van in front.

'It keeps me amused,' Miss Hunroe replied. 'I like to see the law of odds in action. There's a fifty-fifty chance that I should or shouldn't overtake, yet somehow this coin always lands on what I've guessed it will land on. So I always overtake! It's as if the coin wants to get back to London as quickly as possible!'

And so on they drove, as if in some sort of a race, upsetting the other traffic on the road, causing other drivers to raise fists and blast their horns. Molly stared at the straight road ahead, as she knew that an eye on the horizon would help her carsick feeling. She watched a cat-shaped cloud turn into the shape of a dragon and kept watching the clouds until her stomach felt better. Every so often Micky began a conversation with Miss Hunroe. These went something like, 'Butanoic acid. Miss Hunroe, isn't that the name of the colourless liquid that causes that nasty rancid smell in butter?' or 'That word CACHE . . . Miss Hunroe, do you spell it like that? Does it mean "a secret place where a store of things is kept hidden"?' Or, when Micky had moved on to his special book of riddles, he started to test Miss Hunroe:

'The beginning of Eternity,
The end of time and space,
The beginning of every end,
And the end of every place. What am I?

Shall I tell you, Miss Hunroe? . . . The answer's E. The letter E. Clever, eh?'

'Sorry, dear, I can't talk. I'm driving,' was usually Miss Hunroe's answer to whatever question or riddle Micky threw at her and so he went on with his puzzles alone, or he looked out of the window or craned his neck to talk to Molly or consulted his compass to see in which direction they were heading.

*

AH2 drove behind in his sleek black car, keeping his distance. His locater box was switched on so that, however crazily the emerald-green sports car drove, he could always tell where the alien girl, Molly Moon, was. He sucked on cool mints and listened to space-age ambient music that twanged and tocked, reminding him, he thought, of the size of the universe. He wondered how far away Molly Moon's planet was. And he thrilled to think that soon he would be about to meet a real, living extra terrestrial.

Finally the countryside gave way to concrete and brick and soon he was driving over a flyover road, past a glass and steel office block on to the main drag into London.

'Ah the smoke!' Miss Hunroe gasped. 'Culture and art! Heaven! Nearly in! Kensington and Chelsea soon! And the weather doesn't seem to be bad at all!'

Both sides of the road now became punctuated by black taxis with their famous old-fashioned curvy design. Big, red, double-decker buses chugged past. Some were open-ended at the back so that people could jump on and off at traffic lights. And quicker than Molly had expected, they came to their destination.

As the car drove alongside the tall iron railings of a giant Victorian building with four gothic towers, Miss Huroe announced, 'So here we are! The Natural History Museum! This is where lessons start.' She swerved the car into a DIPLOMATS ONLY parking space.

'What's a diplomat?' Molly asked.

'It's a special person,' said Micky, 'who works for the government of a country. Their job is to go and live in *another* country where they sort out stuff for the people of their *own* country in that *other* country, if you see what I mean.' Then he looked at Miss Hunroe as though through a magnifying glass. 'You're not a diplomat, are you, Miss Hunroe?'

'Oh no!' Miss Hunroe answered, adjusting her wavy, blonde hair and turning the car's rear-view mirror to put on her red lipstick.

'Um, then won't you get a ticket?' Molly asked.

'Definitely not. I've made arrangements,' declared their new tutor mischievously, slotting a pass of some sort into a plastic holder on the windscreen.

They all got out. Molly's legs felt very stiff when she stood up straight. She shook them out.

The previous day Molly had been sitting in one of the attic rooms of Briersville Park, on a wide window ledge with her legs pulled up to her chin. Rocky, the boy she'd grown up with in the Briersville orphanage, Hardwick House, had been leaning against the wall whilst Micky sat in a red armchair, with Petula, their black pet pug at his feet. He'd been scouring the papers for interesting news and reading bits out from a book of riddles to Molly and Rocky. A fire crackled in the hearth. They were all in dry clothes now that they were back inside from spending all afternoon with Amrit, their pet elephant, who loved to play in the pool.

Molly remembered how ill Rocky had looked. How he had flopped down in the furry chair and pulled a cushion on top of himself. His brown skin appeared greyer. He looked like he was catching the flu, the same flu that Ojas, their Indian friend, had caught. It was then that the phone had gone. Molly had picked it up. It was Lucy Logan.

'Hello, Molly, it's me.'

'Oh, hi, Lucy.' Molly couldn't quite bring herself to call Lucy Logan 'Mum' even though she was her mum. She was of course Micky's mum too, and Rocky and Ojas's adopted mum, but all of them called her Lucy. She had been away with Ojas and Primo for a night in Yorkshire.

'How are things?'

'Fine, well, sort of. Rocky's ill. Is Ojas better?'

'Not really, and now your dad, erm, Primo's, feeling bad too. We'll be back tonight, but, annoyingly, after dinner. The weather is shocking. It's as if there's been a freak storm. We're in a terrible traffic jam. Apparently a huge lorry full of milk skidded and turned over. It's completely blocked the motorway.'

'Well, you know what they say?' Molly replied. 'Don't cry over spilt milk!'

Lucy laughed down the phone. 'Well, we won't, but it is a bit boring. We could practically walk back quicker. But listen, don't forget, the new tutor is coming for supper tonight. Be polite. Show her around. And we got the elephant chair . . .'

In the background, Molly could hear Ojas's voice. 'The howdah,' he corrected Lucy.

'Yes, the howdah. We think it will fit Amrit perfectly.'

When Molly put the phone down, Micky glanced up from the papers. 'Says here there's a flu epidemic happening.' He wrinkled his nose crossly. 'Wish I'd remembered to pack some medicine before I left the twenty-sixth century.'

'Wish you had,' Rocky moaned. 'I bet there was brilliant medicine there.'

'Sure was,' Micky agreed. 'They have a cure for practically everything in five hundred years. Suppose we could always nip forward and get some pills. Fancy a quick trip, Molly?'

This may seem a strange way for someone to talk, as if they came from the future, but in Micky's case, it wasn't. For Micky did, in fact, come from the future.

'I'd love to take you, but Primo and Lucy say I'm not allowed,' Molly replied. 'I told you, they've confiscated my time-travel crystals and my time-stopping crystals. Can you believe it?'

This also may seem like an odd thing to say. But in Molly's case it was entirely apt. For Molly was a time traveller and a time stopper. She was also a world-class hypnotist. The odd thing about Molly, however, was that even though she had all these amazing skills she had never found that she had any talent for schoolwork. So that afternoon she'd stared out of the window, dreading the new tutor who was coming.

'I'm a bit worried about this teacher,' she confided. 'Bet she hates me. All teachers hate me.' She sighed. 'Always. Mind you,' she added more quietly, wiping the misted-up windowpane with the sleeve of her sweater, 'I usually hate them.'

'Oh, she'll be fine,' said Rocky, raising himself from his slump. 'She won't be anything like the teachers we used to have, Molly. Lucy and Primo *chose* her. Even Forest says she sounds cool.' Forest was the ageing hippy that Molly and Rocky had met in Los Angeles in America, who also now lived in the big house that was Briersville Park.

'Talking of teachers,' said Micky, folding his newspaper into a huge paper dart, 'will you teach me how to hypnotize again, Molly? I'm sure I'll pick it up quickly, since I used to be so good at it.'

Molly nodded. 'Of course. Whenever you want.'

A week or so before, Molly and Micky had been a few hundred years in the future, where Micky had been put on a mind machine. It had sucked all his knowledge of how to hypnotize out of his head.

'Or,' Molly suggested, 'there's the book in the library downstairs. You could use that. That's how I learned to start with. It's called *Hypnotism: An Ancient Art Explained*. Are you still getting nightmares about the mind machine?'

'Not really.' Micky threw the newspaper dart into the fire, where it burst into flames.

'My head really hurts,' said Rocky. He pulled a blanket off the sofa and lay down on the carpet in front of the fire beside Petula. Petula dropped the stone that she had been sucking and snuggled up to him.

Molly shut her eyes. *Hypnotism: An Ancient Art Explained.* The title of the old book swam around her head. That book had changed her life. And ever since she'd found it she'd been travelling. Travelling all over the world and through time.

'You gotta calm down, Molly,' Forest had said. 'Gotta like get into the groove of yer *own* time.'

That was when Lucy and Primo had hidden her special chain with the time travel crystals on it.

'Just so you won't be tempted,' Lucy had said. 'You really should stay in this time for a bit, Molly,' she had recommended. 'And try not to use the hypnotism. Live like an ordinary girl. It'll be good for you.' She had given Molly a new chain with four animals on it – a black pug, a silver elephant and the two blackbirds. 'You can wear your pets instead. They're sweet, aren't they?'

Molly had felt happy to start with, like a bird glad to be back home safe in its nest. But then something started to happen. Molly found herself longing for excitement and wanting to spread her wings again. You see, for most of her life she'd been cooped up in an orphanage. She loved the freedom of adventure. And so, quite soon, life started to feel a bit boring. She wanted to see more of the world. She wanted more

13

unpredictability. But her parents and Forest had insisted that a normal time was needed. This was why a teacher had been hired.

Primo, Lucy and Forest said that Molly, Micky, Rocky and Ojas couldn't carry on as though life was one big holiday. They needed to have routine working and playing. Lucy had promised that the tutor who was coming was *very* nice, but Molly was dreading lessons. As far as she knew, lessons were when you watched the clock, or got picked on by a teacher or where you got punished for not knowing the right answer. Micky and Rocky were both natural students, good at learning, and easily able to work. Ojas was keen as mustard. He'd never been to school, ever. 'You don't know how lucky you are, Molly,' he had told her. 'Where I come from some children can't even read. Don't you want to get more and more clever? Don't you want to know things?'

Molly did, but she didn't want a teacher having anything to do with it. All the teachers she'd ever known had been small-minded and mean. 'I'd rather teach myself and learn directly from the world,' she'd said.

Molly was a straight talker, but there was one thing that she had kept secret from everyone at Briersville Park. She sat on the secret like a chicken on an uncomfortable egg.

On her trip to the future, Molly had discovered that she'd developed a new skill. But it wasn't a skill that she could ever tell her friends and family about. For Molly's newest skill was *mind reading*.

Imagine if your friend could read your mind! You might start to avoid seeing them, for you might worry that they'd see something in your mind that you didn't want them to see. Even though Molly had decided not to use her new-found powers on her family and friends, she knew that, if they knew what she could do, they might start to mistrust her. They might assume that she was probing into their heads to see their thoughts. And so Molly had decided to keep sitting on her spiky egg of a secret.

Of course this didn't stop Molly looking into other people's minds. Maybe Molly would have a little look into the tutor's head when she arrived and see what she was *really* like. To the left of the attic room window Molly saw white lights twinkling far away at the gate lodge. A car began making its way along the dark drive.

With Lucy and Primo stuck in a traffic jam, Molly, Micky and Rocky found themselves being hosts, looking after their guest, their new tutor, Miss Hunroe.

It all began a little strangely for Miss Hunroe. For Todson, the new butler (who preferred to be called plain 'Todson'), had forgotton to put Cornelius Logan away in his stall for the night. Cornelius was Molly's uncle. He too had hypnotic powers, but he had used his hypnotism for bad ends. Molly had been forced to hypnotize him into thinking he was a lamb, and then 'lock' that hypnotism in, so that he wouldn't revert to his bad ways.

Cornelius was harmless as a lamb and spent the afternoons with the llamas in the front field, eating grass and running about. Todson looked after him, bringing him his meals, and in the evenings putting him to bed. But tonight Cornelius hadn't been put away. Bristling with excitement, Cornelius came trotting into the sitting room where Rocky, Molly and Micky were giving Miss Hunroe a cup of tea.

Before anyone could do anything about it, Cornelius was kicking his legs. He knocked over a table, upset a vase of flowers and leaped excitedly on to a sofa. Then he ran round and round the chair where Miss Hunroe was sitting, finally lying down at her feet like a pet.

'Er, sorry about him,' Molly said. 'He's my, um, uncle. He's not quite right in the head. He was in a special home,' she lied, 'but we brought him back to live here. Don't worry, he won't hurt you.'

'He seems to like you a lot,' said Rocky, wiping his nose.

'Oh, don't worry,' Miss Hunroe replied. 'He's sweet!'

And so Cornelius sat at Miss Hunroe's feet until she went upstairs to change for dinner.

The round-tabled dining room was being used that night. Todson had brought out all the Georgian silver and polished it. Every place had two knives, three forks and two spoons, with a bird-shaped name-card-holder perched next to each person's water glass. Two tall eight-armed candelabra stood proudly between the shiny peppermills and the salt and mustard pots. The candles were lit and a stack of pinewood burned in the grand fireplace so that the room danced with orange light, and the faces in the old gilt-framed portraits on the walls flickered and moved as if coming to life.

'Well, isn't this lovely!' exclaimed Miss Hunroe as Todson helped her into her chair. 'And something smells delicious.'

'That's a relief,' said Todson, grunting. 'New cook.'

Molly looked around the table. Everyone had made an effort tonight. Forest had got home and was sitting the other side of Miss Hunroe in a bright, lime-coloured jumper and a smart green woollen sarong with pine-apples on it. His long dreadlocked grey hair was tied in a plait. And he had a jungly bandanna tied round his forehead. Micky sat beside Molly in a proper tailored turquoise blue shirt. Rocky sat opposite, shivering in a thick navy coat. Molly was wearing a clean T-shirt. Her hair was fairly detangled as she'd spent twenty minutes attacking it with a comb. Todson stood behind each in his smart butler's uniform, holding the soup tureen for everyone to ladle themselves helpings of carrot soup.

'You smell of flowers or somethin',' said Forest, obviously enamoured by the beautiful new tutor. 'Is it like, um, narcissus?'

'No, it's rose,' Miss Hunroe corrected him, smiling a pearl-toothed smile. 'But good try.'

'I'm really sorry,' said Rocky, suddenly pushing his chair back, almost upsetting the soup tureen all over Todson. 'Oh, I'm sorry, Todson. I've got to go to bed, you see. I feel terrible.'

'I've lost my glasses,' said Todson, 'but I can still detect, Master Scarlet, that you look distinctly worse for wear. I'll bring you some hot water bottles and a mug of hot lemon and honey.'

'Thanks, Todson.' Quietly Rocky plodded out of the room.

'It's this terrible flu,' said Miss Hunroe. 'People are falling like flies from it.'

Outside, the wind battered the windowpane. Todson went round the table with a basket of bread. When he came to Forest, he tripped on the edge of the rug. Four pieces of white bread flew past Forest's shoulder into his soup.

'Erm, so sorry, sir, lost my glasses,' muttered Todson. 'I'll get some more bread.'

But Forest was so enchanted by Miss Hunroe that he didn't notice. 'Yes, the flu, man, it's bad,' he agreed. 'It's this weather. All this damp air. Not nice 'n' warm like LA. If only we could control the weather, then we'd have far less of this kinda thing. I mean peace to all creatures, man, but it would be kinda cool to stamp out the flu bug population.'

A small smile played on Miss Hunroe's rose-shaped

red lips, and then they twitched as though she was about to laugh but was controlling herself. She seemed to have a good sense of humour.

Molly couldn't resist. She knew it was nosy and she shouldn't probe, but she wanted to take a little look and see what their new teacher was thinking. No one would know she was doing it. No one would be able to point a finger at Molly and complain. Molly felt like a thief about to steal something, for she knew Miss Hunroe's thoughts were her own. Yet Molly was determined to learn a little more about her new tutor. With butterflies in her stomach from the excitement of it, Molly focused her mind. She silently thought the question to Miss Hunroe, *What are you thinking?*

Immediately one of the hazy bubbles that always appeared when Molly wanted to know someone's thoughts – popped up over Miss Hunroe's head. In it were pictures – various images that merged as Miss Hunroe's mind wandered and flitted about. First Forest's soup bowl, full of bread, shimmered into view.

'Yes, it is dreadful,' Miss Hunroe agreed. 'The flu has no mercy. It forces people to bed for days and days. No mercy.' Then she laughed. 'And I'd love to be able to control the weather too. What a charming idea!' Above her head the bubble filled with a moving picture of Miss Hunroe standing on a hilltop with tall, teardrop-shaped stones all about her. She had a baton in her hand and above her the sky flashed with lightning as she conducted the weather. 'It would be fun, don't you think, Molly?'

'Er, y-yes,' Molly stammered, feeling as if she'd been caught looking through a keyhole. She let the bubble above Miss Hunroe's head pop. 'Yes, um, snow and blizzards one moment, hot sun the next.' Molly nodded with a smile. 'And it would be nice to make it rain in countries where they have droughts.'

Miss Hunroe leaned towards the table and sipped her soup elegantly from her spoon.

Opposite her Forest slurped. 'Man, this soup is very, er, bready! Must be a new recipe.'

And so the meal went on, a little stilted as everyone was on best behaviour with the stranger in the house, but Miss Hunroe was good natured, and, as the minutes ticked by, the ice melted.

'So what are your plans for our education?' Micky asked as Miss Hunroe passed the peas to Forest. 'I'm very good at physics,' he added, matter-of-factly. 'Well, I'm good at *all* sciences really. My knowledge is *more* than up to date.' Micky paused as he saw Forest give him a raised eyebrow. Micky had been told that he was forbidden to let Miss Hunroe know that he was from the future. 'But,' Micky went on, 'my knowledge about the twentieth century and its history is full of holes. I would like to know more about this time.'

'Gosh! You sound like an alien who has just arrived from another planet!' Miss Hunroe observed.

'I've always been completely useless at school stuff,' Molly interjected, feeling that she ought to get things straight from the start.

Miss Hunroe frowned.

Molly crossed her arms and looked down at her plate of chicken, potatoes and peas. 'Sorry. But that's the way I am. I thought you should know.' She looked up at Miss Hunroe, who was smiling at her. And her smile was so nice that Molly found herself promising, 'I will try, though.'

Miss Hunroe put her knife and fork down. 'Well, I do have a grand plan,' she began. 'And it begins with a gentle entrance to the classroom. I have spoken to your parents and they are both agreed that an educational trip to London would be a lovely way to start the school term. And so, tomorrow morning, we are going to London. We will come back the next day and we are going to pack a *lot* in. The Natural History Museum, the Science Museum, art galleries. What do you think of that?'

Molly and Micky nodded, amazed.

'I'm afraid dogs aren't allowed in museums so your Petula will have to stay behind, but it looks like Rocky is ill so they can have each other for company.'

'I'm sure Petula would prefer to be here,' Molly suggested, reaching down and massaging Petula's firm neck.

I'd love to go,' said Micky.

'Sounds like a brilliant idea,' Molly said, really

relieved that Miss Hunroe wasn't like the other old-trout-like teachers that she'd known.

'Well, that's settled, then,' said Miss Hunroe. 'Pack your bags tonight. Your parents will let Ojas know to pack his. We will be staying in a nice place, by the way, but the location of that is going to remain a secret.' She winked conspiratorially.

'It sounds real cool, Miss Hunroe,' Forest remarked, stroking one of his dreadlocks. 'Wish I was coming too.'

'You're most welcome to,' said Miss Hunroe.

'Maybe you should come,' suggested Molly.

'Yeah,' agreed Forest, 'the bright lights of Buckingham Palace, the Tower of London. I've heard the Queen throws groovy late-night parties!'

'Oh yeah,' said Molly. 'Forest, the Queen has *garden* parties, daytime parties with cucumber sandwiches and scones and cream and smart guests with fancy hats – not late-night parties.'

'Hey, Mol, don't tread on my daydreams!'

'OK, Forest,' Molly said, smiling. 'If you say so – the Queen is a funky dude.'

'Well, it would be great,' said Forest, 'but I have a feelin' Miss Hunroe here needs to size you guys up. Besides, I've gotta do some big time yoga tomorra.'

'Perhaps tonight, if there is time, we shall have a little music,' Miss Hunroe said, pulling a gold coin from her pocket and eyeing the piano that she could see in the drawing room next door.

When everyone heard Todson trip up the front stairs and heard a tray with breakable things on it smashing to the floor, Miss Hunroe made a 'goodness gracious me' face. 'Do you think he's all right?' She pushed back her chair and went to see.

'Oh, my dear!' Molly, Micky and Forest heard her exclaim as she helped Todson up.

'Don't worry about me,' came Todson's reply. 'I'm always falling over.'

'She's a nice lady, ain't she?' said Forest. 'Cool. Wish I'd had a teacher like her when I was a kid.'

Todson tripped up twice more, once over Petula when he was carrying a big fruit jelly. It nearly nearly shot off the plate. The other time he tripped carrying the cream, so that it splattered out of its jug and actually put out a candle.

'Bravo!' Miss Hunroe laughed.

Molly and Micky went to bed, leaving Miss Hunroe and Forest by the grand piano. As they went upstairs, they heard Forest suggest, 'Hey, Miss Hunroe, would ya like to hear a new song I wrote? It's all about the planet.' Chords hit the air, and then Forest's song began.

'Oh, everyday folks, where ya going?
If your eggs had no yolks, would you be singing?
The bees they are dying, the deserts are frying,
And you keep on wasting an' driving an' buying . . .'

His words floated up the stairs, following Molly and Rocky to their rooms. Fifteen minutes later, the music changed style. Evidently Miss Hunroe was a skilled pianist. She played beautifully. Though Molly only heard parts of the piece that Miss Hunroe was playing, the sweetness of the music lulled her to sleep.

The next day the sun had broken through the rain clouds. However, the atmosphere in Briersville Park had grown heavy. In the night, Ojas, Lucy and Primo had arrived back but, after a sleep, they and Forest had *all* caught the flu. Todson had taken them morning tea in their bedrooms and found them very sick indeed. Only Micky, Molly and Miss Hunroe had escaped. So, as the others slept in, Molly, Micky and Miss Hunroe gathered in the kitchen for breakfast.

'It's such a pity that Ojas and Rocky can't come,' said Miss Hunroe, leaning against the kitchen counter with a cup of coffee in her hand. 'But there will be other trips. And lovely Todson is here to look after everybody. So we don't need to worry about them in that respect.'

'What if we came down with it while we're in London?' Micky asked, glancing up from a maths puzzle in the day's newspaper.

'Well, then you come straight home.'

'Miss Hunroe's right,' Molly agreed, biting into her ketchup sandwich. Splodges of red shlop oozed out and fell on to her lap. She took a slug of concentrated orange squash from her glass. (Ketchup sandwiches were Molly's favourite food whilst concentrated orange squash was her favourite drink.) 'This place is crawling with flu germs. We're probably better off going to London.'

Before they left, Molly and Micky dipped their heads into different bedrooms to say goodbye. Molly found Petula, who was dozing in her basket in the pantry, and kissed her velvety nose.

'We won't be gone for long, Petula. I'll bring you back something nice.' She joined Micky in the hall.

'It's like the plague,' Molly observed as they walked down the nine white steps outside the front door. 'Let's buy everyone a get-better present in London.'

They crossed the circular white gravel drive, passing a topiary bush in the shape of an eagle. Miss Hunroe was already inside her green sports car, revving the engine.

'Nice car, Miss Hunroe,' Micky commented. 'A classic Porche, isn't it?'

'Yes, well, we all have our weaknesses,' Miss Hunroe replied, her rose perfume filling the cold morning air as she opened the car window. 'I'm afraid it's a bit small, though. It's only really designed for two people. One of you will have a tight ride in the back.' She held out her coin. 'Toss?'

Molly took the coin. It was heavy – solid gold, Molly suspected. And it wasn't like a normal money coin. It was plain, except for the picture of a musical note embossed on one side. It fitted snugly into her palm and felt really nice to hold.

Molly lost the toss and so climbed into the back. In a minute or two they were motoring up the drive past the llama fields where the animal-shaped bushes stood dotted about like leafy zoo creatures. Ahead of them the morning sky smouldered with pink light.

Miss Hunroe reached out to the dashboard. 'Let's see what the weather's going to be like today,' she said. With the flick of a switch, the car's radio was on.

'. . . *the skies should be fairly clear over all the country*,' a weather man was saying, '*though there are blustery winds and cloud forms building near London. Quite a bit of rain may be on the way. We recommend . . .*'

'Damn!' Miss Hunroe snapped the radio off. 'How irritating. I'd wanted it to be perfect weather today. Someone's interfering with it. Ha.'

Chapter Three

Miss Hunroe clicked her fingers, encouraging Molly and Micky to follow her towards the Natural History Museum.

She led them through two tall black gates in the museum's railings and down a slope past a large rectangular outdoor skating rink. A white expanse of glinting ice sparkled in the grey noon light and a few happy skaters wobbled or glided about in bobble hats, coats and gloves. A slim Japanese woman, in a red felt tutu and smart red boots, pirouetted and then came to an abrupt halt when she spotted Miss Hunroe.

'Hurry, Miss Teriyaki!' Miss Hunroe called to her. 'The meeting's now!'

'What meeting?' Molly asked.

'The meeting to meet you, of course,' said Miss Hunroe mysteriously. 'I've got quite a few surprises for you two today.'

Molly looked at their tutor and then at the stylish

woman out on the ice. No wonder she had never enjoyed school before! Miss Teriyaki was now skating very fast to the rink's exit. Too fast. For in the next second a large man stepped nervously on to the ice. She crashed into him and fell, her leg twisting horribly beneath her.

'Ow. That looked nasty.' Molly winced. She and Micky stopped to watch the woman being helped up. She was obviously in pain. 'Miss Hunroe,' Molly called after her. 'Your friend . . .'

Miss Hunroe walked briskly on, oblivious of the accident. She was already a hundred metres ahead, climbing the broad stone steps to the museum's main entrance. So Molly and Micky followed. They admired the building's brickwork. They pointed at the animals and the imaginary creatures and monster-face gargoyles that were carved in stone under the tall, first-floor windows.

'Spooky,' Molly commented, and she and Micky stepped in through giant brass ornamented doors into the building's entrance vestibule. They walked up the steps through interior doors that led them into the museum proper.

Once right inside, the ceilings were enormously high, high as the building's vaulted roof. The walls were built with orange and white bricks, which made the hugeness of the interior seem pretty and almost cosy. Then at the end of this tall exhibition room was a very wide set of stairs that rose and parted like two branches of a tree going left and right up to balconies. And in the centre, between the staircases, jarring all sense of cosiness, was the massive black skeleton of a diplodocus dinosaur.

Molly and Micky paused to absorb the atmosphere and to look at the lonely, ghostly remains of the dinosaur, but already Miss Hunroe was steaming up the stairs, her cream patent boots clipping on the marble steps. Molly and Micky followed. They had both suddenly become slightly irritated by Miss Hunroe's speed. Both had now been reminded that with a teacher, even a glamorous teacher, a student does what they are told.

'I'm not used to being led about like a kindergarten kid,' Molly grumbled to Micky. 'You know, the last time I went to school was over a year ago.'

'Well, I've been bossed about *much* more recently that that,' said Micky. 'It stinks. Hope she doesn't turn into a dictator.'

'A what?'

'A dictator.' They took the left branch of steps that went upstairs. 'A dictator is a leader of a country who just does what they want, who tells everyone how things are going to be without asking them, without anyone voting for anything.'

'Yeah, well, let's hope she doesn't turn into a dictator,' Molly agreed. 'You know, I don't think Miss Hunroe is quite as unteachery as we thought she might be. I think she's got a great big thumb and wants to keep us under it.'

They walked up to the museum's upper gallery level.

Here they passed display cases full of stuffed apes. Some were glaring with snarling mouths, others stared with doleful eyes.

'Incredible to think we're descended from them,' Molly said. 'I suppose they're just like us, though – some are mean and selfish and some are kind and thoughtful.'

They walked past glass boxes full of examples of insects. A model of a termite the size of Petula raised its ugly pincers at them.

'Urrgh! Look at that ant!' Molly said.

'It's a termite,' Micky corrected her. 'I like termites – they're cool. They make huge mud-castle constructions that they live in.'

At the end of the balcony corridor were half a dozen steps veering to the centre of the building. Here the ceiling was very low. It was panelled, and painted with examples of plant species.

'*Atropa belladonna*. Deadly nightshade,' Miss Hunroe declared, sweeping her hand towards the paintings. Beside the letters was a picture of a herb with oval leaves, dull purple flowers and black berries.

'That's a nasty one, isn't it?' said Molly.

'Yup,' Micky answered. 'If a person eats that, they get poisoned and they can't walk properly. And that one too.' He pointed to a picture of a plant with white flowers. '*Conium maculatum*. Hemlock. That paralyses you if you eat it. Amazing, it looks so pretty, doesn't it?'

'Don't judge your flower by its prettiness,' Molly agreed.

'Hurry up,' tutted Miss Hunroe, only visible for a second as she poked her head back through the door in an oak partition in front of them. It was the entrance to a section of the building called 'The Botanical Library'.

'I suppose this is one of the surprises,' said Micky. He pointed to a sign that read BY INVITATION ONLY. PLEASE OBTAIN PASS.

He and Molly looked at each other and began to trot as they tried to catch up with Miss Hunroe. They followed her into a long room with desks laden with books and papers along each side of it. Miss Hunroe hurried past the desks towards two large wooden-framed glass doors. These swung back behind her as she blasted her way through them, one catching Molly's shoulder.

'Ow! Slow down, missus,' Molly muttered, rubbing her arm.

Now they were in an arched, high-windowed space that housed columns and columns of fitted oak filing cabinets. These rose from the ground to the ceiling everywhere. A block of tall wooden cabinets even punctuated the centre of the room.

'The archives,' stated Miss Hunroe, without a backward glance.

Molly saw that in front of each window was an alcove with a desk and a chair. And here museum workers busied themselves on computers, all of them too buried in work to bat an eye at the visitors.

'First a diplomat's parking permit, then access to all this. Miss Hunroe seems to know people,' said Micky. 'What's she doing now?'

Miss Hunroe stood at the end of the room in front of a set of drawers.

'Crumbs. Looks like lessons start here,' said Molly.

As she and Micky arrived at Miss Hunroe's side, their new tutor smiled so that her hazel eyes shone. Then, with a naughty expression on her face, she pressed the drawer beside her so that, instead of popping out, it went *in*. And to Molly and Micky's immense surprise the whole of the double-fronted cabinet before them turned on a pivot, becoming yet another door – this time a secret one.

'Oh my giddy aunt,' said Molly.

'Your what?' asked Micky.

'It's an expression,' whispered Molly, following Miss Hunroe through.

On the other side of the door, which now snapped shut, the space was similarly filled with towering filing cabinets. Like a businesswoman late for a board meeting, Miss Hunroe quickened her pace and marched through it.

'Miss Hunroe, I think you should know,' Micky said, 'your friend had an accident.'

'Sounds like her!' the tutor replied.

'Where are you taking us, Miss Hunroe?' Molly

asked, beginning to feel uneasy. She'd had enough experience with strange situations to know that this one didn't feel entirely right. 'It's all a bit mysterious, this. I'd prefer it if you told us what was going on.'

Micky flicked his hair from his eyes. 'Molly doesn't like surprises, you see,' he explained. 'In the past she's had a few nasty ones so . . .'

'Oh, don't worry, you two,' said Miss Hunroe, flinging her words over her shoulder. 'This is all completely above board. Just a few more steps and nearly everything will be revealed.'

She came to another door and turned its porcelain handle, leading Micky and Molly into yet another room. They both stepped warily inside.

'Now we're in one of the museum's towers!' Miss Hunroe announced excitedly, closing the door, locking it and quickly pocketing the key. 'Do you see – the roof is pointed! Lovely and light, isn't it, with its big windows? It's a sort of very smart library.' She pointed up some stairs to a balcony above where bookshelves hugged the walls. 'Exquisite, isn't it?'

The library was indeed splendid and luxurious. Its furniture, shelves and balconies were made of polished walnut decorated in Art Deco style with inlaid ebony motifs of leaves, flowers and humming birds. On the level where the twins stood was a fireplace with a large framed picture of a feather-shaped tree above it, and in front of this a big, low coffee table laden with books. On the other three sides of this table were three sofas.

Molly noticed that the window's panes had stained-glass patterns and back-to-front writing etched there too. Writing that was designed to be read from outside, she supposed. Yet how anyone might read it when the tower was so high, she didn't know.

'Make yourselves comfortable,' Miss Hunroe invited. Then she reached into her suit jacket pocket and took the gold coin out. She flipped it, guessing, 'Heads!' and then looked at the result in her palm. 'Heads you win. Would you like hot chocolate?'

'Yes, that would be great.' Micky shrugged.

'Unless . . .' Molly faltered. 'Unless you have concentrated orange squash?'

'Concentrated orange squash! Certainly not! Wait here on this ottoman, and I'll be back in a trice.' She disappeared through a door in the corner of the room and Molly heard her clapping her hands.

Micky picked up a glass paperweight with a black narcissus flower inside it, then he wandered over to the bookshelf by the fireplace, where he began to look at book titles.

Molly walked across the room to look out of the window. It was a blustery day. A sheep-shaped cloud above the leafless trees in front of the museum was changing its form and beginning to look like a wolf.

'We're very high up,' she said to Micky.

An elderly voice with a French accent suddenly piped up behind Molly, making her nearly jump out of her skin. 'We are, in fact, 'ere.' The end of a silver walking stick tapped the glass of an old drawing of the museum that hung on the wall. 'We're almost in ze top of zis tower.'

Molly turned to see the smile of a brown-faced old lady with a blue rinse hairdo. A string of pearls white as fresh snowballs hung round her neck. The wrinkly woman was dressed in an ankle-length, grey-blue suit embellished with waves of frills from top to bottom. She smelt very strongly of lavender. She peered enquiringly through silver spectacles.

'I didn't give you a 'eart attack, did I?'

'Of course you did, Miss Suzette,' said Miss Hunroe, returning. It was then that Molly and Micky saw the others. Like cats entering a room, two other women had also come quietly in. They settled on a long sofa under the balcony.

'Now, Molly and Micky, sit here,' Miss Hunroe continued, gesturing to the sofa in front of her, 'and let me introduce you to everyone.'

Molly and Micky observed the women. Taking up most of the room on the long sofa was a large, muscular woman in a wide, tent-like, seaweed-green dress and white gloves. She had a mop of blonde hair that was scraped into little buns on either side of her head, so that she looked as though she had strange second ears above her own. Her face was ruddy and scrubbed-looking. Squeezed next to her was a small, heron-thin lady with thin straight black shoulder-length hair, parted down the centre of her head. She was still in her coat – a charcoal, woollen one. Her hands were soapy white, the veins on the back of them were blue and pronounced.

There was a knock at the door. The Japanese skater, who was still in her red tutu, but with moon boots on instead of skates, hobbled in, helped by a maid in a blue apron. She was assisted towards the sofa, where she too sat.

'So sorry. I slipped. Had a bad fall. Twisted my ankle,' she said. She took her right boot off and the maid lifted it up on to a stool. Another maid came in with a bag of ice and a towel and gave it to the Japanese woman, who packed it round her swollen ankle. Molly noticed that she had a long, straight scar up her right forearm and wondered what accident had caused that. The two maids left and the Japanese woman leaned back.

The large woman in green pulled a small harp out of her bag and passed it to Miss Hunroe. 'I collected it from ze menders,' she said in a deep German-accented voice. 'Before I forget, here it is.'

'Oh, thank you,' Miss Hunroe said, taking the harp. 'Do we have to do bandages now?' she asked the Japanese woman, frowning at her.

Molly nodded politely at the gathering, but not feeling at all comfortable, moved back towards the fireplace, near Micky. 'Weird,' she said under her breath to him. When she turned back, she found that the lady with the blue-rinsed hair was now perched on the arm of the long sofa with the others and Miss Hunroe had moved to stand proprietarily beside it. Each of the women smiled warmly across towards the twins. Suddenly a nervous giggle rose in Molly's throat. The situation was so *odd*. And the peculiar women looked so *funny*, as though they were birds roosting on the branch of a tree. But they weren't trying to be funny, she knew, and this made Molly want to laugh even more. She didn't dare look at Micky because, if she did, they both might start to giggle, and they were supposed to be on best behaviour today.

'So,' began Miss Hunroe, rather more grimly than Molly expected. 'Prepare yourselves. We have some surprises for you.'

Micky glanced at Molly and he put the glass paper-weight down. It clunked loudly on to the table top, nearly cracking it.

Molly nodded. 'Um . . . OK.' She and Micky eyed the well-heeled ladies suspiciously. Then, to their amazement, a wide white screen began lowering from the balcony behind their heads. As it did, to pass the time, Miss Hunroe gave her small harp a few strokes. Lovely music filled the air.

Then Miss Hunroe spoke, all the while plucking and strumming her miniature harp. 'How to start. It's difficult. But I'll be as quick and as to the point as possible. This is Miss Oakkton . . .' She pointed to the big muscly woman.

'Nice to meet you,' Miss Oakkton said in a German accent.

'And this is Miss Speal.' The thin woman in the grey coat smiled weakly. 'You met Miss Teriyaki, on the ice, and Miss Suzette, who just gave you a fright.'

'How do you do?' Molly and Micky said uncertainly.

'Hello. How do you do?' the cluster of women replied. Molly felt like laughing again.

'This is mad,' she whispered to Micky.

'Yeah,' he agreed.

'These ladies already know about you,' Miss Hunroe continued. 'In fact, rather more than you might think. They know for instance that you, Molly, are a hypnotist, a time stopper and a time traveller. And we are here today to talk about what you can do.'

'This is where I say, "Oh my giddy aunt,"' Micky said under his breath to Molly.

And Molly, though shocked by Miss Hunroe's revelation, replied, 'A load of giddy aunts, I think.' She didn't care whether the gaggle of women heard her or not. Suddenly she was *very* suspicious. A cynical frown creased her forehead. And suddenly Molly didn't like the music or the women's smiles or the elegant room or the idea of the hot chocolate that was coming her way. 'Do you mind,' she said to Miss Hunroe, 'putting down your harp? It's just a bit weird.'

Miss Hunroe stopped immediately and put the instrument down on the desk.

Just then a fair-haired maid dressed in a blue uniform with a white apron entered. She was carrying a tray with two mugs on it and had the obedient look of a well-trained dog. In fact, Molly thought, she looked hypnotized.

Miss Hunroe smiled at the maid. 'Thank you, Sally.' Then she tossed her gold coin and let it land in her left hand. Then, as though its landing musical note side up had directed her, she declared, 'Now, Molly and Micky, maybe you have guessed or maybe you haven't guessed. My good friends here and I are all hypnotists.'

Chapter Four

Outside the Natural History Museum, shielded from the high tower that Molly and Micky were in by bare winter trees and a 'Beefeater' hot-dog stand, AH2 stood shivering in the winter sun.

'She's definitely up there,' he was saying to someone on the other end of the mobile phone. 'Unless the device is faulty.' The other person said something to which AH2 replied with a wry chortle. 'Yes, she's well and truly trapped. She's like a fox in a hole now. I'll get the proof and then we'll confront her, or, I should say, we'll confront *it*.' He laughed happily. 'Over and out.' AH2 slipped his phone back into his pocket and rechecked his tracking machine.

He felt good for, like a fisherman after a clever fish, he'd been trying to catch Molly Moon since he'd first come across her in New York City. And today here she was swimming near his net. Molly was extraordinary.

As soon as AH2 had encountered this Moon girl,

he'd known exactly what she was. Even her name gave it away! He didn't believe the outlandish story that she was named after the box of Moon's Marshmallows she'd been found in as a baby. Nonsense! No, this girl had superhuman, unearthly talents. She could make other people do *exactly* what she wanted. AH2 had concluded that, without a shadow of a doubt, this Molly Moon was *not* human. No, it was very clear that this 'girl' was definitely neither *he* nor *she* but instead an *IT*. For she was, as sure as hot dogs were hot dogs, an alien.

AH2's real name was Malcolm Tixley. He was twenty-five and was in the Royal Air Force and he'd been an alien hunter since he was five years old. His obsession began when he'd seen a green alien sitting on the wing of an aeroplane. He'd been travelling with his parents to visit relations in Tanzania, and the plane had been cruising at twelve thousand metres, but the alien had been there all right. It had even winked at him. His mother had seen the alien and so had the flight attendant. Ever since then he'd been hooked.

At ten, he'd joined the Y.B.A.H.A (the Young British Alien Hunting Association), and had risen through its ranks he was Deputy In Command, thus his title AH2 – Alien Hunter Two. At eighteen he had joined the air force and become an excellent pilot. He enjoyed his work but, deep down, his main reason for flying was to see an alien again. At night he took classes in space studies.

'Strange weather we've been havin', haven't we?' the fat-faced hot-dog man asked, holding out a bun and sausage. 'Hailstorms with stones the size o' ping-pong balls and then bright, bright sunshine.' AH2 was so deep in thought he didn't hear him. 'Hungry for it, are ya?' the man asked.

'W-what? For what?' AH2 stammered, caught off his guard in his daydream.

'For the hot dog, of course. Are you hungry for it?' The hot-dog seller wiped his hands on a chequered cloth.

AH2 took the hot dog and squirted some mustard on it. 'Actually,' he said, dropping some coins on to the tin counter, 'I'm hungry to catch an alien.'

'Ah. Right. I see,' said the hot-dog seller. 'Very nice.'

'So you're hypnotists too,' said Molly slowly. She paused as the maid placed her hot chocolate in front of her. 'I don't think I'll be drinking that hot chocolate, then.' She eyed the well-dressed collection of women before her. 'Am I right in thinking, Miss Hunroe, that you aren't a tutor at all?'

Miss Hunroe nodded. She looked down shamefully and fiddled with her gold coin. 'I do apologize for misleading you both, and your parents and family,' she said, 'but it was necessary. Your parents would never have let you come if they knew my real reason for wanting you here.'

'Unbelievable.' Molly glanced sideways at Micky. As

the full impact of Miss Hunroe's deception became clear, a steely anger filled her. 'You had no right,' she said. 'You wouldn't take *normal* kids out of their family house by posing as a teacher. If the police knew, they'd lock you up. Who do you think you are?' Molly turned and walked towards the door. 'Where's the key for this? I noticed you locking it. It did cross my mind that that was a weird thing to do. We're going home. Now.'

By now Micky was standing beside her. Both of the twins felt extremely anxious. The truth was they were clearly in a tricky situation because these five women, all hypnotists, seemed to have the upper hand. But this didn't stop Micky and Molly from saying what they felt.

'You've acted in a really underhand way,' Micky said.

'Completely out of order,' Molly agreed.

Miss Hunroe was totally unruffled. 'I do understand your reaction,' she said. 'And if this is really how you feel of course you are free to go. But I have one favour to ask. Please just listen to why you are needed here. If you still feel the same way afterwards, we respect your decision and you can, of course, return to Briersville Park immediately. We will get a chauffeur-driven car to drive you home as soon as you would like.'

Like birds cooing around her, the other women voiced their agreement.

'Yes.'

'Yes, we will.'

Molly looked at Micky, and raised her eyes to the ceiling. He narrowed his eyes at the female crowd, then made a tiny gesture of a shrug to Molly. Molly breathed out irritatedly. 'It better be good,' she said, returning to the third sofa and leaning against its back.

'And quick,' Micky muttered, joining his sister.

'Well, we spotted you quite a while ago, Molly,' Miss Hunroe began. 'Word got to us that you had moved into Briersville Park. We were suspicious to start with. We were aware of the huge success you had had in America starring in a Broadway show and we calculated how much money you had made.' Miss Hunroe pulled some cuttings from newspapers out of an envelope. They were from American newspapers.

'"*Moon is out of this world!*"' Miss Hunroe read. '"*. . . Molly Moon has eclipsed Davina Nuttel and taken her part in* Stars on Mars. *Last night the whole of Manhattan was alive with the gossip. Who is this Molly Moon? Nobody knows . . .*" And so it goes on.'

Molly hung her head. She was slightly ashamed of how she had conned her way to the top in Manhattan.

Miss Hunroe continued. 'At first we thought you were a bad egg. But then we saw how you used the money to help the other children in the orphanage that you grew up in. We saw your loyalty to them, especially your good friend Rocky, then it all clicked into place. We realized that that huge twenty-five-roomed house, Briersville Park, was in fact your family home. For though you are called Moon, you are really a Logan – the great-great-granddaughter of Dr Logan who wrote the phenomenal book *Hypnotism, An Ancient Art Explained*.'

Molly bit her lip. It was really odd how these women knew so much about her life.

'I don't know whether you realize this, but the world is full of hypnotists,' Miss Hunroe stated. 'Full of people who have mastered the ancient art.' She paused. 'It has to be said, very few are as good as you. It's an honour to meet you,' Miss Hunroe said smoothly. 'My friends and I are elite members of the National Society of Hypnotists. Only a small proportion of these registered hypnotists are truly talented. There are very few time stoppers and there are even fewer time travellers. What's more, I have yet to come across a mind reader . . .'

A shiver went up Molly's back as she spoke. She wondered whether Miss Hunroe somehow knew about Molly's secret mind-reading skill. Molly really didn't want this to be exposed now. Her heart now galloping, Molly decided to read Miss Hunroe's mind again. She knew that what she was doing would be invisible to everyone in the room, and yet she found her nerves were on edge as she did it. As though, this time, she was going to be caught. *What are you thinking?* Molly thought to Miss Hunroe.

A bubble popped up again over the blonde-haired woman's head and, as she continued to talk, pictures in it illustrating her words appeared.

45

'As you might suspect, Molly and Micky,' Miss Hunroe continued, 'not all hypnotists are good, kind people. Hypnotism can be used for a person's own fulfilment, and if that person has no morals, and they don't know the difference between right and wrong, these bad hypnotists can use their powers entirely for themselves. They can easily become powerful, influential, *rich*. Yes, bad hypnotists can be destructive without a care for the damage or suffering they are causing others.'

Above Miss Hunroe's hair the thought bubble filled with pictures of different people in wonderful surroundings – a grey-haired woman in a large, lavishly furnished room, a Mexican-looking man sipping a cocktail on a yacht on a calm sea somewhere hot and tropical, and a tall ugly man posing in front of a casino called BLACK'S CASINO with a cigar in his hand. Then fast cars shot through the bubble, as well as racehorses and jet planes.

'I believe that you learned how to hypnotize from your ancestor Dr Logan's book. Am I right?' Now above Miss Hunroe's head was the picture of a bespectacled man with a potato-shaped nose, in Victorian clothes.

'Yes, that's right,' Molly admitted.

Miss Hunroe continued. 'That book holds lessons for hypnotizing animals, then people, long-distance hypnosis, crowd hypnosis, that sort of thing, doesn't it?'

'Yes, that's true,' Molly agreed. And now, to check

on the other women in the room, she opened thought bubbles over their heads too. All were thinking about what Miss Hunroe was saying, except for Miss Suzette, who was thinking about a jam-and-buttercream-filled cake and then a chocolate cake, as though she was hungry and making her decision about which she would buy at the local café when this was all over.

Miss Hunroe flipped her coin, then she asked lightly, 'Did you know, children, that your great-great-grand-father wrote a second book? Volume Two?'

Both Molly and Micky were taken completely by surprise at Miss Hunroe's announcement. Molly saw that above all the women's heads, their thought bubbles filled with the images of a heavy book, with oval shapes in each of its corners.

'Which makes it all the more amazing,' Miss Hunroe went on, 'that you, Molly, have actually learned some of the lessons from *that* book. You seem to have learned them intuitively, without the book.'

'Hmmm,' agreed the large German woman, Miss Oakkton, on the sofa, smiling encouragingly and rub-bing her white-gloved hands together. 'It's arbsoluteleeey extraordinarrry. It is as if you have a natural gift.'

'What lessons?' Molly asked, though deep down she had already guessed what some of them might be.

Miss Oakkton answered. 'Time stopping and time travelling are lessons in zat book. Mind reading is in it too.'

'Mind reading . . .?' Molly, determined to keep her

own mind-reading skill a complete secret, frowned. 'That sounds tricky.'

'And morphing,' said Miss Hunroe. Above her head, a person appeared to turn into a cat.

'Morphing? What's that?' asked Micky.

'Oh,' Miss Hunroe sighed. 'It is perhaps the most dangerous of all the hypnotic arts.'

Above Miss Hunroe's head, a horse turned into an owl, then the owl into a short hairy man. Then that man turned into a baby. It was too much for Molly. She wanted to listen intently to Miss Hunroe, to concentrate on this new thing, 'morphing' but she couldn't whilst mind reading at the same time. And so she let the bubbles above Miss Hunroe and the other women's heads dissolve. She would put her suspicions of them to one side for a moment. Besides, Molly's suspicions of them were beginning to fade. These people weren't entirely angelic, she could tell, as they did have their maid hypnotized, but then Molly had kept Cornelius back home hypnotized to think he was a lamb. They probably had good reasons, just like her.

Miss Hunroe picked up a remote control and pointed it at a projector with a slide wheel above her. It began to purr electronically. Miss Speal, practically curtsying to Miss Hunroe before she did it, shut the room's blinds and dimmed the lights.

'If you can morph,' Miss Hunroe elaborated, 'you can change from a cat –' on the screen up came a picture of a black cat – 'to a dog.' Now a photograph of a shaggy sheepdog appeared. A succession of animals followed – mice, a whale, an elephant, a bird, even insects: flies, beetles and a red ant. 'A morpher can only change into an animal that he or she can actually *see*. The morpher borrows their body for a while, so some people prefer to call morphers "body borrowers".'

Molly was now even more taken by the whole idea. To be able to borrow a bird's body and fly, or be a fish and swim was fantastic! But Molly kept very still and quiet and didn't show her excitement.

'How do you know about this stuff?' Micky asked. 'Do you have a copy of the second book?'

From the sofa, Miss Teriyaki laughed.

Miss Hunroe smiled. 'Oh dear, no. If we did, well, all would be fine and you two wouldn't be here. Now where was I? Ah yes, to move from *animal* to *animal* is the elementary form of morphing. But do not think for one second that it is easy to do.'

'Can you do it?' asked Micky.

'Oh, I wish,' sighed Miss Hunroe.

'How do you know about it?' asked Molly.

Suddenly, the wren-like voice of Miss Speal, the skinny, tiny, dark-haired woman with the thin face, piped up. She stood and spoke quickly, in a half whisper, as though frightened that if she spoke louder something horrible would happen. 'My parents were hypnotists. They looked after the book for a while when I was about seven years old. But it was a dangerous thing to possess for its contents are extremely powerful.'

Molly found the hairs pricking up on the back of her neck. Miss Speal's face was so pale and bloodless that she looked like a ghost, and now, talking about the book in this way, she was even spookier.

'I remember finding it once when my parents were out. I wasn't that good at reading but I knew the book was very, very special as I'd heard my parents talking about it, and so I opened it and made an effort to understand it.' The woman stroked her black, limp hair as she remembered. 'It was a very heavy book. Four flat stones were embedded in its thick leather cover, one in each corner. One was orange with red streaks in it, one was light grey with white and black cloudy parts to it, one was green and brown, like the colour of plants and earth and the last was blue with white flecks in it, like waves and white foam.'

Miss Speal then pursed her lips and suddenly reached into her coat pocket.

'Miss Speal,' cautioned Miss Hunroe soberly. But, ignoring her, the thin raconteur pulled a small piece of blue stone from her coat pocket and thrust it up towards the children's eyes so that they both could see it. It was a watery-blue-coloured stone mottled with patches of white.

'This is the blue stone from the book!' the woman announced. 'It fell out and I'm glad it did, because a few days later the book was stolen.'

Outside, a crack of lightning broke through the sky.

'Miss Speal,' Miss Hunroe cautioned again. 'Please try not to get over-emotional about this. The children need to know about the book. Do you want to tell them, or shall I?'

Miss Speal sniffed and her eyes darted to look at the sky outside. 'Yes, yes. Well, inside the book was the title, *Hypnotism. Volume Two. The Advanced Arts.* There were about ten chapters, but I can't remember what all the skills were. It was intoxicatingly exciting and I read it as though I had opened some sort of spell book.' As she spoke, she rubbed the blue stone. It was as though it was a talisman that brought memories of that precious evening back to her. Outside, thunder rumbled.

'MISS SPEAL!' Miss Hunroe now scolded the woman. 'Please control yourself.'

Miss Speal put the flat stone back into her pocket and looked nervously at Miss Hunroe, rather as a dog with its tail between its legs might look at its master. 'Yes,' she finished, her attention now on her audience. 'As I said, the book was stolen . . .'

'Before you learned any of its lessons,' Miss Hunroe added, helping her along.

Miss Speal looked bewildered for a moment, then her eyes widened. 'Y-yes, yes, before I learned any of its lessons. I read the list of lessons but never learned them.'

'Who stole it?' Molly asked.

Miss Speal shook her head. 'The devil knows.'

'But the important matter,' said Miss Teriyaki impatiently, 'is where it is *now*.'

'First things first,' insisted Miss Hunroe, reprimanding Miss Teriyaki and tapping her sharply on the wrist with her remote control. 'I haven't finished explaining morphing.'

Miss Teriyaki put her hands together and humbly bowed to Miss Hunroe. 'Sorry, sorry,' she said subserviently, readjusting the ice pack round her ankle.

Miss Hunroe pressed the button on her remote control again. 'As I said, the elementary stage is to morph into an *animal*, but the sophisticated level . . .' She turned towards the children and said very seriously, 'The thing is that the second level of morphing is being able to change from *human to human*. And, as you can imagine, anyone who could do this could become very, very powerful and influential. Why, a person with this skill might choose to morph into the President of the United States of America!' Up on the screen came a picture of the President of America talking to an important-looking army official. A line of soldiers stood behind them both, saluting. 'Or they might morph into the body of the President of *China*.' Now on the screen was a picture of thousands of soldiers standing to attention, saluting the Chinese President. 'Once inside another person's body, they'd have control over that person's very *mind* and so of course their *actions*. Do you see how dangerous this could be?'

'Of course,' said Molly, spellbound.

'And so,' guessed Micky, 'you're telling us that the Prime Minister of this country is really someone else – that an evil hypnotist has morphed into his body.'

'No, not yet. At least I hope not.' Miss Hunroe crossed her arms. 'But, we *do* know that the book – *Volume Two* – has passed into the hands of a very undesirable person. We know that he is highly likely to try to learn the book's lessons for bad ends.'

Miss Hunroe pressed a button on the slide controls and up on the screen came a photograph of a leathery-faced man with a mop of dark hair. His skin was rough and pock-marked. He wore a smart pinstriped suit with a red tie and a brimmed Homburg hat. Molly recognized him from the thought bubble that had appeared over Miss Hunroe's head earlier.

'His name is Theobald Black. He's a hypnotist. He uses his talents to embezzle money.'

'Embezzle. What's that?' asked Molly.

'It means,' Micky quickly explained, 'when you get something – usually money – through trickery.'

'Yes, that's right,' agreed Miss Hunroe. 'Mr Black here picks on easy prey – rich old ladies or gentlemen. Here are some photographs we got of him in action. In this one he is hypnotizing a very rich heiress who owns gold mines.' Up on the screen came a black and white photograph of Mr Black on a park bench holding a pendulum up in front of a small, middle-aged woman in a hat with a stuffed bird on it. 'And here he is taking control of an old man who has made a fortune in marmalade . . .'

'And jams, very good jams,' Miss Suzette interjected. '"Wiltshire Jams" is de company's name.'

Now, another picture came up. It was taken through the window of a café, and showed Mr Black sitting at a table with an old man in a bowler hat. Their faces were very close and Mr Black was staring into the man's eyes as though hypnotizing him.

'He runs a casino, Black's Casino.' On the screen, Mr Black dressed in black was talking to the casino doorman. 'He has a daughter called Lily.'

Now a photograph of a girl of about seven with short, dark, curly hair came up. She was dressed in a smart pink peacoat, with boots to match.

'As far as we know, she is not a hypnotist. But she is quite a number.' In the next picture, Lily was outside a restaurant with a furious look on her face. She seemed to be stamping her foot and her hands were clenched in fury by her side. 'She was angry in this picture because her father couldn't get a table at The Orchid.'

'But if he's a hypnotist surely he can get a table at any restaurant,' Micky said.

'I was at school with Black. I know what he's like. Selfish. No doubt he wanted to go home and didn't care what his little girl, Lily, wanted.'

'Lily Black – what a name,' Molly said. 'So how do we come into all of this?' she asked, already half knowing the answer.

A new picture came up on the screen. Molly reckoned that a concealed camera must have taken it for it was a photograph of the inside of Black's Casino. Uniformed croupiers stood behind roulette wheels and game tables, dealing cards to their customers. And stacked on the green baize tables were little towers of brightly coloured gambling chips.

'The place is crawling with guards,' Miss Hunroe explained. 'And there are cameras everywhere. There is no way that any of us –' she let her hand turn like a soft wing over the assembled women near her – 'could get in to retrieve the book. We'd be spotted instantly. You see, we tried once before to get Black's time-travel crystals off him, but failed. In fact Miss Teriyaki has a souvenir from that attempt.'

Miss Teriyaki lifted her arm and showed Molly and Micky the long scar there.

'Didn't you call the police?' asked Micky.

'The police! We don't want them involved now! Black would only take further precautions to hide the book. Then we might never find it. Besides, we were trespassing. It was four in the morning when the casino had closed. He could probably prove that we were attempting some sort of robbery. And, don't forget, he's a hypnotist. Who knows what sort of witnesses he could drum up. He could hypnotize them to say whatever he wanted! We might find ourselves in prison!'

'You could always hypnotize your way out,' Micky tested her.

'True, but Black would always be a step behind. And

get us put back in prison. We might end up there forever.'

'Indeed, it's not worth the risk,' Miss Teriyaki agreed.

'So,' Miss Hunroe continued, 'the long, the tall and the short of it is that now Black is well aware of us. He knows that he needs to protect himself. Even if all five of us went in, using our hypnotic skills, we wouldn't stand a chance. He has taken precautions.'

A picture on the screen focused on one of the casino guards' pockets and zoomed in. Poking half out of it were some dark glasses with a swirling pattern on them.

'Anti-hypnotism glasses,' Miss Hunroe explained.

Molly nodded. 'Seen them before,' she said. 'I saw a version that were like normal glasses with white swirls, not so dark as those ones. They work.'

'Yes, and when the guards put them on they look simply like dark glasses,' said Miss Hunroe. 'So, when anyone suspicious approaches, they wear the glasses.'

'If you don't mind me adding, Miss Hunroe,' said Miss Teriyaki, 'we also think that Black has given the guards voice-scrambling devices to put in their ears. Because we think that if Black has worked out how to counteract hypnotic eye-glare it's highly likely he will also have thought of voice hypnosis and how to block that.'

'Yes, correct, Miss Teriyaki,' said Miss Hunroe, visibly irritated by Miss Teriyaki's interruption.

'So *how*,' demanded Micky, 'can *we* be of any help?'

'I expect,' said Molly, 'it's got something to do with the daughter.'

'Yas, you are right!' cried Miss Oakkton, slapping her knees.

'Yes,' Miss Hunroe agreed. 'You see, the thing is this. The *only* people who the guards ever interact with normally are the children who are Lily's school friends. They never put on their anti-hypnotism glasses when Lily's friends come round for a play date.'

'Of course,' Miss Suzette explained, 'we could have hypnotized one of zese children to go in to fetch ze book, but we felt zat to use an innocent child would be unfair . . .'

'Yas, most unfair,' Miss Oakkton agreed. 'Poor little sings.'

'Our great hope,' Miss Teriyaki interjected, 'is that you two could go to the casino with the excuse that you have to see Lily, your school friend.'

Miss Hunroe unfolded a sheet of paper with an architectural diagram of the casino on it. 'Once inside the building,' Miss Hunroe said, 'you could access the private areas of the premises. With this map you can see the vents and conduits that carry the pipes and cables from room to room, and you can access Theobald Black's office. You could use your special crystals to freeze time and get the office keys.'

'I haven't got my crystals,' Molly replied.

'But aren't you wearing your crystals now?' Miss Hunroe asked, eying her neck. 'You have some sort of pendant.'

Molly pulled out the chain with the black pug, the silver elephant and the two blackbirds on it. 'Oh no. These are just our pets.'

Gasps of disbelief and disappointment erupted from the ladies opposite.

'That's a pity,' declared Miss Teriyaki. 'We ought to fetch the crystals.'

'No time!' squeaked Miss Speal. 'Oh lord. We're already risking it. What on earth are we going to do?' She began wringing her little hands as though she was trying to squeeze water out of wet socks. 'Maybe your parents could send them up on a motor—'

'NO!' interrupted Miss Suzette. 'They might ban Molly and Micky from helping us.'

'Even though it's for the bigger cause?' asked Miss Teriyaki.

'They wouldn't be happy about letting us help,' said Micky. 'They think Molly needs a bit of time being normal.'

'Which is why they advertised for a tutor,' added Miss Hunroe. Then she pursed her lips. 'Oh dear. Molly, Micky – I'm really not comfortable about this any more. If your parents wouldn't approve, then I don't feel we should go against their wishes.'

Molly considered the assembled assortment of women. She could see why they were worried. The idea of a maniac learning how to morph into another person was scary.

'How do you know he's not a morpher already?' Molly quizzed.

'We don't.' Miss Hunroe flipped her coin as though the coin's action of turning like a tossed pancake in the air was a comfort to her. 'We know the book came into his possession a month ago. Since he's only had it for a short time the chances are he can't morph ye—'

'How—' Micky asked.

Miss Hunroe cut him short. 'An anonymous person called us.'

Molly studied the ladies in front of her. 'If you don't mind me asking,' she said, 'how come you lot know each other? How come you are involved in all of this?'

'Well,' Miss Hunroe began, her lips pausing for a second to blossom into a brief rose shape before moving to talk again, 'as I said, there is a society of ordinary hypnotists. We met there. We were invited to form a group of *elite* hypnotists – though it has to be said we are all merely hypnotists, not time travellers or time stoppers. We vowed to use our powers to help people in the world. We try to sort out any foul play.'

'We want to catch the dodgers before they dart,' whined Miss Speal.

'Grab ze codgers before zay grunt,' finished Miss Oakkton.

'We are like Wonder Women, I suppose,' explained

Miss Teriyaki, smiling. 'We root out crooks like Mr Black. It is such a pity you haven't got your time-stopping crystals. What's more, there is not time to get them.' She turned to Miss Hunroe as though the situation had now moved on, and Molly was now irrelevant. 'I will go in, Miss Hunroe.'

'But surely Molly can still could go in wizout her time-stopping skills,' Miss Suzette commented.

Miss Teriyaki gasped. 'Don't be ridiculous!'

'Listen,' Molly interrupted. 'Micky and I really don't need time crystals for this. It's a cinch. This job can be easily done without them.' Next to her she could sense Micky's eyes widening. But her appetite had been whetted. This little trip into Black's Casino to retrieve the book looked like it might at least give her a taste of the adventure she'd been craving. 'Besides, I'm very interested to get a look at that book. We could take it down to Briersville Park and keep it in the library there. After all, that's where it belongs.'

Micky shrugged. 'I suppose that's true . . .'

'Zat's ze spirit!' Miss Suzette exclaimed, twiddling her silver cane enthusiastically. 'Just ze idea I'd had for ze book myself!'

'Vunderful!' Miss Oakkton echoed, thwacking the coffee table with her white gloves.

Miss Hunroe clapped her hands. 'Absolutely not!' she decided vehemently. 'I'm sorry, Molly and Micky, but I've acted like a fool and completely improperly. You've said your parents wouldn't want you to get involved with this risky business and we cannot ignore that.'

'But, Miss Hunroe,' Miss Teriyaki interrupted, 'Molly herself thinks that she and her brother can retrieve the book easily. Maybe this is our only chance.'

'Miss Hunroe, it is madness not to accept ze children's help.'

'No, Miss Oakkton, I've been influenced by you enough. These children cannot be involved without their parents' consent.'

'Listen,' Molly interrupted, 'we want to help. And our parents have only just *become* our parents. Micky only met them recently. I haven't known them that much longer. We've lived our lives for a long time without them. So, we aren't like normal kids. Maybe Micky hasn't made his mind up about it yet,' she added, smiling, 'but I have.'

'Oh, I don't know,' Miss Hunroe said, her decision hovering. She pulled her gold coin out again and turned it over and over in her fingers.

'I zink zay *must* help,' Miss Suzette advised. 'Zese children, Miss Hunroe, are not ordinary children. Molly has special abilities, and Micky eez probably gifted too – after all, zay are twins. Wiz Molly's gift comes special responsibilities. Zis is a critical problem zat needs specific solutions. No one can help as Molly can. What is more, eef we don't get Molly's help, ze whole world may suffer ze consequences.'

Miss Hunroe's coin flipped through the air and

landed in the palm of her hand. She smacked it on to the back of her left hand.

'Heads you win,' she said.

A hundred and eighty miles away, Petula woke up from a midday sleep. She'd had a nightmare of Molly leaving her all alone in Briersville Park, which was silly, she knew, because, apart from Molly and Micky, everyone else – Rocky, Ojas and the adults, were all there. She shook her head, and her ears and her lips flapped and the sparkling name tag on her collar rattled. But it was odd, she thought, that her sleep had been so undisturbed. Petula had been out the night before down on the neighbouring farm where her friends the sheepdogs lived. She'd stayed with them until well past midnight. Then she'd trotted home under a starlit sky, barked at the local fox, who she could smell was in the llama field, and she'd got back in late. Now she would go and visit everyone and see how they were. It was peculiar, as normally at this time of day she'd hear the butler, Todson, laying tables for lunch. But all was quiet.

So off she trotted from her basket in the pantry, along the corridor to her basket in the hall. There, she picked up a small pebble in her mouth and, chewing and sucking it, made her way up the wide hall stairs to the first landing that led to the house's master bed-rooms. Portraits of Molly and Micky's ancestors looked curiously down, their eyes seemingly fixed on her.

'Don't you know it's rude to stare?' Petula barked at them.

On the first floor the hundreds of clocks that lined the passage ticked like clockwork crickets. Petula nudged open Primo Cell and Lucy Logan's bedroom door. The room was dark, as the curtains were closed. Both Lucy and Primo were sitting in bed. They were leaning backwards on cushions, staring upwards. For a moment Petula thought that perhaps they had bought a very modern television screen that was set in the ceiling. But as she trotted into the room she could see that there was nothing on the ceiling. What was more, neither said hello to Petula. She dropped her stone and barked. Primo and Lucy were still. Petula put her front paws up on the side of the bed. She whined at Lucy and pawed at the silk bedspread but neither of the humans uttered a word. Then Lucy took a sip of water. She didn't even glance at Petula.

Something was wrong, very wrong. Petula barked again and then some more, but it was useless. Petula suddenly felt very scared. She'd seen humans in this state before. It was as obvious as an unburied bone: Lucy and Primo were hypnotized. But by *whom*? Petula looked about her to see whether her barking had summoned anyone to the room. Turning on her heels, Petula fled.

Panic rushing through her, she bowled along the passage of clocks until she came to the small flight of stairs that led to the children's quarters. She must let

Rocky and Ojas know what had happened and get their help! Her claws slid and scrabbled up the polished wooden steps. Skidding to stop herself, she reached their bedroom. The room was empty. Petula turned and began to run along the corridor to the attic stairs. Her heart lifted as she approached the children's den. The sound of jingles on the TV escaped through the crack of the closed door. Everything was normal, she thought. Rocky and Ojas were watching TV. But when she pushed the door open her hopes were dashed. For there in the dark with the curtains shut, reclining in armchairs with glazed expressions on their faces as they gawped at the TV, were Ojas and Rocky.

Petula leaped in Rocky's lap and barked right into his eyes but he was like someone half dead. The light from the television screen danced across his brown face. Petula jumped to the floor and pounced at the TV. An advert was on. Three pots of mustard, each with a smiling face, jigged about in front of a barbecued sausage. This should have seemed funny but today, as though in some nasty dream, the pots of mustard looked sinister.

Petula growled and tried to hit the OFF switch. Having no success, she attacked the television plug, and eventually pulled it out of its socket. Now the room was pitch black except for the light from the passage. Frightened and confused, Petula left that room too. Forest the hippy or Todson or the new cook *must* be all right, Petula thought as she sped along the carpet to

64

the main stairs. Inside she felt desperate. A howl of fear was building up in her. For surely Forest or Todson would have called Molly and Micky back home if they knew what had happened to the others. Then a horrid thought occurred to Petula. Perhaps Todson or the new cook were the guilty hypnotists.

Down in the sitting room, Forest was so still he looked like he'd rooted to the floor like a human tree. Even the children's pet blackbirds sitting on his shoulders had been hypnotized. Petula was scared. As quietly as she could, she crept to the kitchen. She found Todson and the Thai cook sitting in armchairs with their eyes closed.

Petula's head swam as the nightmarish reality of her situation sank in. She crept to her special low chair. This was a chair that she could hide under, where no one would find her. Finally, under its velvet-fringed bottom, Petula caught her breath and tried to think straight.

She thought of the strange, glamorous woman who had smelt of red lipstick and rose perfume. Before, Petula had detected a scent of thorn in the perfume. Now she realized that the perfume had been the rose smell and that it covered the woman's true scent, that of sharp *thorn*. Petula remembered how the woman had whisked Molly and Micky away, and a horrid mixture of anger and worry rose in her guts.

Emboldened by this detective work, Petula made her way to the drawing room, where she knew Lucy Logan had hidden Molly's collection of time-travel and time-stopping crystals. She nudged the inlaid mother-of-pearl box from its low shelf near the fireplace until it fell on the floor and burst open. Nothing fell out of it. Nothing was in it. Someone had stolen the crystals.

Now Petula saw things clearly. This woman stealing Molly's crystals meant she knew about Molly's talents. The woman was obviously a talented hypnotist for she'd switched every person in the house into neutral. But what about Molly and Micky? Perhaps, just *perhaps*, they weren't in real danger yet.

Petula shivered. She felt small and hopeless and all alone. But there was nothing for it. Molly and Micky must be helped. If Petula didn't go to their rescue, who would? Petula made her way down to the kitchen, to the back door. With a deep breath she nudged the wooden dog flap with her forehead and stepped out into the cool, damp air. Raising her black nose to the wind, and cocking her head to sense Molly and Micky's whereabouts, she set off up the long drive.

Chapter Five

Miss Hunroe stood alone beside a high round
table in a large grand room with a very tall
triangular ceiling above her. Her and her acquaintances'
lavish apartments were all situated in the uppermost
parts of the four towers that punctuated the top of the
Natural History Museum building. Miss Hunroe's
rooms were in the Art Deco style. The black lacquer
chairs had curved solid-wood backs and smart cushions
with a leafy garland pattern on them. There were etched
mirror tables and at the far end of the room was a
concertinaed, freestanding, pale wood screen with a
long-legged leaping dancer inlaid in darker wood on it.
Behind this was an oval-shaped double bed. The walls
were green and decorated with gold brocade. A tall
maple cabinet displayed a collection of ancient gold
plates and goblets, and on the floor in front of the
thirty-six-paned window a giant rare solid-gold vase,
taken from the Egyptian department in the British

Museum, stood proud, filled with magnificent sun-flowers. A gorgeous gilt harp stood to the side of the vase, whilst, above, a massive golden chandelier hung from the apex of the room like a giant honeycomb.

The walls were hung with paintings. One echoed the sunflowers on the floor, and was by a world-famous painter, Van Gogh. Miss Hunroe had 'borrowed' this from its museum home in Amsterdam. Languidly, she sat down at the harp. The sound of the strings as her fingers plucked them was like the sound of a heavenly waterfall. Then Miss Hunroe pinched one of the strings tightly and slid her pinch from the top of the string downwards. This made an unearthly screeching noise. Smiling, Miss Hunroe abandoned the harp and swivelled round on her stool. Crossing her legs, she pulled a clear crystal out of her pocket and held it up to the light.

'If *she's* mastered time travel and time stopping,' she said, 'I don't see why I shouldn't.' There was a knock at the door. 'Come in.'

Miss Speal and Miss Suzette entered, each looking modestly proud, as though they were about to receive gold stars from the head teacher.

'They've gone!' Miss Speal squealed suddenly, unable to control her excitement. She rubbed her hands together. 'I just saw them off in a taxi.'

'*And* zay fell for it hook, line and sinker,' gushed Miss Suzette. Then she added flatteringly, 'Miss Hunroe, you were brilliant – a tour de force! You should receive an Oscar for your performance! I loved ze part where you refused to let zem go.' Here Miss Suzette imitated Miss Hunroe's words. '*I'm sorry, Molly and Micky, but I've acted like a fool and completely improperly. You've said your parents wouldn't want you to get involved with this risky business and we cannot ignore that.* It was inspired, Miss Hunroe. Well done!'

'The girl's impetuous. And the boy seems to follow her lead. I knew it wouldn't take much,' Miss Hunroe said, brushing off the praise.

'Expect zay'll be at ze casino in ten minutes,' enthused Miss Suzette.

'They are nearly there,' said Miss Speal, with her eyes shut.

'Let's hope it works,' said Miss Hunroe, plucking three strings of the harp with her long-nailed fingers.

'Oh, play us something, please, Miss Hunroe,' Miss Speal sighed.

Miss Hunroe cast her eyes to the ceiling and then she played. Heavenly music drifted about the room and the women fell quiet, in awe.

Then Miss Hunroe suddenly stopped. 'But, Miss Speal, you should be ashamed of yourself, losing control like you did. I've asked you not to rub that piece of stone while we are here. You behaved like an idiot. It was as if you wanted them to know our secret!'

'I'm sorry, I couldn't help myself,' the thin spinster mumbled, staring at the ground. Miss Hunroe tutted nastily and then narrowed her eyes and impersonated her. '*I couldn't help myself.* Pathetic.'

An awkward silence filled the room. Miss Suzette broke it, trying to change the subject. 'I'm sure ze Moon girl ees a mind reader,' she said excitedly, bobbing about from foot to foot like some over-keen lapdog so that her frilly clothes started to flap. 'Did she mind-read you, Miss Hunroe? Did you see ze way she looked at us? It was very good we knew how to take precautions and bar her probing mind from our *true* zoughts.'

Miss Hunroe nodded matter-of-factly and replied sourly, 'She was most certainly attempting to read my mind. I felt it. It was as though a window had been opened into my head and a breeze was coming in. It took all my strength to invent the things she should see and keep her out of my real thoughts.'

'Yes, yes! For me it was a tickly feeling all over my forehead!' Miss Suzette declared. 'Do you think she's a natural morpher? Do you think she can body-borrow?'

'You couldn't learn without that book,' Miss Speal replied. 'Unless you had a teacher. For instance I taught you all to morph into animals, but I originally got my lessons from the book.'

'Where *are* the cats?' Miss Hunroe asked impatiently. She looked at her watch.

As if on cue the door opened and, led by a beautiful short-haired, blue-eyed, white Burmese cat, the two other hypnotists, Miss Oakkton and Miss Teriyaki, entered. Miss Oakkton held two cats, a big ginger tom and a grey hairless sphinx cat, whilst Miss Teriyaki,

70

with a crutch under her right arm, held a fluffy white Persian cat under her left arm. A grey Siamese followed her.

Miss Teriyaki spoke: 'Oh, Miss Hunroe, you were so clever to make the story up that my skiing-accident scar was from a trip into the casino! I'm sure those gullible children believed it completely!'

Miss Hunroe blinked at Miss Teriyaki, then glared at Miss Oakkton. 'You're late, Miss Oakkton. Just like you were last week when we were in Black's Casino. May I remind you that your lack of punctuality then upset our whole plan. If it hadn't been for *you*, we would have the book by now. Because of *your* sloppiness then, we were caught inside the casino. Because of *you*, the guard *you* were supposed to deal with was left unhypnotized. But there was a reason, wasn't there? Ah, now, what was it you were doing? Buying tobacco? So all in all, because of *your* dirty pipe habit, we have had to go to *ridiculous* lengths to persuade these horrible Moon children to help us.'

'Ze cats ver difficult to round up,' explained Miss Oakkton.

'You always have an excuse,' whined Miss Speal.

'You ought to set your watch five minutes fast, like a child zat is always late,' laughed Miss Suzette patronizingly. 'Zat would teach you!'

Miss Oakkton growled at her under her breath.

Miss Teriyaki passed the big-eyed Persian cat to Miss Suzette and bent down to pick up the grey Siamese.

71

'Oh, daaaahleeeng!' Miss Suzette exclaimed, pressing her nose up to her pet's.

Miss Oakkton kept the large, hairy orange cat firmly tucked under her arm, whilst giving the thin, hairless sphynx to Miss Speal.

'Ready?' Miss Hunroe asked, as her white Burmese cat rubbed against her ankles. The women murmered yes. Miss Hunroe frowned irritatedly. 'Not you, Miss Speal. I've ordered the plane. It takes off at five thirty. You should be in the chamber by eleven tomorrow morning our time.'

Miss Speal dropped her head apologetically. 'Thank you for forgiving my stupidity, Miss Hunroe.'

'We will meet you there as soon as our business is finished here,' Miss Hunroe added. Then she turned her attention again to the other three women. They were all now staring at a patterned rug on the floor. 'Let us go,' Miss Hunroe decided. In the next second an astonishing thing happened. She and the women staring at the rug disappeared as instantly as blown-out flames. All that was left was their clothes – a pile of frills of cotton and silk, of wool skirts, trousers, shirts and jackets, of old-fashioned bras and pants of varying sizes and of nylon tights. Scattered about under the mounds of material was an odd assortment of shoes as well as a crutch. Four cats sat on the belongings as though they owned them.

The cats stared at the floor as they adjusted to their insides, for each of them now had *two* beings inside them: the original cat beings, and the women, who had just entered, and who were now taking them over.

The real cat characters shrank back and down like sea anemones reduced from blooming flowers to tiny balls. Miss Hunroe, Miss Teriyaki, Miss Suzette and Miss Oakkton took control of the cats' minds as quickly and as thoroughly as an eggcup of black ink might colour a small mug of water.

The white Burmese was the most difficult of the feline creatures to take command of. And today, as was often the case, it resisted Miss Hunroe's control. It fought hard, refusing to let its identity be squashed and replaced by Miss Hunroe's personality. But it was no use. Miss Hunroe won the tug of war and the blue-eyed cat succumbed to her.

'Miaow,' Miss Hunroe mewed. And then in the language of cat, for once in an animal it was possible to 'speak' to other animals of the same sort, she asked, 'Are you ready?'

Miss Speal, sitting on a stool with her hairless sphinx in her arms, watched as the four cats twitched their tails and nodded to the white Burmese. Then she stood up and opened the door for her feline friends.

The cats descended a straight, steep, thirty-step staircase and came to an open fire exit on to the main roof of the museum. Nimbly, they leaped out on to the slate tiles there and, in an ordered fashion, trotted along the full length of the roof down to the museum's central towers. Here, traversing the triangular peak of the roof, they came to the front of the museum, where they nego-tiated a wrought-iron fire escape that descended until they were at first-floor level. They each jumped on to a balcony, and walked along a thin, granite windowsill before hopping from the head of an ugly stone gargoyle to the bare branch of a tree in front of the museum. Soon the procession of cats had snaked their way down to the cold pavement of Brompton Road.

A big red double-decker bus stopped at the lights and all four cats sprang on board.

'Oh my word!' exclaimed the Jamaican bus con-ductor.

'Ah, look at those sweet cats!' cried an eight-year-old girl on her way home from school.

A wobbly-chinned woman, surrounded by shopping bags, looked up. 'How extraordinary!' she said.

'MIAOOW!' screeched Miss Oakkton, the orange cat, swiping at the child with her claws. Miss Teriyaki, the Siamese, hissed and darted forward aggressively. The girl shrieked and stumbled backwards so that her purple felt school hat fell off.

'Blood clot!' the conductor gasped. 'Like a bunch of witches' cats, I'd say. Are you all right, sweetheart? Best to leave 'em alone.'

And so the bus pulled away. The people on it eyed the feline passengers nervously. The four cats, the white Burmese, the grey Siamese, the fluffy white Persian and the huge orange cat, sat beside the stairs near the vehicle's open back. Then at Knightsbridge they stood up, raised their noses to the air and disembarked.

AH2 pulled his collar up as another gust of cold air blew through the street. He'd followed Molly Moon and the boy who looked like her brother out of the Natural History Museum. He had hailed a cab to tail theirs, but with the heavy late-afternoon traffic his black taxi had lost them. With his tracking device, however, AH2 could of course deduce exactly where Molly Moon was. And so he had switched it on and made his way through the crowded pavements after her.

It was odd. Molly Moon and her accomplice were inside a smart old building that bore the sign, BLACK'S CASINO, ESTABLISHED 1928. What an eleven-year-old girl could need to do inside a casino was beyond AH2. Then again, he considered, digging his hands deep into his pockets, she was *really* an alien. And the brother was probably an alien too. Maybe the place was a nest of aliens. As AH2 grew dizzy watching early gamblers entering the casino through its cylindrical rotating door, his imagination took flight. It would be incredible, he thought, if he were to uncover an alien headquarters. AH2 imagined himself interviewed on news programmes, his face transmitted to televisions all over the world. He'd be a hero.

'*All those years of knowing aliens were here with no one believing you!*' he pictured the news journalist saying. '*How did you cope?*' AH2's mind spun off into a fantasy.

'*I had a very strong gut feeling,*' he imagined himself saying. '*And, coupled with the proof I was collecting, I was confident that I'd be able to prove to the world that aliens had arrived.*'

'*Well, it's truly impressive,*' the interviewer would reply. '*I'm sure everyone watching would like to personally shake you by the hand and thank you.*'

AH2 was woken from his daydream by something gliding past his feet. He looked down to see an *extraordinary* sight. Four cats, two white, a ginger and lastly a grey, slipped quietly past him as though following each other. Hiding in the shadows for a moment until the casino doorman had his back turned, they then all leaped towards the tiny alley that ran alongside the casino. One, two, three and finally the fourth cat disappeared round the corner of the alley before anyone else noticed them.

AH2's fantasy that this place was a den of aliens suddenly became concrete.

'Bingo!' he said, under his breath.

Twenty minutes earlier, a cab had dropped Molly and Micky off at the end of the street.

'There it is, luv,' the cockney cabby had directed them. 'Gambling's not good for you, though. Don't spend all yer pocket money!'

Micky and Molly paid him and thanked him. They

paused as he drove away and stood still to watch the casino entrance.

'Here we go,' said Molly. 'Remember, Micky, we're Lily Black's friends, so behave like a seven-year-old.'

'This is crazy,' Micky replied. 'If just being kids doesn't work, use your hypnotism, will you, Molly?'

Molly looked at her brother. He was licking his lips nervously. 'If you don't want to come in, don't worry, Micky. You could wait out here and I'll go in on my own. It won't take long and you'll be safe here.'

Micky shook his head. 'I've read so many adventure stories,' he mulled, 'hundreds probably. From ones set in medieval times to ones set far in the future. Space adventures, cowboy adventures, war adventures, survival adventures.'

'That's why you know so much stuff,' Molly interrupted.

Micky nodded. 'Suppose now is the time to be *in* an adventure.'

'Sure?' Molly said, smiling with amusement at her brother's logic.

'Yes, sure,' Micky answered, with his mind made up. 'Let's do it.'

The siblings ascended the casino's short set of steps where one of the guards stood, brushing dandruff off the shoulders of his suit jacket.

'Excuse me,' Molly began. 'Is this Lily Black's . . . um . . . house? We've come for a play date.'

Micky interrupted her. 'Don't be silly, Matilda. I told

you, this can't be Lily's house. This isn't a house – it's a shop. Oh, Matilda, we're lost. I want Mum!'

The unsuspecting doorman looked down. 'Hey, little fella, don't worry, this *is* Lily's house. She stays here till her dad takes her home, so if you've come for a play date you've come to the right place. Come in!'

'Oh, fanks!' said Micky, smiling up sweetly at the guard. 'Does Lily have sweets here?'

The guard laughed and ushered the kids through. 'Should think so, knowing Miss Lily!' he chuckled. He pointed into the casino. 'Walk straight over there and round that corner and her room is the second on the left.'

'OK, fanks, mister!'

Molly and Micky walked through the revolving door.

'Brilliant, Micky,' Molly said, smiling. 'You've got talent.'

And so the children padded into the casino. Only seven steps inside and they felt as though they were in a twilight world – a place of neither day nor night – for the casino was windowless and devoid of natural light. Instead it glittered with golden lamps and imitation candlelight. The floor's green carpet was filled with a copper-threaded coin pattern, which gave the impression that money had been strewn all over the ground. The walls were a pale green decorated in the trompe l'œil fashion. An artist had painted fake columns with plants on top of them and views of a garden behind.

These views were executed to look three-dimensional so that it really seemed as if the casino was set in a weird paradise. Gamblers of all nationalities sat concentrating on their card games, and shiny silver balls clattered on spinning roulette wheels before they found a resting place. Molly and Micky walked silently by them, along the side passage that ajoined the gambling room.

'Looks fun!' said Micky. 'Pity we can't have a go.'

'Come on, Micky. Cameras are everywhere. We don't want Mr Black spotting us.' Molly pulled her brother behind a slot machine. 'Some people call these machines "one-armed bandits",' she said, discreetly pulling out the casino map Miss Hunroe had given her, 'because the handle you pull is like an arm, and, like a bandit, the machines steal your money.' She quickly looked at the map. 'So we need to go over there.' Molly gestured towards the corner of the casino. 'That's where the vent grille is. Once inside that we can crawl through the vent to Mr Black's office.' She smiled at Micky. 'No locks, no guards.'

'What if Black's already seen us via one of the casino cameras?' Micky whispered, his voice now wobbling slightly with worry.

'If he has, we are in trouble,' said Molly. 'So let's get this thing done quickly.'

The children both took a deep breath and began to cross the casino floor, walking swiftly from slot machine to slot machine towards the corner of the room.

However, when they got there, to their horror, another guard, shorter and brawnier than the door guard, stepped from behind a pillar to obstruct their way.

'Hello, you two. Come to see Miss Lily?' he asked.

'Erm, yes,' Micky said. 'The man at the door told us her room is round that corner.'

The guard shook his head. 'Not exactly. But I will take you to her. First, though, you have to say good afternoon to Mr Black.'

Molly gulped. Micky's eyes widened. Molly saw that her hypnotism was needed. She only hoped that Mr Black hadn't hypnotized this man so that he was *un*-hypnotizable. She wondered whether the man was suspicious enough of them to put his anti-hypnotism glasses on. She could see them poking out of his jacket's front pocket.

'And will Mr Black give us some sweets?' Micky asked, buying Molly time.

Molly looked at the man and considered his frowning forehead, his muscly body and his official-ness. Feeling what it was like to be him, she found it easy to stare up at him and tune in to him. Then Molly turned her green eyes on. At once, their hypnotic power shot towards him straight into his eyeballs. His eyes widened. Molly felt him bridle. There was some resist-ance there. But now she'd started she couldn't give up.

Micky watched as Molly's eyes strained and as the skin between her eyebrows furrowed. He saw her jaw clench as she bit her teeth together trying to concentrate.

Molly could feel a slight weakness in the man, as though the instructions that he'd been given, of *not to be hypnotized*, weren't one hundred per cent firm. Black had obviously thought that the quality of his hypnotism would be enough to bar any of Miss Hunroe or her friends from controlling his guard. But Black hadn't reckoned on Molly. Perhaps he hadn't come across a hypnotist with Molly's power before. She hoped Black's instructions weren't locked in.

As far as the guard was concerned, Molly's green, close-set eyes were like alluring beacons that he could neither ignore nor resist. Like super magnets they pulled him in. Their green throbbing pulse seemed to match the speed of his own heartbeat and fixed him to the spot.

Molly felt the fusion feeling warm her body.

'Brilliant,' she said under her breath.

'What?' Micky whispered.

'I'm getting the fusion feeling – it's a kind of warm tingling all over my body that tells me I've managed to hypnotize someone. You'll get it too when you learn. I'm looking forward to teaching you how.'

'So is he hypnotized?'

'Yup. Cooked.'

Whatever this messy-haired girl suggested the guard had to agree with her. He wanted to treat her like a princess and her friend like a prince.

'Yes, certainly,' he found himself saying. 'Lots of

sweets. Toffees, truffles, boiled sweets. I can get them for you now.'

'Don't worry about the sweets,' Molly said, keeping her eyes firmly on him. 'Micky, tell him what we want him to do.'

Micky's eyes widened for he hadn't expected this. 'What, like hypnotic instructions?' he asked.

Molly nodded. 'Make it quick.'

'Um, OK. Right. Um, so, mister, listen to this. We are going to climb through a ventilator shaft. We want you to take the cover off it, then to stand guard and put it back on when we come back through. And after that, once we are out of your sight, you will forget that you ever saw us here; you will forget that you were hypnotized.'

The man nodded obediently.

'Nice.' Molly smiled encouragingly at Micky. Then, without batting an eye, the guard led Molly and Micky to the wall where their chosen vent was. Soon, he was tugging at its cover and pulling the metal grating off it. Hurriedly the twins climbed in. The space was only just big enough for them. Micky pulled the vent cover in behind him and placed it on the inside floor of the tiny passage, so that the opening was unobstructed for their return. Outside the vent, the guard resumed his position.

'Don't kick my face,' Micky said as he crawled with Molly's trainers almost hitting his nose. 'I can't believe we're in here. It smells.' Micky sneezed.

'Shh,' Molly whispered. 'Sound travels in these pipes.'

The duct was dark now, but ahead was a glow where another grille brought in light from the casino from the floor below. And so the twins began to crawl towards this. When they reached it, Molly stopped, and since the vent went in two directions, she and Micky were able to sit, side by side.

Molly pointed through the vent to a roulette table below where three rich Chinese people sat. Two smartly dressed businessmen and their velvet-suited lady friend sat on smooth-backed stools with piles of Black-marked betting chips stacked on the green baize table before them.

'Look! That chip's worth a thousand pounds!' Molly observed. 'And she's got about fifty of them.'

'And,' Micky noticed, 'if the ball lands on a black number, she'll win quite a few more.'

The croupier, a man in a dark waistcoat and a starched shirt and black trousers, stood calm and official behind the spinning roulette wheel. The little silver ball tittled and tattled, as though gossiping with the numbers on the roulette wheel as it spun. Then it stopped. For a few seconds it was impossible to see what colour it had landed on, for the wheel was still a rotating blur.

'Red, fifty-two,' the croupier announced. Without a glimmer of emotion, he swept all the gambling chips off the numbered felt towards a slit in the table's surface, through which the chips disappeared.

'Black must make a fortune!' Molly whispered.

'Just like a one-armed bandit,' said Micky.

'Yup. He's an ugly bandit,' Molly agreed. 'Come on, let's get the book.'

The twins followed the duct up a slope and round a corner. Now it was dark again and to make things worse a cold breeze was blowing as the casino's air conditioning blew through the system. It made the tight passage like an arctic wind tunnel.

Finally they reached the grille. And, loyal to Miss Hunroe's plans, this vent looked down on Black's casino office. Molly and Micky peered down. A glass kidney-shaped lamp with a brass stem lit the room, its warm glow making the green-leather-topped desk and the panelled walls tinge with gold. A narrow slit window on to an alley outside let in a little more light from the street.

'Empty! Perfect,' Molly exclaimed, and she and Micky began easing off the metal grille.

'Bet I can punch it through,' Micky decided. 'You hold it so it doesn't fall out into the office.' Seconds later the grille had given way and Molly was quietly pulling it into the duct.

'After you,' Micky said.

Manoeuvring herself so that her legs went first, Molly dropped into the room. Micky followed and at once they set to work. Molly began to quickly lift pictures off the walls, peering behind them to see where the safe was.

'Maybe it's under the carpet,' Micky whispered, lifting the corner of a Persian rug from the floor.

Molly opened the central drawer of the desk. And, as though the heat of an oven had just hit her in the face, she stumbled backwards.

'What is it?' Micky asked worriedly. Then looking into the drawer himself he uttered a sigh. 'Wow!'

For there, almost so carelessly deposited that it seemed like it must be a trap, lay the book. Its brown leather cover, heavy with inlaid stones, had golden embossed words that read:

Hypnotism

Volume Two

The Advanced Arts

Molly ran her fingers inside the indentation in the top right-hand corner of the leather cover and remembered Miss Speal's stolen stone.

With a shaking hand and full of respect for the book, Molly opened it.

Chapter Six

Molly glanced around the room suspiciously. 'Can't believe he left it in such an obvious place. Do you think it's a trap? Or maybe the book's a fake.' Something buzzed past her nose. 'What was *that*?'

'A ladybird, Molly. You're just jumpy because you're nervous,' Micky said, jittering himself. 'They're crawling all over that plant.'

Molly pulled the heavy book from the drawer and opened it up. 'Let's check it's the real McCoy.'

The pages inside the book were yellow from age. Molly found the title page, *Hypnotism. Volume Two. The Advanced Arts*, inside, and read on.

'*By Dr Logan, published by Arkwright and Sons, 1910* . . . I can hardly believe that our great-great-grandfather wrote this,' Molly whispered. 'Can you? The first book was written in 1908. So he wrote this one two years after he wrote that.'

'It's very fancy-looking with those stones stuck on the front,' Micky observed.

'Yes, much fancier than the first volume,' Molly agreed.

'Don't expect there are many copies exactly like it,' Micky said. 'Maybe it's unique.'

'Let's hope so,' Molly replied, running her fingers along the headings. 'Do you think Black has photo-copied it? *Chapter One,*' she quietly read, *'Recapping Hypnotism Chapter Two, Time Stopping. Chapter Three, Time Travelling* . . . Ah, now this is more interesting. Look. *Chapter Four, Morphing – Animals. Chapter Five, Morphing – Humans. Chapter Six, Mind Reading. Chapter Seven, Hypno-dreaming.* Wonder what that is. *Chapter Eight, The Logan Stones. Chapter Nine, Possibilities.* Wow.' Hurriedly, Molly flicked to the first page on morphing.

Unable to control their curiosity, the twins began to read the book's instructions.

'*Morphing or body borrowing,*' read Micky, '*like hypnotism, is best learned in two steps. Just as I encouraged you to master the art of hypnotizing animals before humans, you must learn to morph into an animal before you will be able to morph into a human. It is very important that you choose your morphee with care for, if you choose an animal or person that knows about morphing, or one that has a very strong character, when you change into them they will resist your presence in their body and swallow you up entirely.*

87

Animals are usually easy subjects. It is people that you must choose very carefully. Be respectful to the creature you are morphing into for – remember! – you are borrowing their bodies. You are a body borrower. And it is imperative that you read right to the end of this chapter before you begin morphing at all!'

'Imperative? What does that mean?' Molly asked.

'Don't know. But I like the idea of being a body borrower.' Dr Logan's words ran before the twins' hungry eyes and Micky read on.

'*Bring yourself into a semi-trance.* How do you do that?'

'It's just like going all daydreamy and letting the world drop away from you.'

'Oh, OK.' Micky read on. '*Find a pattern. This may be in a wallpaper design, in some upholstery furnishings, in material or even in flooring. Clouds can also be useful for this exercise. Stare at the pattern or shape. Let it take over your visual fields until it begins to move and change. You will begin to see other forms in the pattern. Two leaves in a plant motif, for instance, may begin to look like a teapot. It is of no significance what the new picture is that you see, so long as it is there. At this point consider the animal you would like to morph into. You must be able to see it. With the image of (let us say) this leaf-made teapot, held in your mind, focus on your animal and enter its being.'*

'He makes it sound so easy,' said Molly with a chuckle of amazement.

The eager twins read on, completely oblivious to the eyes that were upon them.

Lily Black crouched in a cupboard in the office, peering out through the crack where its two doors met. Her heart was thumping against her ribcage and her breath sounded to her like a steam train in the confined space as she tried to quieten it. Her expensive white wool dress itched horribly as she was so hot.

She could make out two children in her father's office, and she could hear them.

'*Morphing to humans is much more difficult to accomplish*,' the boy was reading out in a low voice. '*It requires a controlled but also a playful mind. Follow the steps for morphing to animals. In the same way, find a trance-like state and then with intense observation of a pattern find a picture in it. However, because you are morphing to a human, you need to do something different. If that human is an adult, you must imagine them as a child; if the human is a child, imagine them as a baby; if the human is a baby, imagine them as an egg. It is very difficult to hold in your mind both the picture of (let us say again) the teapot and to also imagine an adult as a child. Do not underestimate how difficult this might be for you. Once you are seeing both images at once, the teapot and the child's face, then you can morph into the human subject. May luck be with you!*'

Lily was in two minds as to what to do about the

intruders in her father's office. She wanted to blow the whistle on them, but she couldn't because she wasn't supposed to be there either. Moments before they'd arrived, Lily herself had been reading the hypnotism book. That morning she'd found the spare key to her father's 'forbidden room'. It had been hidden under a china soap dish in his bathroom. After school she'd come to the casino and waited near the corridor outside the office until the guard there had needed to go to the loo. She'd unlocked the door at once, slipped inside and locked the door behind her. She'd found the book, and skimmed through it. Then she'd heard noise coming from the vent above the office and that had scared her stiff. Faster than she'd known she could move, she'd bolted to the cupboard and hidden there. If her father found out what she'd done, he'd go berserk. And Lily would be in such trouble that she didn't dare think of it.

But there was another reason, a more important reason. This reason was that Lily had high suspicions that the children were hypnotists like her father. Lily had no talent for hypnotism herself, but she knew all about it. She didn't want to step out into a firing line without armour. She wasn't a brave person at all, but she also wasn't an idiot.

'He makes morphing into humans sound like a piece of cake,' the boy was saying.

'Just don't morph into a piece of cake,' the girl replied with a wry smile.

As the girl spoke, something caught Lily's eye. There was movement in the high slit window behind and above the twins. To her amazement, four *cat* faces were peering down at the children. Each cat was a different breed and a different colour. Lily shrank back, feeling suddenly scared, because four cats standing on the outside sill of a slit window peering into a casino was very odd. Even though she was completely hidden, Lily felt very conspicuous, as though the cupboard door was transparent and made of glass. Now she really regretted that she'd ventured into her father's office at all. She wished she'd stayed at school to do homework.

Four cats vied for position on the narrow sill to see what was going on in Black's office. 'Just take the book now and *leave*, you idiots,' the white cat that was Miss Hunroe urged nastily. Then she noticed both Micky and Molly stop reading and turn their heads towards the door. 'You fools!' she spat.

'Someone's coming,' Molly hissed to Micky. 'Quick!'

She shut the book and slipped it back into the drawer. Grabbing the sleeve of Micky's sweatshirt, she pulled him towards the floor behind the sofa.

'We're so stupid, Molly. We should have—'

'Shh.' Molly strained her ear to the shuffling noise outside the room. Someone was opening the door.

Up on the window ledge the fluffy white cat that

was Miss Suzette and the grey Siamese that was Miss Teriyaki leaped away, leaving the white cat that was Miss Hunroe and the ginger cat, Miss Oakkton. They stood still as statues at the edge of the window, waiting to see what would happen next.

In the cupboard Lily pushed the door a centimetre open to watch Molly and Micky disappear behind the sofa, then she quickly shut it again. Her father was going to be in the room soon. If she told him about the twins, at least he'd know that they were there. But then he'd be very, very cross with her. Lily winced. She hated the idea of being scolded. He hardly paid her much attention as it was, and she didn't wanted her ration of the day to be taken up with him telling her off.

Theobald Black entered. From her hiding place, Molly caught sight of a black shoe and the bottom of his green velvet trouser leg. She bit her lip and gripped Micky's wrist tightly. Micky pointed to a couple of ladybirds on the ground. Molly gave him a puzzled look. Micky then tapped the knotted boards of the wooden floor, pointing again, this time more emphatically, to the ladybirds. Without waiting for a response, he began staring intently at the pattern on the floorboard. Molly guessed what he was doing. It was a crazy thing to be attempting but, if morphing was real, it was definitely a very neat way of getting out of the room.

Then, before she'd expected anything to happen,

Micky, amazingly, disappeared. His wrist vanished from Molly's grasp as fast as a light turning off. Instead of him, Micky's clothes lay bodyless in a heap on the floor, like a snake's moulted skin. Molly's eyes scrutinized the pile to try to see a ladybird. And there it was. It seemed to be jumping about. In fact, Molly could have sworn it was shaking its little legs as though it was doing a jig. Then it spread its wings and flew straight towards her, landing on her nose.

From her perch above, Miss Hunroe the white cat, saw all of this. She splayed her claws in annoyance. Now her eyes were trained on Molly.

Molly felt the sofa move as Black dumped his full weight on it. He began to make a call. Molly listened to his heavy, congested voice as he spoke to someone.

'I'll look for it, Terry. Probably dropped it here somewhere yesterday. Yes, then I'll get him for you.'

Molly shivered and crossed her eyes as she tried to look at the ladybird on the end of her nose. She didn't want to be caught red-handed in Black's den. He was three times bigger than her and a hypnotist. He'd be too alert to *be* hypnotized and he'd easily use his physical power to overcome her. Molly wouldn't stand a chance.

She stared at the floor. Now Molly was desperate to follow Micky's example. She concentrated on the weave of the wood of the floorboard. It was oak, streaked and knotted with dark brown marks. She focused on the pattern. She thought of nothing else. For a moment her mind faltered. All she could see were brown woody marks. There were no pictures, and she had to see *pictures*. If the book was right, that was the only way into morphing. Molly gulped, took a deep breath and breathed out slowly. With an enormous effort of will she tried to forget about Black and levitate her mind into a trance. She turned her scared feelings into careless feelings, light and easy. She let her mind drift away from the casino office.

And soon her concentration brought a result. Black's voice began to sound distant and small. Molly let her eyes linger over the pattern again. Now the lines began to move and twist as Molly's imagination opened. And a hugely obvious picture sprung out from the lines and grooves – the image of a long finger with a painted fingernail poking a worm.

Molly smiled. Now, still thinking of this picture, she concentrated on the ladybird that was walking up the wall.

The words of the book echoed in her head: *Focus on your animal and enter its being*. Molly considered the ladybird. She imagined what it felt like to have the six tiny legs. Then she thought of its curved shell with heavy folded wings on top. She let herself conjure up this feeling of what life must be like as a ladybird. She imagined antennae projecting from her head and she thought about wanting to fly. And as she thought, still holding on to the image of the finger and the worm, she dropped into the essence of the ladybird. And she threw herself forward towards the insect.

A peculiar feeling, the likes of which she had never *ever* felt, shuddered through her. And Molly the human disappeared.

Chapter Seven

For a second Molly was all air and *then* she was *in* the ladybird. It took a moment or two for her senses to adjust. She flowed into the insect's body like water into a glass, her legs multiplying, her arms vanishing and her back extending so that the creature's wings were hers. And as she looked out through her compound eyes, she saw how minute she was. The area behind the sofa was like a valley and the room was like a country. But the other strange thing that she hadn't expected was that underneath her feeling of being herself was the feeling of another being – that of the ladybird!

The ladybird's real self had been pushed down, packed down like sand into the bottom of a bucket. Every second it was squashed more as Molly's character took over its body. Molly could sense it squeaking in horror. But she was the supreme force now and though part of her knew that overcoming this other creature was wrong the other side of her understood that now she was there she had to be in charge, or *she*, Molly, would sink below the ladybird and she'd be lost underneath its spirit forever.

So, though she could sense the miniscule bleatings of the insect, she ignored them, and concentrated instead on being the ladybird herself. She remembered the book's words, about how she would be 'body borrowing', and Dr Logan's advice to be respectful. As she took possession of the insect's body, she tried to communicate apologies to it.

I'm really sorry, she found herself thinking to it in as ladybird a way as she could. *I won't be here forever. I'm just borrowing you for a bit. Thank you.*

And as she thought this the ladybird relaxed and let her in. From way down in the bottom of its brain, it looked up and saw into Molly's mind. It saw some of Molly's memories and thought processes. But its brain was far too basic to be able to understand what it was seeing. Molly on the other hand was able to comprehend the ladybird's tiny mind. It had no concept of how big the world really was in a human way. It had no perception of the world being a globe and yet it sensed where the moon and the sun were, even though neither was visible. It also had an instinct for water. Molly felt a tug from the other side of the sofa,

Where there was a glass of water. Perhaps it was on Black's desk. Molly the ladybird knew the water was there with the same certainty that she knew she was awake. She could also sense the heat coming from Theobald Black's body. It was a very strange sensation.

Then Molly nearly jumped out of her shell. A massive ladybird, like some sort of monster from a horror film, landed beside her. As suddenly as the surprise arrival of this creature had hit her, the shock subsided.

'Don't know why we're called *lady*birds, I mean I'm a boy.' Micky's voice sounded high-pitched and thin, as though it had been whizzed up in an electric voice blender. 'How many spots have I got?'

'Six, Molly replied, studying the red glossy shell of his wings.

'You sound really funny!' Micky laughed, his buzzing giggle like a sound effect off a synthesizer.

'You sound normal,' Molly replied.

'Really?'

'Of course you don't, you numbling. You're the size of a lentil!'

'Did you say hello to your ladybird? You know, sort of introduce yourself before you took over?' Micky squeaked.

'Yes. Well, it seemed like the kind thing to do,' Molly replied.

Just then there was an enormous wind-like noise in the room as Black coughed. The ground shook as he walked to his desk. He opened a drawer.

'Let's see what he's up to,' Micky suggested, his voice so comically high that Molly began to laugh.

'How?' she spluttered. Now her own voice made her laugh too. On top of this, Micky's seriousness was making the situation even funnier.

'Fly of course,' Micky said. This reply had Molly the ladybird on her knees. 'Why are you laughing?'

'I don't know! It's just that we've both turned into ladybirds and you're behaving as though . . .' Now Molly was laughing so much she could hardly talk. 'You're behaving as though it's completely normal and you sound like a cartoon character.' Molly was in stitches.

'Molly, pull yourself together,' said Micky. This made Molly laugh even more as now having a bossy ladybird tell her what to do was even funnier. 'It's probably the shock of being a ladybird,' Micky said with the coolness of a doctor analysing a patient's illness.

At this point, Molly rolled on to her back from mirth. And there she lay, laughing, with her feet up in the air.

Micky stayed quiet and after a while she calmed down. 'Now you're stuck, aren't you?' he said. 'That was a bit stupid. Haven't you ever seen how ladybirds can't get up from their backs?'

'Oh!' Molly spluttered a bit more and then tried to sober up.

'Lucky I'm here.' Micky went round to her side, and rocked her back on to her feet.

'OK, OK, I won't laugh any more,' Molly promised. 'Oh. Phew. So how do we fly?'

'It's easy,' Micky replied, 'because as a ladybird, you were born to do it. Just stretch out.' He extended his wings, and Molly copied him. 'And just kind of reach for the air, cup it in your wings and push it down to the ground with them.'

'Like thi—?' Before Molly could finish her sentence she had shot up into the air.

'Yes,' Micky said, now flapping beside her. 'It's great, isn't it?'

'Amaaaaazing!' Molly yelled back as she dived upwards. 'It's a bit like swimming underwater! Except the air is thinner and easier to push than water.'

'It's brilliant!' he shouted, laughing as he landed on the top of the sofa back.

Now they could both see Black beside his desk.

'Book, book, book,' he grunted under his breath. These words weren't actually decipherable to Molly and Micky because they now only spoke Ladybird but they could understand exactly what Black was doing. He had slipped the hypnosis book into a large black shoulder bag and was gathering his coat from the back of the chair.

'We'd better follow him,' Molly buzzed. 'Before he shuts the door.'

Micky wiggled his front legs in agreement.

From her window-ledge vantage point Miss Hunroe twitched her tail furiously.

'Black's got the book,' she hissed angrily to the fat

ginger cat. 'And, somehow, those children have morphed.'

'All is not lost,' Miss Oakkton replied. 'Zay probably read ze lesson on morphing into humans. We can at least get zat information from zem. Zay have no idea who ve are yet so ve have ze advantage. If ve can learn zose lessons from ze brats, ve are halfway to achieving our aims.'

'We just need to follow Black,' purred the fluffy Miss Suzette, who had hopped back up beside them.

'Shh,' miaowed Miss Hunroe, highly irritated by the turn of events. 'Follow me.' Turning, she leaped off the window ledge.

Micky and Molly took flight and, still a little unsteady, followed Black out of his office, slipping past him as he switched off the light. Micky, it had to be said, was better at flying than Molly. She tipped from left to right like an erratic see-saw. She found the noise of her wings much louder than she'd expected. Not as loud as the blades of a helicopter, but the whirring, flicking noise meant she could hardly hear Micky when he called over to her.

'Relax, Molly. You look so serious!'

'How can you tell?' she yelled back.

'Your antennae are too stiff!'

Molly noticed there was a distinct smile on the black glossy face of Micky the ladybird. Now it was his turn to laugh.

'OK, I'll try to relax!' she shouted, and she gave a sigh as she flew. Immediately the flight improved. 'Less turbulence now!'

Molly and Micky flew high in the casino room, dodging the massive golden chandeliers that now seemed as big as buildings. Molly looked down. The green baize card tables seemed like green fields and the casino customers were like huge giants. Ahead of them, Theobald Black's head bobbed slowly up and down as he negotiated the crowds and crossed the room.

'Quick!' Micky shouted as Black reached the revolving door. 'We have to get through.'

He dived kamikaze-like towards the revolving segment of the door with Black. Molly misjudged her speed and hit the glass. Surprisingly, the collision didn't hurt as much as she thought it might, but it did cause her to tailspin.

'Pull out, pull out!' Micky screeched, and like some sort of super-bug he jetted below Molly and budged her upwards so that she moved forward as the door turned. In the next second they were blown out into the cold night air of the street.

'Thanks! I could have been squashed there, Micky. Thank you.' Molly shuddered as she regained control of herself. Both ladybirds trod air and watched Black set off. 'The best thing to do would be to land on him, and get a free ride.'

'Good idea!'

*

Opposite the casino, standing in the marble porch of a very smart jewellery shop with his brown collar up, AH2 heard his red tracking device beep. Pulling a glove off, he quickly tugged it out of his pocket to consult it.

Molly Moon was coming out of the casino. AH2 looked up expectantly but, to his puzzlement, saw only a dark-haired man in a camel-hair coat. As he stepped out to turn right, so AH2's gadget told him that Molly Moon was also turning right. In fact, she seemed to be following him. She was *invisible*. AH2 gulped. If Molly Moon was an alien, perhaps the true alien form was like this – invisible! Why, if this was true, there might be millions of aliens living on Earth without humans having the slightest knowledge of them!

Then something else grabbed AH2's attention. Those cats! There they were again! They'd come out of the alley and were darting from shadow to shadow in pursuit of the man. AH2 waited until Black, the Molly Moon alien phantom and the cats were all a safe distance away and then he began to follow.

Up in Black's office, Lily sat in the dark cupboard. Her father had left the room and turned off the light. She thought about the cats. She wondered what the twins were doing. And she waited for them to start talking in low voices again. But they didn't. Minutes ticked by. Tick tock. Tick tock. Lily's legs began to feel cramped and the cupboard started to feel uncomfortably small.

Lily considered her predicament. She didn't want to be hypnotized by the children, yet she didn't want to sit in this cupboard all night either. It was so quiet. Were they there any more?

Full of trepidation, Lily silently and slowly opened the cupboard door and slipped out. The room was dark except for some light from the street that was coming through the slit window where the cats had been. She glanced up at the open air vent. Perhaps the two children had escaped through the vent, or maybe, just maybe, they were still behind the sofa. With her heart pounding and her mouth dry, Lily tiptoed aross the room. She could, she knew, simply unlock the door and run, but now her curiosity had got the better of her. In the semi-dark, she peered over the sofa.

The twins had gone. Vanished. Now Lily rushed back to the desk and turned the lamp on. There on the floor behind the sofa were two heaps of clothes. The clothes that the children had been wearing!

For a moment Lily was confused, then she realized what had happened. Those kids had morphed. There was no other way they would have left the room, leaving all their clothes behind.

Lily scrambled over the sofa and rummaged through the clothes. She delved in the jeans pockets for anything that might tell her who these children were. But the pockets were empty. Whoever they were, it was clear they were after the hypnotism book. Lily's temper began to stir and then a guilt began to smoulder like a fire inside her. She wished she had warned her dad when she had had the chance. Because of her, the book was in danger of being stolen. Maybe *he* was in danger.

Hundreds of miles away, Petula walked along a muddy country road. She followed her senses, for she could feel where Molly had been. It was as if there was a radar inside her head, and that Molly glowed there.

When Petula had set out, she was so full of determination and fury that this had kept her going for a good few miles. The country lanes edged with brambles and the fields full of sheep or cows or horses kept her amused for a while. She sniffed the air as she walked past unfamiliar farms where strange dogs barked. She raised her nose as she went through cottaged villages. There were hundreds of different smells, from baking to engine oil to hives and honey. How had she not guessed that the woman might be a threat? She shook her head at herself as she walked, making her collar rattle. When she stopped at puddles to drink, she saw her black reflection and frowned at herself. She always prided herself on the way she kept an eye on her friend Molly. How had her guard slipped? She dropped the pebble she'd been sucking into the puddle so that her reflection was cut up by ripples.

'Stupid!' she barked at herself.

After ten miles Petula really was beginning to flag. Her legs were aching. Fit as she was, Petula wasn't used to marathon walks.

She felt as though she had hardly made any progress. She realized that she was going to have to get some help. She sniffed the air for inspiration, and noticed that she was approaching a farm, an establishment that smelt of flowers. This one had high wooden gates. A battered sign with writing on it, and pictures of flowers, hung to the left of this. Beyond the gates was a large yard with a big corregated-roofed building and, to the side, huge greenhouses. Three men were lifting boxes into an open-backed lorry. The boxes, Petula could smell, were full of flowers. Cautiously, she went closer to get a better look. It was then that she saw a white bulldog sitting on a pile of sand. At the same time he saw Petula. After raising his nose to the air to catch her scent, he began to make his way over.

'Good afternoon. Interested in April showers?' was how he introduced himself.

And that was how Petula met Stanley.

Now Petula was forty miles outside London, sucking a small pebble in the back of the open lorry, her black ears flapping in the wind. They were en route to the flower market in London. Petula had found out that 'April showers' meant flowers. Stanley sat beside her, and all about them were boxes full of freshly cut flowers tied together with rope.

'Thank you for giving me a lift,' said Petula, watching the tarmac drop away from under the back wheels of the truck.

'My pleasure, sweet 'eart,' replied the handsome bulldog. 'Would have taken you days to walk to London.'

'It was so lucky I came across you,' said Petula. 'How often do you pick up flowers, erm, April showers for the flower market?'

'Well, it depends. My man drives out to the country dependin' on what people are buyin'. They like their April showers in the Old Smoke.'

'The Old Smoke?'

'That's cockney rhymin' slang for London.'

'So you come from London?'

'Oh yeah. Born and bred. My man is a barrow boy.'

Petula frowned and put her nose up to the dark late afternoon air to feel for Molly. 'Is the market in the centre of London?' she asked.

'Not far. Near the 'Ouses of Parliament. Just the other side of the river.' Stanley scratched his ear with his back paw.

'How long do you think it will take to get there?' Petula asked with a shiver.

'Oh, I dunno, we've covered quite a bit of ground already. I reckon it'll only be another forty minutes. You look like you're a bit taters in the mould.'

'Taters in the mould?'

'Potatoes in the mould. Cold.'

Petula nodded. 'I am. It's a bit windy out here.'

'Wish you had told me, luv. Could 'ave easily helped you with that. Wait there.'

'Don't worry, I'm not going anywhere,' Petula said. She watched as Stanley dragged an old sack from behind a crate. He nudged it around her body. Petula smiled. 'Thanks.'

The bulldog watched her. Then he asked, 'So, these dustbin lids that you know that are in trouble, you say you can feel where they are?'

'Dustbin lids?'

'Kids.'

'Oh yes. Yes, I can. And the closer we get to them, the stronger the feeling of them gets.'

'You must have a strong connection with them then. And this woman that you say has taken them, can you feel her?'

'No, I've only come across her once. Wish I'd bitten her ankles when I met her, and drew blood. She smells of roses and thorns.'

'Well, she sounds a babbling brook,' Stanley commented.

'A babbling brook?'

'A crook. I mean, that's downright wicked, stealin' a couple of dustbin lids. But don't you worry now, Petula. I've got a friend who's joinin' us when we get to the market. The arrangement was we were going for a good ol' sniff about. But now plans have changed. He knows central London like the back of his paw and he's got a nose like a hound on him. We'll have a butcher's with 'im.'

'A butcher's?'

'A butcher's hook, a *look* – we'll have a look for your friends with him. Magglorian will help you find them.'

'I hope he can,' Petula said. 'You see it's all a bit more complicated. Erm. Do you know what hypnotism is, Stanley?'

Chapter Eight

Miss Oakkton the ginger tomcat was out of breath. She watched the white cat that was Miss Hunroe as it slipped ahead chasing Mr Black, and she side-stepped into the entrance of a closed delicatessen shop. In a few seconds she had materialized back into her human self, this time in an olive-coloured, ankle-length tweed coat with a hat and bag to match, carrying two baskets. The tomcat sat dazed by her feet. Miss Oakkton put down her baskets and put the ginger tom into one of them. She reached into her pocket and pulled out a tortoiseshell pipe and an ivory tobacco box. Packing the pipe with tobacco, she lit it. For a few minutes she stood smoking, enjoying the peace and quiet. Then her phone rang. Lazily, she pulled it from her bag.

'Zank you, Miss Teriyaki. Yes, I vill be zhere in a few minutes . . . No, I am not smoking my pipe! What an idea! I stopped because a voman picked me up . . .

Well, of course not! No vun has picked *you* up, Miss Teriyaki, because your cat is not as attractive as mine . . . You don't need to nag. I am coming.' Tutting, Miss Oakkton snapped her phone shut. 'Interfering nag!' Then she refilled her pipe and lit it again. As she exhaled, a cloud of smelly smoke filling the shop alcove, a teenager drove his motorbike and sidecar into a parking space in front of her. Miss Oakkton stepped towards him.

'Excuse me, young man,' she began. The biker pulled the keys from the ignition slot and looked up. Immediately Miss Oakkton's large eyes had a hold on him. He couldn't look away, and for some reason he felt he ought to do whatever this big muscly woman said. So, when she asked, he passed his motorbike keys to her.

'Now get off zat bike,' she said. The teenager did as he was told. Miss Oakkton put her two baskets, one with a cat into it, into the sidecar, and climbed on to the motorbike. It sank down under her weight. She started the engine. Then, laughing like a woman fresh out of the madhouse, she revved up the engine, and drove away.

Flying along a London street on a blustery winter's night as a ladybird is difficult, as the tiny Molly and Micky were discovering. Huge double-decker buses driving past them made cyclone-like swirls of air that buffeted and knocked them. Then one gust blew to their advantage. It caught up with them and cast them forward inches from Black. With a few sturdy flaps of their bug wings, the twins had soon landed on his right shoulder, and were standing knee-deep in the fuzz of his camel-hair coat.

Underneath them, Black's giant body parted the night air with ease. His massive feet thudded on the pavement.

Around, the streets were heavy with light. Beautifully designed shop windows with dummies dressed in the latest fashions and photographs of glamorous people having fun in the same clothes behind, shone out into the night. Late-night shoppers passed Black, their arms laden with bags, some brushing shoulders with him, so that Molly and Micky had to grip the camel-hair strands with all their might.

Cafés glittered invitingly, cars with white headlights and red brake lights beamed brightly. Red, orange and green traffic signals blinked. And everywhere the noise of engines hummed – buses, lorries, cars, motorbikes, accompanied by the sound of bicycle bells. Clonk, clonk, shuffle, thud, tap went the people's feet on the street.

'The human being certainly dominates the world!' Micky observed.

'I know. It's frightening when you're only four millimetres high, isn't it?' Molly replied, wiggling her antennae.

As they settled down again, a mountainous building

loomed up. Its stucco walls and pillars rose into the sky to a lofty grey slate roof. Dozens of windows punctuated each floor. They looked like eyes, and hanging underneath them were their balconies that looked like wrought-iron mouths. On the wall, in shiny gold, was the sign, THE GLITZ RESTAURANT. Two torches with flames in their sockets burned either side of it. A large window followed the corner of the building around so that the restaurant faced both the hat shop on one corner and a bus stop on the other.

Black paused before entering. He swung his bag off his left shoulder, tugged his coat from his arms and, seeing two ladybirds on his lapel, brushed them off with his hand. And then he entered the Glitz.

Molly felt like she had been charged by an elephant. She tumbled through the air as light as a lentil and as helpless as a frog in a flood. She tried to flap her wings and regain her balance but instead she flipped round and round so that the world was a blur. Then finally she hit the wall of the entrance. With crumpled wings she fell to the ground and bounced from her back to her front legs. Dizzy and stunned, she lay still.

A few minutes passed as Molly's senses slowly came back to her. She shook out her wings, then packed them into her shell-like outer layer, and checked her body for injury. Surprisingly she was fine – a bit shaken, but not hurt. Now she looked worriedly about for Micky.

Micky had landed closer to the pavement where

dangerous feet trod past and he was spinning round on his back. Molly scuttled towards him and with her face under his wings heaved him over.

'I don't like being a . . .' Micky didn't finish his sentence for a massive feathered monster was standing over them. A scruffy, mangy pigeon stared down at Molly and Micky, cocking its head as it contemplated the two tasty morsels.

With a sudden vicious movement it lunged. Its beak hit the paving stone between the two ladybirds, grazing Molly's left wing.

'Oh no . . .' Micky was speechless.

'Hide!' Molly screamed.

Micky and Molly dived for cover where a small broken piece of masonry had left a tiny hole in the wall. But even in the crack they weren't safe, for the pigeon was hungry. It began to peck relentlessly at the stone, determined to oust its supper.

'I don't want to be eaten by a *pigeon*!' Micky screamed. 'I don't want to be chomped up by a . . . by a . . . beeeeak.'

'Just . . . just control yourself, Micky,' said Molly, squishing into the hole as far as she could. Then another beak began to peck at their hiding place too.

'Two of them! Jeepers!' Micky screeched. 'You know birds are related to dinosaurs! T-rexes, velociraptors, allosauruses!'

'Calm down, Micky,' Molly pleaded, starting to feel desperate herself.

'What do you mean calm down? Those beaks are like car-sized pickaxes.'

Molly's insides lurched with fear.

Calm. Calm. Molly tried to find some amidst the terror of the moment.

'I know!' she gasped. We should just morph *into* them!'

'What?'

'Morph, you ningbat. Like before.'

'But . . . but we have to find a pattern – there isn't one.'

'Yes, there is,' Molly gulped. 'Look the wall.'

Micky raised his eyes. It was true, the stone was covered with green mildew.

'OK, OK, OK,' he stuttered. 'OK. I'll try to turn into the scruffy one.'

Molly and Micky grew quiet and focused for they knew their lives depended upon it. Both stared at the green algae, ignoring the horrible pecking that threatened to snap them up. Molly saw a picture first. The strange pattern of algae began to look like a dog. Immediately holding this image to the side of her mind, she thought of what it was to be a pigeon. She looked at the beady cold eyes of the bird that pecked so intently. She considered its feather and wings.

And, amazingly, she found it quite easy to find the essence of pigeon.

Goodbye and thank you! she managed to think to the ladybird.

For a milli-moment she was nothing. Then she got the watery 'tipping' feeling as her mind and her spirit washed into the pigeon. The creature stopped pecking. Like a gadget suddenly without batteries, it stood stock-still. Its pea-brained mind registered Molly's arrival. For a moment, it attempted to push her out. But its efforts were a futile grapple.

In the next second, Molly eclipsed its personality and had taken charge of its body. She flexed her new scrawny bird legs with claws on the end and stretched out her muscly wings. She peered out of its beady black eyes over her new pale, dirty beak. Below her, the lady-bird whose body she'd borrowed stood stunned as it recovered from Molly's body borrowing.

Molly shook her feathery self and observed the inside of the pigeon's mind. She saw rooftops and streets as though from a bird's-eye view. She saw a great white sculpture of a woman with no arms, on which the pigeon liked to sit on sunny days.

Then she noticed that the other pigeon was still pecking at the ladybirds and knew that Micky hadn't managed the morph yet. Quickly, Molly gave the scruffy pigeon a sharp jab in the neck. For a moment she thought the creature would peck her back, since he was bigger than her. But instead it went very quiet.

'Is that you, Micky?' Molly asked.

'Just made it,' the scruffy pigeon replied, his voice a coarse trill. 'Let's fly up to that corner balcony before we get into any more trouble.' With the ladybird flying lessons under their belts, the twins flapped up to a first-floor balcony.

'Scary being a ladybird, wasn't it?' said Micky as they landed. 'Suppose it's fine if you're on a rose bush in the summer, eating aphids.'

'Yes . . .' Molly agreed, folding her wings. 'And then, scary to be an aphid.'

Below, the traffic flowed past – a river of machinery.

'You know we're in trouble, Molly, don't you?' Micky suddenly said. 'We can morph from animal to animal, but we don't know how to morph back into *ourselves*. I mean, we have to choose the creature we want to morph into, don't we? But Molly and Micky, the *real* us, aren't here . . . The question is, where *are* our bodies, Molly?' A cold wind ruffled the feathers on his neck. Instinctively, he puffed himself out to keep warm.

'Maybe,' Molly said, 'we have to morph into a *human* first and then perhaps we'll feel how to do it.'

Molly peered down at the two streets below. Near the hat shop was an alley where she could see some rats foraging near a smelly bin. She looked down at the main street.

'That old couple waiting for a bus,' she said. 'How about them? You be the man; I'll be the woman.'

The old woman was dressed in a brown and yellow tweed coat with a green home-knitted wool hat on.

She was sucking on a boiled sweet and was clutching her brown handbag tightly with mittened hands. She had a weather-beaten face, pink cheeks and little brown eyes that glittered behind round spectacles and her grey hair was as thin as candyfloss.

The old man wore a flat dark blue beret and a nylon raincoat. Molly saw that imagining the old woman as a child wasn't going to be as easy as she'd thought. She wondered whether mind reading would help, so pulling her thoughts together Molly sent out the message:

Old lady, what are you thinking? However, to Molly's disappointment, a bubble didn't appear above the woman's head. It was as if mind reading was something Molly could only do in her Molly Moon body. Molly shrugged her bird shoulders. She supposed it didn't really matter. The book hadn't said that mind reading would help a person to morph.

'Are you ready?' Micky the pigeon asked. Molly nodded. And they both began. Molly looked about for a pattern. The bus shelter was good as it had glass on the front of it that was stained with old watermarks. The drips definitely looked like mountains. Holding these in her mind, Molly did her best to imagine the old woman as a child. She would have been smaller and thinner, Molly thought, and much less wrinkly, of course. She would be wearing a child's coat and hat, with a satchel instead of a bag. Molly's eyes considered the old lady's face and drank it in. And as though she had a magic rubber, her imagination erased the crow-lines around her eyes and the puppet-like 'marionette' lines round her mouth. The creases of her brow and the puckering round her chin dissolved and the old lady's mottled skin was replaced by the fresh complexion of a child.

Molly pulled the image of the water-stained mountain range into the centre of her mind. And as the two visions merged Molly aimed her being at the old lady. She felt herself shiver and quiver and suddenly she lost all sensation of her claws, her wing tips and her tail.

'Goodbye and thank you!' Molly managed to cry as she whizzed away. In a split second she couldn't feel her pigeon body at all. But this moment was miniscule for in the next the pouring feeling swished through Molly.

'EEK!' the old lady shrieked.

Molly had done it! She'd morphed into a *human* body. The idea of it was so miraculous and the sensation so spectacular that for a moment Molly was half stunned with amazement.

'Are you all right, dear?' her husband asked concernedly.

Molly floundered for a second as the shock of her situation overwhelmed her, then, seeing that the old woman's personality was stronger than she had reckoned, she concentrated hard. Molly felt like she was wrestling with the pensioner's spirit, trying to pin her down. Molly was winning, but not entirely. Finally, Molly took control and the woman's personality was submerged. As soon as Molly felt she was in charge, she thought apologies to her, explaining what was happening. At once, she felt the person who she was in relax.

Molly felt strange. It was extraordinary to be in another human body, and it was an extra shock to be in an *old* one. Her bones were creaky and stiff and she could hardly register her muscles. Her bottom was fat and bulgy and it was very peculiar having two lumps on the front of her chest.

On top of the physical sensations were the mental ones. Molly was at once familiar with the woman's life and her personal history. She didn't see every memory at once, of course, for there were billions of them tucked away in the old lady's mind. But Molly knew that she was called Sofia and that the man beside her was Wilf, her dear husband, whom she had married fifty-four years ago in a church in Rome.

'I said, are you all right, Sofia?' her husband repeated.

Brought to her senses, Molly was now in the moment. She saw two buskers, one with a violin, the other with a flute, who were sitting near the bus stop filling the evening air with their music, and she saw the man, Wilf, looking concernedly at her.

'Yes, I'm fine,' Molly as Sofia said, an Italian accent rounding her words. 'I think something stung me, that's all.'

'Stung you? Where?'

'On my nose,' Molly said. Then she added, 'Um, are you there, Micky?'

'Micky? What are you talking about, Sofia?'

'Nothing, nothing, you just look like Micky Mouse in that hat.'

The man looked very confused.

Molly glanced upwards, then saw a scruffy pigeon flying towards her. It flapped over and landed on her arm. She knew at once it was Micky.

'Good lord, Sofia,' her husband exclaimed. 'Get that filthy bird off you.' He lunged towards Micky the pigeon, who fluttered upwards and then back down to perch again on Molly's shoulder.

'Don't worry, Wilf. The poor bird's just being friendly. Now I must use the lavvy in that restaurant, dear. Please wait here.'

Without waiting for Wilf's reaction, and still with Micky the pigeon on her shoulder, Molly waddled to the kerb. She looked left and right, and crossed the road.

A mile and a half away, the truck that was carrying Petula and her new friend, Stanley, pulled into the Nine Elms Flower Market. It drove round the vast covered building and parked. The giant plastic electric doors were in operation, opening and shutting as stallholders wheeled trolleys piled high with boxes of flowers inside. Stan's driver climbed out of his truck, and Petula and Stanley the bulldog heard him greet an old friend.

'How are ya? Cor, me legs aint 'alf stiff. Don't feel like unloadin' this lot now. Fancy a pint?'

'That's the spirit.'

'See you later, Stanley. Good dog.' And then their voices receded into the distance.

Stanley pushed his nose under the tarpaulin at the side of the lorry to check they'd gone. 'Here we go, luv,' he said to Petula. 'Squeeze past 'ere and we'll get you sorted.' He disappeared past some flower boxes and hopped off the lorry. Petula followed him. After a leap on to a bale of cardboard, and a jump on to a crate full of flowerpots, she was down. Stanley had already found his friend.

'How long you been standin' here all on yer Jack Moss?'

'Not long,' said his friend, a small brown and white Jack Russell with a cheeky face and an amused look in his eye.

'Do your people know you're out?'

'The boys were playing a card game with their dad. Let myself out of the dog flap. See you found yourself a girlfriend, Stan.'

'I'd be so lucky! This is Petula. Petula, meet Magglorian. He's got a good loaf a' bread and he'll be able to 'elp ya.' Magglorian smiled and nodded. Petula smiled back, a little bit embarrassed by the introduction.

'"Loaf of bread" is "head", in rhyming cockney,' Magglorian said. 'Talking to Stan here can be like talking to someone who's speaking double Dutch.' Magglorian laughed. 'Nice to meet you, Petula. So how can I help?'

'I'm trying to find the children that I live with. They've disappeared,' Petula began. 'A woman has taken them.'

Magglorian's eyes widened.

And so Petula told Magglorian what had happened. Magglorian frowned and shook his head so that his brown ears flapped. 'Hmmmm.'

When Petula got to the bit about hypnotism, she saw Magglorian give Stanley an 'I see we've got a right one here' look, which annoyed her.

'Look, mister, you can believe what you like,' Petula said. 'I haven't got time to waste trying to persuade you.' She turned to Stanley. 'Thanks for the lift. I should be just fine now. Really, thank you so much, Stanley. Goodbye.'

Petula didn't give Magglorian another glance. She turned and began walking away.

'Magglorian, how come you did that?' Stanley asked, amazed by his friend's behaviour.

'It is a bit far-fetched, Stanley. Come on, you have to admit it – it is a bit crazy.'

'Well, I believe her,' Stanley said. 'And I'm going to help her.' With that Stanley trotted after Petula.

Magglorian watched them go. Then he barked. 'Wait! I'm coming too.' He ran after the other dogs. 'I'm sorry, Petula,' he said, panting, as he arrived. 'I'd search the world over for the boys who own me if I ever lost them. Let me help you find your friends.'

A Glitz doorman in a smart black cap and a red suit with gold braid on its shoulders opened the door to the hotel for Molly the old woman. Molly thanked him, adding, 'Is this the way to the restaurant, young man?'

She hoped that was where Black had gone. She felt very out of place in her shabby coat and her old-fashioned cobbled leather boots, but knew from experience that if you act like you are supposed to be somewhere people usually believe you. As the doorman pointed down the lavishly carpeted orange passage, thronged with golden lamps, Molly noticed Micky, who was still a pigeon, hop behind him.

'Thank you very much,' she said gratefully, and started making her way along to the arched entrance of the restaurant at the end of the corridor. Molly marvelled at what it was like to be eighty-two. Her legs were stiff as wood and her joints felt like bark. As for the woman's memories, Molly could tell that she had only seen a fraction of them. The others, as though in a thousand-mile-deep glacier, were hidden in the deep waters of her mind.

'May I help you?' a slim waitress asked, eyeing Molly's woolly hat.

'A table for one, please,' Molly demanded.

'Do you have a booking, madam?' the waitress enquired.

'No,' Molly replied, realizing that the waitress was about to refuse her entrance. 'And don't give me any of that "we're full" nonsense. I can see lots of empty tables.'

'But, madam, all these tables are reserved,' the waitress replied, sneering slightly.

'What? I'm not good enough for this place? Is that it?' Molly said, and immediately she turned to her hypnotic powers for help. 'Look into my eyes.'

Unfortunately, nothing happened. Just as Molly couldn't mind-read in another body, neither could she hypnotize.

'I'm sorry, madam, really we are full,' the smug woman retorted.

'Everything all right, dear?' Sofia's husband, Wilf, had followed her inside. He stood, looking very out of place in his cap and long black coat. Molly noticed Micky the pigeon hop behind a cheese trolley. She smiled reassuringly at the old man.

'Perfectly all right, Wilf. I think we'll take the table over there.' Pushing past the waitress, Molly gripped her handbag and stepped towards a table. Immediately she saw Theobald Black sitting near the window. He was deep in conversation with a young, smartly dressed, beautiful, auburn-haired woman whose wrists, fingers and ears were adorned with gold and diamonds. *Her* body, Molly realized, was the one she ought to be inside, because she was sitting very, very close to Black's bag, and inside the bag, of course, was the hypnotism book.

'Madam, I'm so sorry,' the snooty waitress began to pester. She smiled but her expression was false and an unkind look came from her eyes.

'Oh, go and stuff your nostrils,' Molly said to her. 'Who do you think you are, Little Miss Poncy?'

The head waiter now stepped towards them. Molly could see that the situation was getting sticky. She didn't want to attract Black's attention, so this wasn't good. But then the head waiter said to the waitress, 'Fiona, this lady is a friend of mine. She and her husband are going to have supper here, and it's on the house.' At once Molly realized that it was Micky inside the head waiter's body.

Fiona, the mean waitress, looked stunned, as though she had just swallowed a peeled boiled egg, in one gulp.

'That means free!' wheezed Wilf in amazement, winking at Molly.

'Yes, sir. Eat and drink whatever you want,' the head waiter replied.

In the portico of the hat shop outside sat the white Burmese cat, Miss Hunroe. Beside her, in their cat forms, were Miss Oakkton and Miss Teriyaki.

They stared across the road at the restaurant window and watched Black and his dining companion.

On the other side of the street was the bus stop where AH2 had just arrived. He was consulting his red tracking machine. Molly Moon, it told him, was inside the grand building opposite. He rubbed his fingers together in excitement. If he played his cards right, he was on his way to making ground-breaking history.

Chapter Nine

Molly hid her old-lady face behind the wine list. She didn't want Wilf to see what she was doing.

'Well, what a choice!' he was muttering. 'Foie gras, caviar!'

Molly stared at the floral-pattern wallpaper to the left of her.

With its twisting vines it was difficult to find another picture there, but Molly knew she had to if she wanted to morph again. So, staring stubbornly, she waited for a shape to emerge. All at once Molly saw a picture in the flowers. A strange-shaped umbrella. Shutting her eyes to make it like a photograph in her mind, she turned her attention to the beautiful, rich woman opposite Black. Her auburn hair was thick and glossy as though she'd just walked out of a shampoo advert. Her slim face had a Caribbean tan and she wasn't wearing much make-up. She had lovely big brown eyes and as they twinkled Molly saw how they must have looked thirty years before.

Molly's imagination, like some sort of magical camera, plumped out the woman's face. Her hair turned lighter and Molly even conjured up the idea of some pigtails. She turned her designer suit into a simple school uniform. The vision was complete. Now juggling this picture with the image of the wallpaper umbrella at the same time, Molly was able to lift herself out of Sofia towards Black's dinner partner.

Goodbye and thank you! she managed to think to Sofia before she left.

As Molly's spirit and personality arrived, the woman sank from her position of control. She didn't stand a chance. With a focused strength, Molly pushed her out of the way, and down. As though from the bottom of a pool, Lady Storkhampton, for that was the woman's name, looked up at who had snatched her body and mind. She saw it was a girl, a girl with a mission.

'My name is Molly,' said the girl. 'I'm borrowing your body for a little while. I won't harm it. I'm sorry if this might make you feel that you have gone a bit mad afterwards.' Lady Storkhampton's body bent forward slightly, like a limp puppet, then Molly took the helm.

*

Two tables away, Sofia, now in control of her body and mind again, shook her head as she took in her surroundings.

'Ooh, Wilf, I just had the oddest experience . . .'

'Lady Storkhampton?' Black frowned at her over his oysters. In his hand he held a piece of paper – a cheque, in fact, that Lady Storkhampton had given to him. Molly took a deep breath. The last thing she wanted was to give herself away. She had no idea whether Black was a mind reader and she didn't want to arouse his suspicion enough that he might try probe Lady Storkhampton's mind.

'Oh, I think the lettuce I ate was a bit too peppery,' she explained, eyeing her plate of prawns and sitting upright with a big smile.

'Do you want some water?' Black poured Lady Storkhampton a glassful.

'Thank you,' said Molly, her accent clear and posh. As Molly drank some water, she got her bearings. Like a person standing in a landscape looking at the surroundings, Molly looked about Lady Storkhampton's mind to see who she was. She was the daughter of a very wealthy ship builder. She was married to an even richer man who owned vast swathes of land in England. She bred miniature horses and kept an aviary full of exotic birds. She spoke four languages, French, Italian, Spanish and Russian, and she loved to ski. Her body felt very healthy, Molly thought. This was because she practised martial arts every day.

'Lady Storkhampton, this really is exceedingly generous of you!' Black was saying. 'Five hundred thousand pounds!' I don't think we have *ever* had such a generous donation! The children's homes will be hugely helped by this.' Black folded the cheque that Lady Storkhampton had just written to him, and slipped it into the inside pocket of his green velvet jacket.

Molly was appalled. So, Black was tricking people into giving him money for *children's homes that didn't exist*! This made Molly really angry. She knew about children's homes first hand. She'd lived in an orphanage until she'd been ten and a half. She knew just how decrepit and run down they could be. Hers had been the worst of all. It made her furious that Mr Black was creaming off this generous woman's money, money that might have gone to *real* orphanages. If this was how Black used hypnosis, she thought, what might he do once he'd learned to morph? She looked down at the prawns on her plate and felt sick. Now wasn't the time to argue. Her main objective, her absolute number one job now, was to get the hypnotism book off him. She tried to judge whether Black had hypnotized the rich heiress or not but Molly found it difficult because she couldn't feel the woman's will at all since it was buried underneath her own.

With huge control of her temper, Molly looked up and smiled sweetly.

'It's my pleasure,' Molly said, her new voice crisp,

each word flowing from her mouth perfectly formed. Then she nudged her handbag so that it fell on the floor. Before Black could offer to get it she dived below the table to retrieve it.

'Got it!' she exclaimed.

Underneath the tablecloth, Molly saw Black's bag. It was close to his leg near the window, its strap hanging loose on the ground. Molly retrieved her handbag and came up for air.

'That was a lightning move!' Black commented admiringly.

'The martial arts keep me alert,' Molly replied. She took another sip of water, and tried to think of a clever way to get Black's bag.

'I'm visiting the Queen tomorrow,' Black said, conversationally.

Molly felt her eyebrows rise. 'The Queen!'

'Yes. She's a close friend of your mother's, isn't she?'

'Indeed.' Molly edged her silk-stockinged leg across the floor to try to hook the strap handle of Black's bag with her foot. In doing so, her body slipped slightly down in the seat. She hoped that to Black her change of posture would simply look like she was relaxing.

'She's given me a morning appointment. Eleven o'clock. I am hoping she will get involved with my children's charity too.' Black smiled.

Molly couldn't believe it! So Black was going right to the top to get rich. It was well known that the Queen of Britain was one of the richest women in the world!

Then the toe of her shoe caught hold of the bag's strap. Without letting Black know what she was doing, Molly began to pull it across the floor towards her.

Black's mobile phone went off. He ignored it.

'Don't you think you ought to answer that?' Molly suggested, eager to have Black's attention diverted. 'I don't mind if you do.'

Black shrugged. 'I suppose I should. I have been ignoring it for the last twenty minutes.' He pulled a slim black phone from his outside jacket pocket. 'Theobald Black speaking.'

Molly felt the bag's weight as she tugged it towards her. She shifted herself more upright on her seat to haul it up.

'You were *where*?' Black was saying into the phone. He looked very concerned. '*What* were you doing in there?' The person on the phone was now gabbling away and as they spoke, Black's expression changed. He glanced worriedly from the waiter, to the other customers in the room, to people on the street outside. Then his eyes fell upon four cats sitting in front of a letterbox. Oddly, the animals appeared to be looking directly at him.

'Cats?' he said disbelievingly. His eyes came back to his table and Lady Storkhampton. Was it his imagination, or was she squirming in her seat?

On the other end of the line, Lily was frantic. 'Why didn't you answer your phone? You are just *so stupid*.

133

You probably saw it was me and ignored the call like you always do. I've been trying to get you for ages. I didn't follow you to start with because I was scared you'd be cross with me. And I was scared of the children. But then I realized it was important. They're after the book. They disappeared. And those cats were spooky! And who knows where they are now. Don't trust anyone! Do you hear me?'

Black nodded. 'I can't chat now, Lily. Thank you,' he said as calmly as he could. 'I'll meet you at the hotel later. Thank you. Goodbye.'

Now on high alert, Black automatically reached for his bag. The strap slipped off Molly's foot.

Micky the head waiter, who had been hovering nearby, saw Black lift his bag on to the banquette beside him. He'd noticed a sudden change in Black – he'd seen how, after his telephone call, he'd glanced nervously about the restaurant. Micky's instincts told him that Molly and he ought to get out of the restaurant now. So, taking a pen from his waistcoat, he quickly found a menu to write on.

'I'll meet you near the bus stop,' he wrote on the menu beside the list of puddings. Then he stepped up to their table.

'Finished, madam?' he asked.

'Yes, I don't feel quite up to prawns today,' Molly answered.

'Maybe something sweet will do the trick, madam,' Micky cajoled. 'May I recommend the iced berries and the white chocolate sauce? Definitely worth *a look*.' He pointed to the list of puddings and to his urgent message.

'Thank you,' Molly replied, at the same time reading his note. 'What a good suggestion. Why not? Mr Black, please excuse me, I need to go to the powder room.'

Beside the bus stop, AH2 held his red gadget up to where he suspected Molly Moon the alien was, and he inspected its reading. Extraordinarily, the glamorous woman standing up in the Glitz restaurant seemed to now be the body of Molly Moon. This was very, very odd. So the alien could disappear into thin air and then change into different bodies! This was beyond AH2's wildest dreams. This was the stuff of science fiction. He was incredibly excited. Part of him was bubbling with delight because he could hardly believe that he, Malcolm Tixley, was actually making this historical discovery. The other part of him was steaming with exhilaration because all he had ever really wanted to do in life was *meet* an alien. And there was one, calmly having dinner.

He wondered what to do. If he spoke to the alien, perhaps he would be able to persuade it to communicate with him. *He* could be the alien's contact with Earth people. He could be the world expert. This would be very, very interesting. And as for the glory! AH2 could imagine his picture on the front page of *every* newspaper in the world! Maybe a movie would be made about his life!

Then his gadget started to bleep and putter. Its silver coordinates were rejigging. It was telling him that the Molly Moon alien was moving through the building opposite. And now the readings showed that the Moon creature was leaving the Glitz restaurant. He looked up. The glamorous woman was crossing the road towards him. A waiter was by her side. They were already standing on the traffic island mid way! AH2 gulped. Did the alien know about him? He'd made up his mind. He prepared himself to speak with it.

Miss Hunroe, now back in her human form, stood with the collar of her thick fur coat wrapped up high round her neck. On her head was a heavy Russian fur hat, so that very little of her face could be seen. Beside her stood Miss Suzette in a cream frilly cashmere cape with a collar; Miss Teriyaki in a red patent mac with a smart silver crutch under her arm and Miss Oakkton in her long green coat with two baskets of cats.

'You,' Miss Hunroe said to Miss Teriyaki and Miss Suzette, 'will follow Theobald Black when he comes out of the hotel.' Miss Oakkton passed Miss Suzette the basket with the Siamese and the Persian cats in it. 'And remember,' Miss Hunroe warned. 'He is far more masterful a hypnotist than either of you and will turn you to putty before you can blink. Don't attempt to challenge him or hypnotize him. Miss Oakkton and I will deal with the Moon children.'

'What a good idea,' gushed Miss Suzette.

'Very sensible,' said Miss Teriyaki, her irritation with Miss Suzette showing in her voice.

Miss Hunroe nodded at them. 'Don't argue; it's not attractive.' Then she turned to cross the road.

Miss Teriyaki sneered at Miss Suzette. 'Why am I always stuck with you?'

The head waiter put his arm under Molly's. Once over the street, they began to walk as quickly as they could along the pavement away from the Glitz. But as they passed the bus stop, a man in a dark anorak obstructed them.

'Excuse me,' he said, addressing Molly as Lady Storkhampton. 'I'd like to introduce myself. I am AH2. My real name is Malcolm Tixley.' He gave a little bow. 'Do not be alarmed. You can trust me. I know your secret and I want you to confide in me. I want to be your contact on Earth.'

Molly looked bewilderedly at Micky.

'I am a sympathetic human being,' AH2 insisted. 'You can tell me all about your planet, your own species, your purpose here on Earth. I will keep the information confidential until a mutually agreed time when you want to talk to the other Earthlings.'

'Listen,' Molly said. 'I'm not sure what you are talking about. Please leave me alone.'

But the man in front of her shook his head and put his hand on her shoulder. He was beginning to look desperate.

'Get *off* me,' Molly said, twisting away from his grip. This time the man grabbed both her shoulders.

Miss Hunroe was almost across the road when she saw the strange situation in front of her. She drew closer.

'You *must* confide in me, Molly Moon,' AH2 hissed. 'It's imperative that you do.'

Miss Hunroe heard the name and was at once absolutely alert. Her mind catapulted. Who was the man ahead? Was the rich woman the Moon girl? Was the waiter beside her the Moon boy? Had they learned how to morph into *humans*?

Miss Hunroe faltered and her heartbeat quickened as she considered what to do. Amazingly, the twins had already mastered the art of morphing. And so they had the secret that she was desperate for. Miss Speal as a child had only learned animal morphing and so this was all she had been able to teach Miss Hunroe. Morphing into other *humans* was so much more useful! If she could get the secret from Molly or her brother, she'd be able to easily get the hypnotism book from Black. And then, why then! . . .

Micky could see that things were getting out of hand. He didn't want this madman drawing attention to them.

'Police! Help!' he yelled, seeing a police car crawling nearby.

138

In a moment two officers had jumped out of their car. They pushed past the people near the bus stop and seized AH2.

'All right, all right, what's this all about?'

AH2 hardly saw the policemen. He clung on to Lady Storkhampton as though his life depended upon it.

'GET OFF ME!' Molly shouted. 'YOU'RE CRAZY! GET OFF!'

The police snapped two handcuffs on to the young man's wrists and restrained him.

'You don't understand!' AH2 cried desperately to them. 'This woman is an alien.'

'I'm sure she is,' said the first officer. 'You can come and tell us all about it down at the station. With that they began to push AH2 towards their car.

We've got to change,' Micky said to Molly. He pulled Lady Storkhampton away from the police and the people about them, and swiftly he found a gap in the traffic. Darting, between cars, he and Molly crossed the road once more.

'Excuse me, you two,' called one of the policemen after them, waving a notebook at Lady Storkhampton. 'You need to come back to give me a statement.'

Micky and Molly ignored him and hurried into the side street near the hat shop.

Miss Hunroe left her hiding place to follow them but for her, negotiating the traffic was difficult and crossing impossible.

'Ve vill have to push srough,' said Miss Oakkton,

returning from another secret cigar break.

Looking ahead, Molly saw the alley where she'd spotted the bins and the rats before.

'Quick, Micky!' she said, 'Follow me. I've had an idea.'

Theobald Black was now leaving the hotel. His eyes moved to the small crowd that had gathered on the other side of the street where a police car had stopped. One of the policemen was talking to a man inside the car who was shouting like a lunatic. Black did not feel comfortable at all. First Lady Storkhampton had disappeared and now there was this trouble outside. He turned his attention to getting home as quickly as possible.

AH2, Malcolm Tixley, sat in the police car. He watched the woman in the fur hat and her large companion with her basket of cats as they made it across the road. Then his eyes darted across the street to look for the glamorous woman who was Molly Moon. There she was, with her chaperon, crouching on the floor in an alley near some rubbish bins. AH2 held his breath, expecting something to happen. He watched as the fur-hatted woman and her friend trotted towards the bins. Suddenly the gadget in his pocket began to bleep. His eyes shot towards the woman who had been eating in the Glitz and the waiter beside her. Simultaneously they both slumped to the ground.

Miss Hunroe and Miss Oakkton were stopped in their tracks. They let the police rush past them towards the two people beside the bins. They could read the signs. These people weren't of any use to them now. For Molly and Micky had left their bodies.

Chapter Ten

Arat was practically the last creature Molly would ever choose to be, so she'd had to force herself to focus on the dirty, mangy, whiskered rodent by the bin.

Now she was flying in a state of nothingness towards it. Within a few seconds Molly felt herself filtering into the rat. And then she became rat. Immediately she was overwhelmed with ratty sensations. She felt her whiskers twitching as they read the air for other rats' whisker messages. Her new skin was numb from the cold, and all over her body was the horrid sensation of itchy bites from, Molly immediately supposed, fleas. Her ears were erect and alert and her ratty instinct was to be almost entirely thinking about food – particularly about the overflowing rubbish bin that cascaded down above her, full of delicious, odorous things.

Molly squished the rat's true character down under her own. It didn't object. Molly apologized as she did it. She tried to ignore the ratty gut feeling that was urging her to climb into the trash to rummage about for old bones or thrown-away half-full Chinese take-away boxes. Then she saw Micky, who had morphed into a darker grey rat.

'Over here,' he was beckoning, his whiskers twitching. 'Fast! Hurry!' he squeaked. Molly scrunched up her nose at Micky, and began to move. As she did, she real-ized how lithe her new body was. She was all tendon and muscle. Her scabby but svelte form moved like the wind. Molly flattened her body from seven centimetres down to three, her bones dislocating into pancake mode and she slid through a crack in the pavement. Her clawed feet gripped underneath the paving stone and she found herself landing gracefully upright underneath the ground.

Black stood by an empty taxi rank, waiting for a cab. Then he noticed a scent of lavender and powder and saw Miss Teriyaki and Miss Suzette hovering in the shadows near him. He was at once suspicious of them, especially when he saw that the fat woman in the cream cape held a basket carrying two of the cats that had been standing by the letterbox. He gripped his bag with the hypnotism book inside it and hailed a cab.

Before climbing into the taxi, he stopped. A tall busi-nessman in a black suit and a bowler hat was walking past, swinging his umbrella and briefcase and whistling the Seven Dwarfs' tune 'Whistle While You Work'. Black

143

caught his arm and stared into the man's eyes. At once his whistling stopped. He was hypnotized and ready to do whatever Black wanted.

'I am getting into this cab,' Black told him. 'The two women behind you – the black lady in the cream cape and the Japanese woman in red – must *not* follow me. You will obstruct them so that they cannot catch a cab for ten minutes. What is more, when they try to hypnotize you, you will be unhypnotizable. Afterwards you will go on your way and forget you were ever hypnotized by me and you won't remember what happened here. I lock these instructions in with the words "Snow White".'

The man nodded and Black climbed into the cab. With a kick of exhaust, it was away. Miss Teriyaki and Miss Suzette immediately stepped out of the shadows. Eagerly they approached the next cab.

'TAXI!' Miss Suzette shouted in a voice surprisingly deep for her tiny, tubby form.

'Follow that cab!' Miss Teriyaki bossily ordered the driver as he wound down his window.

But then the businessman stepped in front of them.

The gutter stank of the smelliest loo Molly had ever encountered yet in her rat body she rather liked the stench. Now it smelt more sugary than sewagey. Eager to escape, she followed Micky further down into the sewer to a ledge near a tunnel that flowed with smelly water. The ceiling above the ledge was tall, making the place feel like a hall. It was lit by streetlights as they shone through the gutter cover above and, here, there were other rats. One bared its teeth at Molly, and at once she felt a pang of fear. Why had she and Micky come down this far under the ground?

'Micky,' she hissed.

But the dark grey rat ahead turned and, in a gruff voice, squeaked back, 'Big water come night.'

And in a flash Molly saw that this rat wasn't Micky at all. She turned frantically towards the ledge down which she had just been led, but there was no Micky there either. Instead a fat, bushy rat with a scarred cheek and a missing ear stood solid as a tree trunk, blocking the way.

'A-oh, darlin'. Like me?' he croaked. The rat's eyes were beady and mean.

'Not likely!' Molly found herself squeaking back. 'Go and jump in the sewer!' and she edged up against the wall. 'Micky!' 'she shouted. 'HELP!'

The fat rat stepped towards her.

'No callin'. No one carin',' he snarled. 'You call again, I bite, missy.'

The businessman was doing a very good job preventing the two spinsters from catching a cab. Time after time they tried. At one point the two ladies split, hoping that this way at least one of them would catch a taxi. But even though Miss Suzette waddled as fast as she could, and Miss Teriyaki did a fast crutch hobble for another taxi, they were too slow for the young man.

'Oh no you don't!' he said. And then he started whistling 'Whistle While You Work', which made him even more annoying. After ten minutes of this game, he stopped, and, picking up his briefcase and umbrella, he sauntered away.

'You stupid woman!' Miss Teriyaki hissed. 'You know I haven't got my hearing aid in today. *You* should have *heard* Black hypnotizing that man. He obviously did it just before he got into the taxi. Miss Hunroe won't be at all pleased with you when she finds out.'

'What are you talking about?' Miss Suzette spat. '*No one* would be able to hear him hypnotizing from ze distance we were to him. It's *your* fault. I haven't got my spectacles on. *You* should have *seen* zat he was hypnotizing the man. You should have been able to guess from his body language, you fool. When I tell Miss Hunroe what really happened, she will be disgusted.'

In the sewer, another rat appeared behind the thuggish rat.

'Molly, what are you doing down there?'

'I thought that other rat was you,' Molly spluttered, choking on her fear as the smelly thug rat crept closer.

'Just try and push past it,' whispered Micky. As he spoke, though, two more rats, both very big, came down the sloped underground path into the hall of the sewer.

Nudging Micky along, the new arrivals were soon behind the twins.

The heavy bull rat lifted his scarred nose to sniff at them. 'Ah, oldies!' he salivated. 'Nice! Like me?' He spoke with a threatening air, a twisted charm that was laced with aggression. But, nasty as his tone was, the new rats weren't bothered by it.

'Get on your way, you stinking piece of salt cod!' snapped the first. Her mouth twitched into a heart shape.

'You 'eard ze lady. Get lost,' barked the second, baring big sharp teeth. With a swift move, she nipped the revolting male rat on his back.

The large rat gave a squeal. Then with a flash of his tail he fled.

Molly's relief was short-lived. In a second it turned to utter confusion. For the light grey rat turned to the charcoal-grey one, and congratulated her: 'Perfectly executed, Miss Oakkton!'

The two rats now turned their coal-black glistening eyes on Molly and Micky.

'Molly and Micky?' asked the pale grey rat, her mouth pinching into a heart shape again.

'Miss Hunroe?' Molly said dumbly. 'It's you, isn't it? And you . . . you can morph?'

The rats in front of the twins smiled and nodded.

'That's Oakkton,' Micky whispered.

'Have you just learned?' Molly asked. 'We really needed your help then. Thanks.'

147

But as Molly spoke she felt that something was wrong, for she wasn't feeling friendliness emanating from the rats that were Miss Hunroe and Miss Oakkton.

Miss Hunroe licked her paw 'You learned how to morph into animal forms *and* human forms,' she said. 'Well done! Most impressive. *Most* remarkable.' She came closer. 'When did *you* all learn to morph then?' Micky questioned. 'You said you didn't know how to when we spoke to you at the museum.'

Miss Hunroe batted her answer nonchalantly back. 'Oh, just now.'

'How?'

'Ze book, ze book taught us, of course,' Miss Oakkton, interjected.

'So you've just seen the book?' Molly asked. 'But I thought Black had it.'

'Yas, ve got it off him,' Miss Oakkton explained. 'But ve only had ze time to quickly scan ze pages on animal morphing. Ve missed ze morphing-to-human part.'

'Would you teach us?' oozed Miss Hunroe. 'You're so lucky to have learned.' She added smoothly with a toothy smile, 'We'd be so terribly grateful.'

Micky glanced at Molly. 'We can't teach you, Miss Hunroe,' he lied. 'We never learned. We only found out how to morph into animals.'

'WE *SAW YOU*,' hissed Miss Hunroe. 'We saw you reading the book. We were looking through Black's office window. Checking on you. Making sure you were safe.'

'As a rat?'

'As a cat!' Miss Hunroe retorted.

'So you *had* already learned to morph into animals. Get your story straight.'

There was silence. Both Molly and Micky knew that Miss Hunroe and Miss Oakkton were lying. The magnitude of their deceit was as obvious as the stink in the sewer and both twins saw how they had been used. As the truth dawned on them, a steeliness, a shared quality in the siblings that was usually latent, now galvanized their replies.

'You're liars,' said Micky through gritted teeth.

'Think because we're children, we're stupid?' Molly asked coolly.

Micky turned to Molly. 'Speal,' he said. 'She must have learned animal morphing from the book when she saw it as a child. And she taught them.' He spat at Miss Hunroe. 'You, Miss Hunroe, have two faces.'

'My dears. What's got into you?' wooed Miss Hunroe, her lip curling. 'It's only fair to let us know – we're so *near* to finding out anyway.'

'You're as bad as Black,' Molly growled. 'You tricked us so that we could get you the book for you to learn to morph into humans. Anyway, as Micky said, we don't know how.'

Miss Hunroe continued, disregarding her: 'I saw you both as *people* just now.' Her voice took on a sing-songy lilt. 'A rich lady and a waiter. Very clever!' Then she snapped. 'TELL US HOW!'

Miss Oakkton pushed her face up to Molly's. She smiled, baring big, yellow teeth. 'Tell us or you vill feel ze bite of my teess.'

Molly thought hard and tried to keep her cool. The simple escape route, she realized, was for her and Micky to morph into these rats that were Miss Oakkton and Miss Hunroe. But this would be very risky, for the women were strong characters and too knowledgeable about morphing. Molly remembered what the book had said – that it was important to choose your subjects carefully, as a strong personality and one that was alert might fight to stop the successful morph. And then where would Molly be? Stuck at the bottom of Miss Oakkton's or Miss Hunroe's minds forever? Her mind raced and then she had an idea.

Instead of attacking, Molly tried another approach. 'We will tell you how to morph into humans,' she bargained, 'if you tell us how to morph back into our own bodies. But *you* have to tell us first. That's the deal.'

Miss Hunroe and Miss Oakkton looked shocked. Then they began tittering.

'What's so funny?' Molly asked.

'You are fools!' Miss Hunroe laughed. 'So you don't know how to meego? That is *hilarious*!' She saw Molly's puzzled expression and added. 'Meegoing is the term for morphing back into one's own body.' She gave a shriek of laughter. 'Ha! You don't know how!'

'Hmm. Well, as I said, that's the deal.'

Miss Hunroe narrowed her eyes. '*Us* telling *you* the meegoing secret before you tell us what *we* want to know is impossible,' she parleyed. 'If we told you *our* secret, you'd never tell us *yours*. You'd be off out of here like a shot. No, the only way round is that you tell *us* the secret of morphing into humans first, *then* we will tell you how to meego.' She laughed again. 'The amusing part of this is that you don't really have a choice. After all, you can't keep morphing from creature, to human, to creature forever. How will you ever sleep? Fall asleep in a body and you've had it. In any case you can't be in another creature for longer than a few hours, for the creature starts to get its strength back. So of course, when you sleep for more than a few hours in another creature or another human, its true owner will rise to take control of itself as you sleep. It will squash you, the sleeping you, deep down under it and you will never get out. You will both be lost. Lost forever in a rat or a bat or a gnat. Ha! No. *You* need the meego secret *far* more than we need the morph-to-human secret.'

Molly gulped and glanced at her brother. She could guess from his eyes that he too had been frightened by what Miss Hunroe had said. And that he too was wondering what other nasty outcomes there were in the world of body borrowing. She started to wish she hadn't morphed at all.

The rat that was Miss Hunroe turned to the large scruffy rat that was Miss Oakkton.

'Until now, I didn't realize what an advantage we had!' Then, impatient suddenly, she spat at Molly and Micky. 'You'd better tell us now.'

'Time to comply,' said Miss Oakkton, muscling forward. 'Tell us! If you don't, zere will be bad, bad consequences. I have no qualms about biting off your ears!'

Molly and Micky dropped their bodies lower on the shiny, cold floor.

'What, tell you so that you can get *whatever you want* in the human world? We'd be crazy to tell you,' Molly snarled.

'You can beat us up all you like,' Micky squeaked. 'We aren't going to tell you.'

'Perhaps I can morph into *you* and get the secret that way,' said Miss Hunroe, her voice sinister.

'Please do,' bluffed Molly. 'You wouldn't dare. That would be the end of you, you old goat.' She stared with hatred into Miss Hunroe's eyes, wishing that she could hypnotize her. Miss Hunroe stared back, her eyes mean and cold.

'I look forward to ridding the world of people like you, Miss Moon,' she said nastily. 'You have no idea how wonderful the world is going to be when I have my way. You have no idea! There will be hurricanes and droughts, and disease will cull. And people like you all over the world, millions and millions of you, will die. And what an empty paradise the world will then be! With only the chosen few left to enjoy it, it will be heaven!'

Molly stiffened. Miss Hunroe's words were cruel and mad but she made her predictions with a horrible certainty.

'Leave zem to me,' said Miss Oakkton, baring her knife-sharp incisors. 'A little torture vill do ze trick.'

Suddenly there was a noise from above. All the rats looked up and froze. A dog had wedged its nose under the side of the drain cover and was now wrenching the grille off.

All of a sudden lots of light poured into the sewer. A Jack Russell stuck its pointy brown and white face down into the gutter. To all the rats he was a monster, a huge killer monster with a nightmare mouth. His growl chilled them to the core. His growl meant death.

Chapter Eleven

The Jack Russell barked ferociously down into the well of the sewer. His jaws snapped with a terrible fury, ready to tear any rodent to pieces. Miss Hunroe and Miss Oakkton fled up the drain. Molly and Micky pushed their backs up to the cold, wet wall of the sewage gully.

'Run!' Micky cried, and turned tail. Molly started to follow Micky then she saw that behind the Jack Russell was a white-faced bulldog and behind him, *amazingly*, a black *pug*! She gasped. She'd recognize that velvety face anywhere.

'I don't believe it!' Molly squeaked. 'Micky! Micky, it's Petula!'

As Micky stopped, so did Miss Hunroe and Miss Oakkton. Molly knew that time was against her. Hunroe and Oakkton were coming back. 'Quick, morph into the white dog,' she whispered to Micky. 'I'll take the Jack Russell.'

And so, slinking flat to the wall to avoid the snapping jaws of the Jack Russell, Molly and Micky focused on becoming two of the canine creatures above.

Molly landed in the Jack Russell's body with such an intensity that as soon as she arrived his personality was flattened. Magglorian was overwhelmed.

Sorry, sorry, sorry, Molly thought to him. Please let me borrow you just for a bit! Molly became aware of Magglorian's brawny, nimble hunting body. His sense of smell was hers now. She was confronted with the pong of the sewer as the Jack Russell smelt it, reading so much more from its foul odours than she had as a rat. And, of course, she smelt rat.

Recognizing Miss Oakkton, Molly growled as though to kill, and then with hate-fuelled determination, she bit. Molly caught Miss Oakkton's filthy rat ear between her teeth and she tugged. She pulled the rat off the ground and shook it like a rag. Then she tossed Miss Oakkton sideways so that she flew, legs splayed, through the air into the stream of pooey water that rushed through the gutter. Molly dug deeper into the drain. With a sharp bite she got a nip of the rat that was Miss Hunroe. Then the two rats screeched and scurried away.

Molly barked viciously after them, watching with satisfaction as Miss Oakkton's tail disappeared down the sewage pipe. With them, Molly realized, had gone the secret of how Molly and Micky might morph back into themselves.

Then Molly turned to see Petula looking at her.

Petula stared at Magglorian. She frowned and put her nose in her paws. *Now* she was feeling that Magglorian had *become* Molly. It must be the stress of the situation. The pressure was getting to her. She shut her eyes, and shook her head.

Then a very peculiar thing happened. Magglorian said, 'Petula. I know this is going to sound very strange, but it's me, Molly.' Petula opened her eyes wide and edged backwards. 'Don't be scared,' Magglorian continued. 'I've learned how to change shape – it's called morphing. And Micky's learned it too. Look, he's morphed into the body of your friend.'

Petula was stumped. *She hadn't told the two London dogs Micky's name*, so this must be true – Molly, her lovely Molly, was *in the body* of the Jack Russell.

'Molly?' she said unsurely.

'Yes, it's me.'

This really was very strange for both Molly *and* Petula. For though Molly with her human mind-reading skills had, on a few occasions, managed to decipher some of Petula's thoughts and Petula, with her dog-given extra-sensory skills, had been able to detect Molly's moods and whereabouts, neither had been able to properly understand one another and *speak* to each other. Now, though, because they were both *dog* they could communicate in dog speak. They looked at each other, stunned. But there was no time to start talking now. Explanations would have to wait.

Molly's eyes shot to the entrance of the Glitz restaurant. Black had gone but with her amazing sense of smell she could tell where he'd been standing. He smelt of ink and books and pinecones. And leather. Then Molly spotted Miss Teriyaki and Miss Suzette arguing on the pavement, and she caught a whiff of the hypnotism book again. Though it was far away its smell lingered in the air. The book had the meego secret and she and Micky had to get it before Miss Hunroe did.

'Petula, we'll fill you in later,' said Molly. 'At the moment, the most important thing in the world is that we follow that smell of pinecones and leather and the cab that's carrying it!'

And so the dogs began to trot. So intent were they on following Black that they didn't smell the two docile hypnotized cats that sat dozing in a basket hanging on a hook outside a hat shop's entrance, waiting for their owners' return.

Luckily the London traffic was dense on this winter night. So although Black's taxi had already driven away, its progress was slow and the dogs were soon able to pinpoint the vehicle and then follow it. It weaved past restaurants, boutique shops and gallery-lined streets.

As the dogs trotted and ran, Petula told them all about what had happened back at Briersville Park and how Miss Hunroe had stolen Molly's special time crystals. While Petula barked and yapped and growled, Molly marvelled at what it was like being a dog. She could smell so much! It was incredible. The ground

157

beneath her feet told stories of who had been there from the smells that they'd left, and the places that they passed all threw up glorious, complex smells that painted pictures. Finally the cab drove into a beautiful square with big white stucco houses surrounding it and a small park in the middle of it.

Here the buildings were very fine, with ornate entrances and tall multi-paned windows. Molly, Micky and Petula stopped behind a red pillar-box and watched as Black climbed out of his cab. Checking up and down the street to see that no one was spying on him, he walked up the steps of a pretty hotel building with three flags above its stone entrance. A porter opened the brass doors for him and welcomed him inside. Out came a warm smell of roast potatoes and vegetable soup and starched linen and lily of the valley soap.

'Who is he?' Petula panted.

'He's as bad as Miss Hunroe,' Molly answered. They watched Black through the downstairs window of the hotel. He stood in the lobby talking to the receptionist. Molly and Micky told Petula all about him and volume two of the hypnotism book. Petula nodded as she took in all the facts.

'That's about all we know,' Molly finished.

'In fact, it's really bad, Petula.' Molly leaned her head on Petula's neck. 'If we don't find out how to do this meego thing, sooner or later we won't be able to keep going. We'll get stuck in someone else's body for good.'

'I'm scared,' Micky confessed.

'Half of me wants to go back to Briersville Park and make sure everyone is all right,' Molly said, 'but—'

'You're not going to do that,' Petula interrupted with a growl. 'Everyone at Briersville Park is much safer than you. This is serious, Molly. You've got to get that book.'

Molly chewed her lip and she looked at Petula. Petula was so very sure of herself and had a sensible quality to her. They watched Black step into the lift.

'Do you think he's staying the night?' Micky wondered.

Molly bristled her fur against the cold air and shivered. 'We could try to get inside. We could follow him.'

'Dog in a lift? A bit risky. Trust me,' warned Petula. 'Before you know it, that bellboy would be calling the dog catchers.'

Then another black taxi pulled up in front of the building. Its door opened and a girl in a pink furry coat with short dark curly hair stepped out.

'That's Lily Black,' Molly told Petula. 'We saw pictures of her. Theobald's daughter.'

As Lily Black stood beside the front passenger window paying her fare, she glanced up and down the street. The dogs could smell that her ordinary smell of popcorn and the scent of strawberry shampoo in her hair was shrouded in a sort of electric lemon. Molly's new dog instincts told her at once that this meant that the girl was very nervous. As her cab drove off, sending a cloud of exhaust into the air, Lily walked round to the side of building, where there was an entrance that led to the back of the hotel. She spent a few minutes checking out the area and then she came back. Glancing up at the trees with a snarling look on her face, she marched up the hotel's front steps and went inside.

'Why don't we go round the back too,' suggested Molly. 'Perhaps there'll be a fire escape and we can walk up it.'

'No!' Petula exclaimed. 'Fire escapes are practically impossible for dogs. They're made of metal and have holes that your paws slip through.'

'Of course they do,' Molly said. 'Oh, Petula, I'm so glad you're here.'

Wasting no time, the three dogs ran to the covered alley beside the hotel. This was the hotel's tradesmen's entrance. They trotted through it, sniffing all about them. Halfway along, there were large hatches in the pavement, opening up to the hotel's basement kitchens. These hatches were used for the kitchens' deliveries. Looking down through one of the grilles, the dogs could see chefs preparing food. A moustached man was whisking a batter, a man in a tall white hat was decorating a cake. And the smells coming from there were unbearably good. The aromas of sauces and gravies, of garlic and fried onions, streamed up out of the hatches and laced the night air. Even the raw meat smelt delicious to Molly now she was a dog.

'Oh, I'm so hungry,' she whined.

'Me too,' agreed Micky.

'Hungry as a wolf!' declared Petula. 'We will sort that out later, but let's track down Mr Nasty first.'

Leading the way with her nose twitching, she led the twins round to the back of the hotel. They came to a small manicured garden with bay trees and crocus-filled flowerbeds. In the centre of the garden was a paved area with a pond, and in the middle of that was a statue of flying cupid. Water gushed from the winged boy's stone spear. The whole garden was lit with blue lights that illuminated the lawn and trees like magic outdoor candles.

The dogs stood on the lawn and looked up at the back of the hotel. Its facade was punctuated with French windows and balconies that overlooked the garden. On the left side a discreet fire escape hugged the brick-work.

'They're up there I think,' Petula said, gesturing to a balconied window on the first floor. 'You, Molly, should be able to smell them better than me – Jack Russells have far superior noses to pugs.'

'You're right,' Molly agreed. 'I can smell them now – it's drifting through those thin cracks of the window. Amazing! He's pinecones and ink and now I can smell wine too. He's drinking red wine. And I can smell the leather cover of the hypnotism book! That's amazing! And I can smell newspaper. I think he's reading the papers. And she smells of strawberry shampoo or face cream or something, and popcorn and felt tips. She's drawing or colouring in with them. That's incredible!'

'Is the human sense of smell so much worse?' Petula asked.

'It's like two hundred times worse. As a human you can only smell present smells and strong ones. Whereas as a dog I can smell that a cat was here at about three o'clock, and that a hedgehog was here last night.'

'And,' added Micky as Stanley, 'that smell of cat is *so* annoying! It makes me want to chase cat. Bite cat. That's a weird feeling.'

'Most dogs can't stand them,' agreed Petula. 'Personally, if I see a cat, my body sort of takes over and before I know it I'm running after it. I'm never fast enough to catch them, though.' Petula smiled. 'Now, you two, I think Mr Bad and Miss Popcorn are staying in this hotel for the night, so there's nothing we can do about them now. Instead we should get something to eat.'

Petula shook herself off and led the dogs to a bin in an outdoor alcove near the hotel's kitchens. The contents of the black bags smelt to Molly almost as good as the food in the hotel.

'As humans,' Petula explained, 'you would never have considered eating from bins, I know, but you'd be surprised – lots of very tasty morsels can be found in bins.' Petula put her front paws against the bulging sack that, like a coconut in a shy, sat lodged in the black plastic bin. 'The only difficulty we're going to have is getting at it.'

'I'll have a go,' said Micky. Leaping, he grasped the side of the bin bag with his teeth and tugged it towards the ground. The plastic bin fell over. Then, with vulpine ferocity, he ripped the bag apart.

Half-eaten steaks and carved-up lamb shanks tumbled out, mixed with the remnants of crêpes and cottage pies, strudels and vegetables.

'Yum!' Molly exclaimed.

Hungrily, the three dogs dived into their supper. They all ate till their stomachs were tight. Then they heard the kitchen doors opening. A kitchen worker was bringing out another bag of garbage. Quickly, the dogs scarpered to the back garden.

'OH NO! I don't believe it!' they heard the man complain. 'Those damn foxes! They've been at these bins again.'

The three dogs lapped up a drink from the hotel pond. Then Petula went to investigate a gazebo-like structure that stood under a horse chestnut tree at the end of the garden.

The hut had a half-open, latticed enclosure that certainly provided shelter from wind and rain. What was more, jute sacks, the sort that gardeners use to collect lawn mowings, were strewn across its floor.

'This will do nicely,' said Petula, 'so long as we sleep close together.'

'Micky and I will have to take it in turns to sleep,' Molly reminded Petula, 'or it'll be like Miss Hunroe said – if we fall asleep too long, we'll get overwhelmed

163

by the dogs who really own these bodies.'

'At least they're nice dogs,' Petula said, finding a white stone on the floor and picking it up to suck.

'Maybe they are, but if we get stuck inside their bodies and under their personalities, maybe they won't know how to let us out even if they wanted to.'

'I can be a night watch dog,' Petula said, collecting some sacks together. 'I can let you both sleep and then wake you up before too long passes.'

So that is exactly what they did.

The three dogs snuggled together and took it in turns to be guard – guard of the hut and a guard of time. Neither Micky nor Molly slept longer than two hours at a time. Then they'd stay awake for half an hour to ensure their control over their dog bodies before going back to sleep again. Petula was the last sentry. When a local church bell struck ten a.m., she woke Molly.

'Time to get up,' she said, nudging her on the shoulder. 'You were tired. It's ten o'clock in the morning.'

Molly yawned and stared at the sky, heavy with grey rain clouds. It was cosy and warm now in the dog nest. Molly listened to the sound of Micky's sleeping bulldog breath and thought how nice it was being snuggled up close to her brother and her friend Petula. And as Molly looked at Petula's black face, she was struck again by how amazing it was to be beside her pet, and to actually be able to talk to her.

'It's really nice to be able to talk to you, Molly,' Petula said. 'You're just how I knew you would be.'

'I know,' Molly said with a smile. 'You are just how I knew you were too. A little bit cheeky and funny, a little bit bossy and very brave. It *was* brave of you to follow us to London, Petula. You are a very good friend.'

'I had to, Molly. That's what real friends do. They help each other out when there's trouble.' Petula rubbed her nose in Molly's fur. 'We've been through a lot together, haven't we?'

For a moment the two dogs lay close to each other, enjoying being together. Petula broke the silence.

'So,' she pondered, 'all you've got to do now is get the book. And, when you do get your paws on it, you have to morph into a *human* in order to read it. *Then* you can find out how to do the morph back to your own body.'

Molly nodded. 'That's exactly right, Petula. You've hit the nail on the head.'

'Or,' Petula replied, 'as a dog might say, I've knocked the cat on the nose.'

Both dogs smiled, then Petula looked serious. 'Molly, it's going to be difficult for me to keep up with you and Micky as you follow Black and the book. But I'll try. I can sense where you are and I'll be there for you whenever I can be. Remember these three barks.' Petula gave a short chirpy bark. 'That barking means I'm safe. If I howl, that means I'm in trouble or that someone else is. If I bark incessantly and urgently, then that means you have to watch out.'

Molly rubbed her wet nose on Petula's velvety black ear. 'Good plan. Look, in a minute, Petula, Micky and I will probably change into birds – those two blackbirds on the lawn. We must get to Buckingham Palace for Black's eleven o'clock appointment with the Queen. He'll be carrying that book around wherever he goes from now on. Magglorian will show you the way. And don't worry, Petula, we'll get through this, and after that we are all going to have a lovely time.'

Petula nuzzled into Molly.

'That's what I love about you, Molly. Your optimism. You always trust that things will work out.'

'They will.' Molly said this far more surely than she felt it. But Petula felt Molly's fear. It rose from her like an electric smoke.

Chapter Twelve

Miss Hunroe was in her lavish rooms back at the museum. She sat in a white negligee and a sky-blue dressing gown having breakfast. Flipping her gold coin over and over the fingers of her left hand, she admired the table set before her. It was laid with a priceless Ming tea set of white and blue porcelain that she had stolen from the Victoria and Albert Museum. Her maid, Elspeth, who was dressed in a light blue uniform, had brought toast, scrambled eggs and a dish of wild blueberries. A dark blue flute lay beside them and Elspeth was pouring Miss Hunroe's tea. The rhapsody of all the blues about her gave Miss Hunroe the greatest of pleasure. She reached for her cup. As she did so, a crack of lightning lit up the grey morning sky outside, giving Elspeth a shock. Her arm jolted and the tea spilt. A few hot drops scalded Miss Hunroe's outstretched hand.

'OW!!!!!' Miss Hunroe shrieked. 'You clumsy FOOL!'

The hypnotized woman dropped her head in shame. 'I'm so sorry, madam,' she begged. 'Can I get you some ice?'

'No, you certainly can't,' Miss Hunroe snapped. She turned to the coin that moved over the fingers of her left hand and with dexterity, and a hard look in her eye, flipped it high into the air. She caught it in the palm of her right hand and smacked it down on the back of her left hand. 'Heads, you lose,' she declared. Then, slowly lifting her mascared eyes to Elspeth, she said, 'For that, Elspeth, you will not eat for . . . hmm . . . for two days.'

'Yes, madam,' the maid said, as though she'd simply been asked to make sure there were newspapers on the table every morning. She curtsied. 'Is there anything else I can do for you now?'

'No.'

With that Elspeth left Miss Hunroe to eat her breakfast. Miss Hunroe ate elegantly and hungrily, and finished by wiping her mouth on her blue napkin.

Then there was a knock at the door.

'Come in.'

Miss Oakkton entered. Behind her, uncertain whether to enter or not, cowered Miss Teriyaki and Miss Suzette.

'*I said come in*,' Miss Hunroe repeated. She picked up her flute and, as though speaking to it, said, 'Miss

168

Teriyaki and Miss Suzette! The two idiots who couldn't follow a taxi. Have you managed to track Mr Black down now?'

'Erm . . . well, not yet,' Miss Suzette stammered. 'We spent ze night outside ze casino. We weren't sure whezzer he went zere or to his hotel home, or—'

'Then get out of my SIGHT!' Miss Hunroe's voice was cutting and vicious. She looked up cruelly. 'And don't speak to me again until you know his exact location.'

The two women fled the room.

Miss Hunroe picked up her flute and began to play.

Miss Oakkton sat down. 'Ahhhh,' she sighed, taking a pinch of tobacco from her ivory box and putting it in her mouth to chew. Then, as though the music had possessed her, she rose up again. The notes from Miss Hunroe's flute floated up to the roof of the museum, and Miss Oakkton began to dance. 'Aaaaah!' she exclaimed, doing a clumsy pirouette, dancing like an absurd cartoon elephant. 'Very nice, very *pretteee*!'

Miss Hunroe stopped playing and clapped her hands crossly. 'Do stop dancing around the room in that ridiculous way! You look unhinged! Stop it!'

Molly and Micky flew away from the hotel garden just as Lily Black came out on to her balcony. She peered down at the garden below. Then she started staring at the stone balcony ledge in front of her. 'Bugs! So you've

169

changed into bugs now, have you, nosy boy and nosy girl? You're going to wish you'd never learned to morph!' With a nasty viciousness, she slapped the stone. 'There, you're dead bugs now!'

For a moment she seemed calm. Then, realizing that the bugs in front of her might easily be just that – bugs – her temper rose again. She threw her angry gaze about the garden.

There were two thrushes now on the lawn. Lily disappeared inside her bedroom and returned with three glass bottles. These she hurled at the innocent birds, laughing as they flew off.

'I'll get you!' she shouted. She turned to two squirrels in a tree. 'And if it's you I'll get *you*, you Squirrel Nutkins.' Her sharp blue eyes shone nastily. A window nearby opened and an elderly man leaned out.

'Young lady, would you SHUT UP. Some people are trying to sleep. If you don't, I'll complain to the hotel.'

Lily narrowed her eyes, wrinkled her nose and stuck her tongue out. 'Could even be you and your missus, Grandpa,' she muttered. Then, looking up at the heavy, water-laden sky, she went back inside her room.

Molly and Micky found Buckingham Palace easily. They flew higher and higher into the rainy sky and landed on the edge of a skyscraper. From here the London traffic looked like a metallic-coloured river and the twiggy tops of trees seemed the size of footballs.

They saw the River Thames and the big wheel, the London Eye, that was for tourists to ride. Micky knew that Buckingham Palace would be fairly near to that, and sure enough there it was, up a long, grand road.

After a smooth, wet, downhill glide, they arrived at the palace's grand gardens, landing on one of its gravel paths. Scores of windows on the rear facade of the building flashed in the dull and cloudy morning sunshine. On top of the roof a flag flew.

'She's in,' Molly twittered as a low, booming bell chimed a quarter to eleven. At the same time, a flash of lightning lit up the sky.

'Who's in?' tweeted Micky.

'The Queen. That flag flying means that she's in. She's somewhere inside, reading the papers, or signing royal documents.'

Molly and Micky flew up to the largest of the balconies on the first floor of the palace. Perching on the iron rails there, they peered through the drip-stained window. Inside was an empty room. They fluttered to the next window. Inside this one was an empty hall with richly brocaded walls and old, fancy furniture. They hopped along to the next balcony.

Beyond pale yellow curtains was a grand sitting room with old, ornate sofas and gilt-legged desks and chairs. Large portraits of past kings and queens, of princes and princesses, hung on the finely papered walls. A crystal chandelier with thousands of droplets of glass was suspended from the ceiling like an eighteenth-century UFO. And underneath it, sitting on a spindly stool, was Theobald Black. He was talking in earnest to a grey-haired lady who sat with her back to the window. A white-gloved butler lay down a silver tray bearing teapots and poured the woman a cup of tea.

'Jeepers, that's *her*,' Molly whistled.

AH2 stepped out of the Cork Street Police Station and zipped his anorak up against the cold. He fished his small tracking device from his pocket and extended its aerial.

A policeman watched from his office window. 'Alien hunter indeed,' he said, polishing the metal button on the top of his bell-shaped police helmet. 'Fruit and nut-case more like.'

AH2 read the gadget screen, and converted it to map form to see where the Moon alien was. He squinted at the results.

'I don't believe it.'

Setting off at a firm pace, he began walking towards Green Park.

On the pavement opposite, two women, one with a walking stick and in a red shiny raincoat, the other tubbier and in a frilly dress, who were pretending to be consulting a map, watched him go. As he strode off down the gallery-lined street, the women turned to walk down it too. One limped, the other waddled. Miss Teriyaki's stick kept slipping on the wet pavement whilst Miss Suzette's voluptuous, frilly scarf kept blowing across her face. This crazy man seemed to know how to find Molly Moon. And Molly Moon, they had both decided, would probably be very near Mr Black and the hypnotism book.

Miss Hunroe was furious with them for not keeping up with Mr Black the night before, so they were determined to get things right now.

'Oh, do hurry, you snail!' Miss Suzette tutted as they hurried through a covered arcade full of chocolatiers and fancy shops that sold leather gloves and luxurious items like moustache combs. 'Try to limp faster or we'll lose him. Like we lost zat cab last night. It was all your fault. If you'd been less lazy and more alert, we would have seen what Black was up to.'

Miss Teriyaki flashed an angry glare at Miss Suzette. 'You're not exactly an Olympic runner yourself, you frog,' she panted, hurrying as fast as she could past an expensive underwear shop. 'Your frilly dress is cooler than my red patent coat. It's easier for you. And you haven't sprained your ankle. Let me remind you that tomorrow or the next day I will be back to my normal fit self. But you have never been fit.' Grunting as she picked up pace she added, 'Oh, I love these shops! They remind me of Paris. When I own Paris, I'll spend all my time in the shops!'

Miss Suzette stopped suddenly and turned with a furious look on her face. 'What *are* you talking about *When you own Paris?*'

'Exactly what I say,' Miss Teriyaki replied smugly. 'When I own Paris. Miss Hunroe has promised me

Paris! Which city has she said you can have?'

'You foolish woman,' Miss Suzette replied scathingly. 'Do you really think she would give Paris to *you*? She gave it to me months ago. I was *born* zere! Paris is in my blood. Zere must be some mistake.' A sly look crossed her face. 'You do know, Miss Teriyaki, zere is also a place called Paris in Texas, America? She was probably offering you zat.'

'No she wasn't.'

'Yes she was.'

'No she wasn't.'

'Of course she was. You know Miss Hunroe *far* prefers me to you. She never would have offered you ze real Paris in France!'

'You old witch!' Miss Teriyaki cried, her feelings visibly hurt. Then her face changed. She thrust her hand at Miss Suzette. 'I don't expect Miss Hunroe gave you a ring like this. She didn't, did she? Ha. Favourite indeed. Miss Hunroe loves me. There you go!'

'Oh, shut up and hurry up, you slug,' huffed Miss Suzette. 'If we don't get Mr Black now, she'll hate us both and then neizzer of us will get Paris or Venice or anything.'

Clip, clip, clip went their shoes and the walking stick on the marble passage floor. Then they were out of the arcade on to the busy street beyond it, just in time to see AH2 disappear through the open gates of the entrance to Green Park. Rain was spitting down, and the skies above were growing greyer.

'I'm sure I heard him say Buckingham Palace,' Miss Teriyaki exclaimed breathlessly. 'Perhaps we should hail a cab.'

'Don't be so lazy, Teriyaki!' Miss Suzette wheezed, wiping some dribble from the corner of her mouth with a lace hanky. She put up her frill-edged umbrella and set off through the park.

Outside high railings in front of Buckingham Palace, a handful of tourists stood watching the changing of the guards. A bearskin-hatted sergeant shouted commands and three, serious, red-uniformed soldiers, also in the tall black furry hats, took it in turns to march up and down the palace forecourt.

Miss Teriyaki and Miss Suzette crossed the road to stand by the railings fifty metres from where AH2 had joined the tourist throng. Miss Teriyaki reached into her handbag for her mobile phone.

'I'm going to alert Miss Hunroe,' she said, beginning to text a message. 'I have a feeling she ought to be here.'

Miss Suzette nodded. 'And I'm going to set up a little Molly Moon trap all of my own.'

Beside her a Chinese woman with dyed red hair and wearing a denim trouser suit raised a camera to her eye and snapped.

'That will be a classic picture,' interjected Miss Suzette with warm charm.

'Oh yes, it will be,' said the Chinese tourist.

'Are you alone, dear?' asked Miss Suzette, smiling.

'Alone? Oh yes, I am,' said the young woman,

completely trusting the sweet-looking, chiffon-collared pensioner.

'You speak very good English.'

'Oh yes,' the Chinese woman replied. 'I have spent ten years at school learning it.'

'Lovely!' Miss Suzette replied. There was a pause as the young woman took another photograph. Then, like a horrid, fat, poisonous spider, Miss Suzette swung her web. 'I say, could you check my eye? I seem to have a speck of dust there – can you see anything?'

The innocent Chinese woman turned. She gazed into Miss Suzette's piggy eye. And before she knew it she was hypnotized.

Chapter Thirteen

'I'll be the butler,' Micky twittered. 'You can be the Queen.'

'The Queen? Are you joking?' The feathers on Molly's head stood up on end.

'Come on,' Micky coaxed, 'she's only another human being.'

'But I don't know if I can behave like the Queen!' Molly tweeted.

'Of course you can. Just be ever so royal and polite. Listen, you'd be helping her.'

'But I can't see her face so I can't imagine her as a child,' Molly objected. 'So how can I morph into her?'

'Your work's been done for you,' Micky pointed out. 'That portrait there with the girl holding the puppy is of the Queen when she was about six.'

Molly and Micky began staring at the edge of the green and white carpet beside the floorboards near the window. It had a pattern of leaves and flowers that twisted round each other. Soon Molly had captured an image of a strange cottage with a tall, spindly roof. She immediately turned her attention to the portrait of the young princess. Micky had been right. The picture was so good it made Molly's task very easy and within seconds she had harnessed the cottagey image, linked it with the princess's face and, as though these pictures were magical charms to pull her, Molly was at once shooting out of the blackbird's body straight for the Queen's.

Like a rolling tsunami wave, Molly crashed into the old lady's mind, overpowering her personality like a breaker swallowing an unsuspecting swimmer. Part of Molly felt apologetic and rude to be pushing into Her Majesty's mind but she knew she mustn't show weakness, for if she did the Queen's character might get the upper hand, and that would be disastrous.

So Molly took charge and as she did she apologized to her. *I'm so sorry*, she thought to her, *erm . . . Your Majesty. It's for your own good*.

Molly was overwhelmed by the Queen's memories and her knowledge. Molly saw giant ships that the Queen had launched, swinging bottles of champagne at their hulls; she saw private yachts and huge stables filled with the Queen's racehorses. She saw wonderful palaces with parks around them where the Queen lived and went on holiday; and she saw memories of all sorts of parades and celebrations that had been given in the

Queen's honour. This was mixed with an unexpected ordinariness of character that made the Queen feel just as normal as the other humans Molly had morphed into. Molly saw how she loved her family, her grand-children, her dogs, her horses and her friends. She saw how she was wishing the butler had brought her a chocolate muffin.

'Cor!' Molly found herself saying. Her accent as the Queen was extremely posh.

'Is there anything wrong, ma'am?' Black asked, something in the Queen's tone putting him on edge. Molly wondered whether the Queen had been hypno-tized by Black. She didn't think she had been, but she couldn't be sure.

'Everything is perrrfect,' Molly the Queen replied, trying desperately to get a grip on herself. '"Cor" is the nickname of one of my corgis – the big scruffy one. His full name is "Cor Blimey". It's cockney, don't you know. He was just being naughty. You didn't see it, but I did. Ha, ha. Oh dear!'

Outside, the sergeant was shouting his commands in the changing of the guard. The marching of the soldiers was perfectly synchronized as their feet hit the ground with concise rhythm.

'Isn't the marching comforting?' Molly said. On the floor by her feet, three corgis turned to look quizzically up at her. The big scruffy one began growling. 'Be quiet, Cor!' Molly tutted.

'You were saying?' Black began.

'What was I saying?' Molly asked unsurely, picking up her teacup and sipping at it. Clumsily she spilled some on her lap. 'Oh. Ah, um, Butler! Have you got a napkin?' Black watched suspiciously as the royal butler came towards the Queen, brandishing a linen cloth. Black eyed the Queen and her snarling corgis. Instinctively, he picked up his leather bag with the hypnotism book inside it.

'There you go, My Highness,' said Micky the butler, mopping away at the Queen with the napkin. Molly pushed him away, knowing that a butler would definitely not start rubbing the Queen's knees. Two of the corgis began to bark.

'You were offering,' Black went on, 'to make arrangements for me to get to the Tower of London to put the book safely there.' Now Black did not feel comfortable at all. Lily's warnings rang loud in his ears.

Molly the Queen eyed his bag. She supposed the book was inside it and she marvelled at Black's cunning. It was very clever of him to be using the book as an excuse to get into the Tower of London, she thought. Why, once he was in there, the riches at his fingertips were immense. The Crown Jewels were kept there, which included the biggest diamond in the world. And she could see in the Queen's memories that she had already been persuaded that the book was very, very precious and dangerous. She already had some knowledge of hypnotism, time travelling, time stopping and morphing, for Black had been explaining it to her.

180

So Black's plan was going well, Molly thought. If he got into the tower, he could use his hypnotism to steal whatever he wanted, and then he could get away with it scot free. 'Hmmm. Yes of course,' said Molly. 'I must say, I am very intrigued by the book. May I see it?'

'You saw it just now,' said Black slowly, his knuckles turning pale as he gripped his bag tightly.

'Yes. Yes. *Again* I mean,' said Molly, trying to dig her way out of trouble. 'Is everything all right, Mr Black?'

Black examined the Queen's lined face and tried to judge whether the girl who Lily had warned him of had invaded her. There was only one way to see. He would read the Queen's mind. So, concentrating hard, he silently asked the question: *What are you thinking?*

Molly felt a tickle above the Queen's eyebrows and all over her scalp, but she thought nothing of it. If she'd been aware, she might have been able to think very proper royal thoughts for Black to read from her mind. But she had no idea that Black could mind-read, and so she had no idea that a bubble had appeared over her soft grey hair. In it were pictures of Black with the hypnotism book and the Queen wrestling Black to the ground. There were other images too of the butler joining in, twisting Black's arm into a one-armed Nelson. For this is what Molly was fantasizing.

'To the tower!' Molly said. 'Butler,' she added, 'please take Mr Black's bag.'

At this point Black got up. 'Oh no you don't. No

doubt you're one of Miss Hunroe's assistants. You're interfering where you shouldn't.'

At once Molly saw that the game was up. Jumping over the corgis – which was quite difficult as the Queen was wearing a straight tweed skirt – she dived for Black's bag, knocking over the tea tray. Teacups scattered and smashed as they hit the ground. All the corgis began to bark frantically. With a swipe, Molly grabbed at the bag but, as Black dodged, she missed and fell head first on to the delicate antique sofa, catching a cushion instead and knocking the whole piece of furniture so that it tipped over, throwing Molly on the floor.

'Get him, Micky,' Molly screeched, and Micky leaped for Black. But, as he did, Black lunged out and walloped him in the stomach. Micky lay groaning in an armchair. Now Black ran for the door.

'Guards!' Molly shouted 'Stop him! He's a thief!'

'Aarff! Aarff! Aarff!' the corgis barked in unison.

The staff and the bodyguards outside the room looked about them, confused. One moved towards where the Queen was pointing, but he could see no one. It was as if Black had become invisible.

'Who, Your Majesty?' the bodyguard asked. The lady in waiting beside him looked equally perplexed. A guard on the stairs was just as puzzled.

For all the staff had been hypnotized earlier by Black – hypnotized not to see him come and not to see him go.

Meanwhile, Black's footsteps grew more and more faint as he hurried further away down the wide palace staircase to the main entrance. Molly glanced back to Micky, who was now standing up, rubbing his stomach. She ran to the room's eastward window and looked out of it, her breath immediately steaming up the glass of its pane. Below was a view of the gravelled palace drive. Two black ravens sat on the windowsill, sheltering from the rain.

'The ravens,' she said. 'Quick!'

In a few seconds Molly and Micky were in the ravens' bodies, blinking, fluffing their feathers and stretching their wings. And then they began to look for Black. There he was, walking briskly, though trying not to look like he was panicked, across the gravel forecourt.

'Now!' Molly cawed.

She and Micky dived. Ravens were far more powerful then either the pigeons or the blackbirds had been. Beating their strong wings, they were like trained missiles. In the next moment Micky tactically flapped his wings into Black's face. Molly snatched the black bag from out of Black's arms and then they were flying off over the traffic with it.

'Good lord, Smuthers!' the Queen exclaimed, clutching the windowsill as she came to her senses. 'Smuthers, I've just had the most disturbing experience, and it strikes me that you have had a similar one!'

'Madam!' her butler, Smuthers, replied, shaking his

head and adjusting his waistcoat.

*

Inside the palace grounds, Black stood in the rain, watching as two powerful birds carried his priceless belonging away. Clumsily they flew, accidentally bumping into each other with their wings. The bag swung like an oversized pendulum beneath them.

'You haven't won yet,' Black snarled, and, ignoring the amazed soldiers, he began to run towards the open gates.

Miss Teriyaki and Miss Suzette now stood by the palace railings beside two cats – a ginger tom and a white Burmese. They all watched the ravens go. At once the cats began running. Miss Teriyaki and Miss Suzette were slower off the mark.

'So what you'll do is stay close to us,' Miss Suzette instructed her hypnotized Chinese tourist. 'When I shout "*Allez, allez!*" you will do what I told you to do. Now, follow me.' The hypnotized Chinese woman nodded, completely understanding Miss Suzette's strange instructions.

AH2's gadget bleeped. 'Ah, so you're ravens now,' he said excitedly. Snapping his machine shut, he too swiftly set off in pursuit of the birds.

'This is so . . . diff . . . i . . . cult,' Molly cawed, gripping the bag with her claws and beating her wet wings hard so she didn't fly into the top branches of a tree.

'It's slipping! It's so heavy!' Micky cried.

Below in St James's Park, a child looked up from feeding the ducks. 'Mama!' he shouted. 'Looooook at de birds!'

Another raven flew past. 'What's in?' he cawed 'Wormsies?'

Molly glanced below and behind and saw Black's large form charging across the muddy grass of the park. 'Oh no, Micky! He's after us.' She didn't see that to his rear, waddling and hobbling as fast as they could, and out of breath, were Miss Suzette and Miss Teriyaki. Beside them trotted their red-haired tourist and ahead of them ran two cats. And a little distance behind them was AH2, who was watching the whole procession in fascination.

With difficulty, the ravens carried the swinging bag through the rain towards Westminster Abbey. Diving towards an arch into a large tree-edged square beyond it, they found themselves surrounded by scores of schoolboys. Then they flapped and fluttered through another smaller arch into what looked like an ancient courtyard.

'This is perfect,' Micky croaked. 'Let's morph into some of these boys.'

They dropped the bag and hopped territorially on to it. In the distance they heard the siren of police cars. A slow clap of thunder rolled through the sky above.

'Maybe the Queen reported Black,' Molly the raven said. 'Maybe he's been caught.'

'Come on, let's change. Who are you going to be?' Micky asked.

Molly picked a boy with dark hair. 'I'll be him,' she said, 'and there's a good pattern in the doodle on his schoolbook.'

'OK,' agreed Micky, 'and I'll be him.' He nodded at a freckle-faced boy. 'And, remember, we have to see them as *babies* because they're not adults.'

In a jiffy, the twins had morphed. Molly became a football fanatic called Max.

For a moment, Molly paused. She was shocked. This was the first time she'd ever been male. And it felt very different. Her body was tougher, with parts she'd never had before. Her blood felt hotter and coursed through her veins in a wilder way. Her feelings were less bothersome and seemed deeper inside her. And when a football was kicked past her, she had an urge to kick it, in the same way that as a dog she'd wanted to chase cats.

Micky (now a boy called Jo Jo) shooed the dazed ravens off the bag. 'Molly? Are you there? What are you waiting for?'

Molly snapped to and picked up the bag. 'Let's get out of here,' she said.

But as she turned Black came charging into the courtyard. To make things worse, two sly cats and Miss Teriyaki and Miss Suzette followed him. It was then that Molly saw that none of the other boys about her were carrying bags, and so the bag she held, with the precious book in it, was easy to spot. Theobald

Black, Miss Suzette and Miss Teriyaki all moved towards her. Molly saw that she was cornered. Students began pointing at the white and ginger cat. Molly thought quickly. She couldn't run, but she could *morph*. A camera-bearing Chinese tourist had meandered into the courtyard. For one thing, she was athletic-looking. For another she was near to the arch that led to the road. She was, Molly realized, the best person to morph into. Molly began to change. As she did, she lobbed the black bag high up into the air, over the heads of the cats, over the schoolchildren, and over Miss Suzette, Miss Teriyaki and Black, towards the Chinese woman. Her plan was to arrive in the Chinese woman's body, *catch* the now falling bag and then run.

As Molly morphed she was unaware of Miss Suzette's words that were shouted into the damp air. '*Allez, allez!*'

As Molly's spirit washed into the redhead's body, she felt her arms reach up for the bag. But at the same time she was aware of something else – something odd. The Chinese woman's character hadn't sunk out of sight. She hadn't relinquished control of her body or her mind *at all*. To Molly's horror, it was as if the woman had expected Molly's arrival.

And she had. For this was Miss Suzette's 'little trap'. She had predicted that Molly might need a perfect getaway body. So she had hypnotized the Chinese woman to expect Molly's invasion. However hard

187

Molly shoved at the woman's mind and tried to spread out in her brain, nothing happened. It was impossible to destabilize the woman's position, to dislodge her and to take command.

'Eeeeeeek!' the Chinese redhead shrieked. To the students in the courtyard, she looked like a person fresh out of the madhouse. She jumped about clutching a big bag, shaking her red locks and wriggling about as though she was doing some sort of crazy dance. And a slim Japanese woman in a red raincoat, walking with a stick, stepped towards the odd Chinese woman. She relieved her of her bag and then calmly made off with it. Miss Suzette waddled after her and two cats followed them, their tails in the air. Molly meanwhile was stuck. Stuck in the Chinese woman's body, able neither to take control of it, nor to leave it. For just as Miss Suzette had hypnotized the woman to withstand Molly's body borrowing, she had also instructed her not to let Molly go – to hold her for as long as she could. The woman was like a dog with a bone.

'I WILL NOT LET YOU GO!' the Chinese woman shouted at the sky. 'I WILL NOT LET YOU GO!' Then Molly felt something else happening. Something super strange. Someone *else* was morphing into the Chinese woman's body *too*.

For a few seconds, Molly was terrified, for she had no idea who had come to share the tourist's mind and body. She simply felt this person's arrival, like a massive downpour of water. It was overwhelming, breathtaking and shocking. And it sloshed in the space that was already uncomfortable with both Molly and the Chinese woman fighting for command. It joined them there like some unwelcome, uninvited guest.

'GET *OUT*!' Molly shouted. These words came out of the Chinese tourist's mouth. 'GET OUT!' the woman yelled at her hands. Students about her thought that she was having a fit. One hurried off to fetch the school doctor.

As Molly struggled it was as if a veil lifted. Because as the person who had joined them settled, so Molly saw *who it was*. The person was *Theobald Black*.

Chapter Fourteen

Molly could hardly believe it, but it was true. Sharing the same head space proved it. Theobald Black was a *good* person.

He really *did* run a charity that raised money for children's homes. He really *had* wanted to put the book in the Queen's Tower of London, so that it was safe. And he didn't own Black's Casino – his brother, Geoffrey Black, did. What was more, he knew about Miss Hunroe and her horrid accomplices. He was a very good hypnotist, but not a time traveller or a time stopper. And he could even read minds. Molly tried to absorb as much information as she could.

Meanwhile Black was trying to help Molly – help her to extract herself from the hypnotized Chinese woman's vice-like grasp. And as he wrestled the Chinese woman's force away from Molly, Molly had a chance to escape. She needed to find the boy Max again. There he was, sitting on a step looking confused. Ignoring the

Chinese woman's efforts to suck her back in, Molly focused on the boy and the pattern on his book. Soon, Molly was whipping through the air and a second later was back in Max's body. Molly looked up at her freckle-faced friend.

'Is that still you, Micky?'

'Yes. Molly, is that you?' As he spoke, the red-haired woman gave a shriek. 'I won't let you win!' she shouted.

'You'll never guess what,' Molly hurriedly explained to Micky. 'Black is in the Chinese lady *now*, and he's a *good* person. We got him all wrong. We've got to help him!'

'You cannot leave!' the Chinese woman was bellowing at her feet.

The shocked pupils who were still in the courtyard could see that this woman really wasn't right in the head. They stepped warily away from her in hushed silence.

Micky eyed a nearby tap and a bucket that was under it. 'I read this thing about fighting dogs,' he mumbled, half to himself. Seconds later he was filling the bucket with water. And a moment after that he was coming up behind the Chinese woman.

In an instant he had emptied the contents of the bucket all over the woman, whose mouth opened to scream, though no sound came out. Shocked, she stood bolt upright.

Everyone was silent. Children gasped in disbelief at

191

Jo Jo's behaviour, and then with admiration – for the drenched woman finally stopped raving. Sopping wet, she slumped to the ground.

Amid the chaos, Black materialized in the wet school-yard holding an umbrella, which he calmly opened.

Half a mile away, Petula, Magglorian and Stanley arrived at Buckingham Palace.

'Cor, can smell the corgis from 'ere,' said Magglorian, his nose puckering.

Petula raised her head to the rain and wrinkled her forehead at the sky. She hated lightning. 'Oh dear, we're too late. She's not here,' she said disappointedly. Her face turned like the dial of a compass towards Westminster Abbey. 'That way!'

'Rightio,' said Stanley cheerfully.

'Let's push on,' said Magglorian. 'It is getting really wet. Over there is near the Houses of Parliament, where the politicians live. That's close to my home too.' And so the dogs set off through the sheets of rain.

Black glared up at the blackening sky. Behind them, a teacher arrived and began comforting the tourist.

'A lot is at stake. We must prioritize.' He nodded over to the Chinese woman. 'She's in safe hands now.' Urging Molly and Micky, who were still schoolboys, to move quickly on, he helped them navigate their way out of the courtyard.

They followed Theobald Black around the school's

tree-lined square. The rain was pelting down. In the distance, they could still hear police sirens.

'I expect you two will be wanting to meego back to your own bodies,' said Black, pulling the neckline of his coat up to conceal his face as much as he could. 'I can teach you.'

'Wow, that would be brilliant,' Molly gasped.

'That would be incredible,' agreed Micky, adding, 'It's amazing how wrong we got you. We had you down as a really bad man.'

'You shouldn't believe everything people tell you about a person,' Black said gruffly. 'You know the old saying – never judge a book by its cover.'

Molly looked up at him. He was unattractive; it couldn't be denied. His thick, greyish skin was ugly and pitted, but now Black looked directly at her Molly saw that there was a kind twinkle in his eye.

'I'm sorry we thought you were bad,' Molly apologized. 'You didn't deserve it.'

'Hunroe and her friends seemed good,' explained Micky. 'They painted you as a dishonest, two-bit slime-ball to fit their story. How much do you know about Miss Hunroe?'

'A lot. I know her very, very well. I went to school with her. She was as nasty then as she is now. Miss Popular, she was, with every teacher thinking she was an angel. She liked to have sycophantic followers—'

'Syco what?' said Molly.

'Sycophantic,' Micky intervened. 'It's when a person

193

blindly follows another person, doing whatever they want like an obedient dog. That's called being sycophantic.'

Theobald Black nodded. 'Hunroe liked her followers exactly like that. They'd all look up to her, and behaved as though they hoped some of her Hunroe-ness might rub off on them. I suppose she was always glamorous. They all wanted to be her and would do whatever she wanted.'

'Sounds like the gang she has now.'

'I'm sure. Miss Hunroe wouldn't be able to exist without her obedient followers. She had a particularly evil thuggy helper at school called Bartholomew. She used him to do her dirty work, to bully people, to get what she wanted. She hasn't changed.' They walked under the old arch at the entrance of the school. 'And now she's got what she wanted – the book. And she's gone.'

'But *I* haven't!' came a smug response behind them. Black and the schoolboys spun round.

AH2 stood behind them, looking proud as a cockerel. Smiling, he thrust his hand forward. In it was a red box.

'Who on earth is *this* person?' Black asked Molly.

'He's an alien hunter,' Molly replied matter-of-factly. 'Somehow that gadget of his can always tell where I am, whoever I am. He wants to be my contact on Earth.'

All of a sudden, Molly got some inspiration. She was

feeling a little guilty about keeping Max from his lessons, since he'd get into trouble for missing them, and she supposed it might be interesting to find out more about AH2. So, quick as a somersault, she morphed into him. As she left Max's body, she thanked him, and then introduced herself to AH2 before pushing his character down below her.

'I'm Molly now,' Molly said to Black and Micky. 'And, Micky, maybe you should be him.' She pointed to a Rasta man who was walking towards Parliament Square carrying a placard that read WAKE UP, CLIMATE CHANGE IS HERE. Above, a flash of lightning lit up the dark grey sky.

'It certainly is,' Black muttered, adding mysteriously, 'and quicker than any of you might suspect.'

'Where to, guv?' asked the cab driver. They were now out on the busy street.

'Blissamore Hotel, please,' Black replied. Above them another flash of lightning splintered across the sky. Heavier raindrops began to fall. 'Good lord, it really has started,' Black said to himself.

They all piled into the cab, dripping from the rain: Molly as AH2, Micky as the Rasta, whose name was Leonard.

'Wow! Everyt'ing is cool in 'ere!' Micky said with a Jamaican lilt to his voice as he settled back into his seat. 'This guy listens to a lot of music. It's flying around his brain like ribbons.'

The cab set off.

'I don't believe it!' Molly gasped as she glanced through AH2's mind. 'This guy shot me with a tracking dart! That's how he always knows where I am. I remember where now. It was by the pool – do you remember, Micky?'

It was then that Molly heard the barking. It was Petula's bark – she was sure of it. Forgetting about AH2, Molly wound down the window. She saw Petula with Stanley and Magglorian. They were running along-side the cab in the rain.

'Stop the car!' Molly cried. And in the next moment she had opened the cab door and was on the street, hugging Petula. Behind, other cabs and buses beeped.

'You better get in,' the cab driver suggested, 'or I'll get done.'

'So has your pet changed into this man now?' Stanley asked Petula, looking at AH2, extremely confused.

'Yes! Thanks, you two. We found her!'

Magglorian sniffed the air and eyed the traffic that was building up on the road behind. 'Talking of pets,' he said. 'I'd better get back to mine. They'll be worrying.'

'Same 'ere,' said Stanley. 'Mine'll be leavin' the market soon.'

Both dogs barked up at Petula.

'Nice meeting you, Petula!' Magglorian barked.

'Good luck, girl!' Stanley added. He dropped a stone into the car. 'And there you go, Petula, I've been meaning to give you that! A little present. Goodbye.' He gave her a cheeky wink and with that the two London dogs scampered away, dodging pedestrians and looking like they owned the streets. Then Petula jumped in the cab, picked up the pebble and shook herself down.

Ten minutes later they arrived back at the hotel where Black had stayed the night before.

'Come on up.' Black led Molly and Micky past a grey-suited receptionist towards the hotel's lift.

'Is this where you normally live?' Molly asked.

'I live in a few places,' Black said, pressing the lift button.

The doors pinged open and they all shuffled in.

'Just explain,' Molly said, tilting her head. 'Why do you live in a hotel and how?'

'This hotel belongs to my brother. He inherited it from our mother when she died. The deal was, I got the equivalent in cash and an apartment to live in.' Molly watched bright numbered buttons light up as the lift ascended through the building. 'He's a businessman now. He owns other hotels too,' Black continued. 'And of course the casino. I don't really approve of that part of his business but he let me have an office there and it seemed a waste to refuse on principle. I mean, he'll continue running that gambling house whatever I say, and it's an excellent location for my charity, so on balance it's a good idea.'

They all stepped out on to a carpeted landing.

Then Micky stalled. 'Before we go into your apartment,' he said, 'I've just got a few questions for you, Mr Black.'

Black nodded. 'Fire away. You need to trust me a hundred per cent.'

'Firstly,' Micky started, 'Miss Hunroe showed us some pictures. In one you were in the park, sitting on a bench with a woman, a woman in a hat with a bird on it, and you seemed to be hypnotizing her with a pendulum. How can you explain that?'

'Oh!' Black exclaimed. 'Mrs Moriarty! She's an antiques dealer. She was selling me that pendulum. I collect pendulums, you see. She met me in the park because I couldn't get to Camden, where her shop is. Hunroe is so devious,' he added. 'That picture must have made me look really bad. I have the bill for the pendulum inside, if you want proof.'

'Hmmm. And what about the man from Wiltshire Jams? There was a picture of you in a café looking deep into his eyes.'

'Yes, I know exactly the occasion you are talking about.' Mr Black smiled. 'I can't believe Hunroe was photographing me then. The old man's name is Sam. We call him Jammy Sam. He's my uncle. I met him for a coffee and he got a bit of dust in his eye. He wanted me to see whether I could get it out for him. I could show you some family photographs, if you like?'

Micky nodded. 'Hmmm.'

Molly interrupted. 'Micky, I promise you, Black is

198

fine. I've seen inside his head. Really, he's *good*. You don't need to worry.'

Micky tilted his head to one side and considered the situation. 'If you say so, Molly.'

A few steps later they were walking into Black's hotel apartment. Molly recognized the French windows that she'd seen before from the outside. It was far fancier than she had imagined.

The sitting room was large with a white carpet. There were two black doors at either end and stone Indian sculptures of gods stood on polished stone stands along the walls. Some wore crowns of gold, others golden necklaces and earrings. One section of the wall was covered with pendulums. Gold, silver and copper, and some pendulums encrusted with precious stones were draped all over the walls. Two huge mirrors at each end of the room made the space seem even bigger and a fire burned in a black slate hearth framed by a white marble fireplace. A strange swirling wire bush of a lampshade hung in the centre of the room like a metal wasps' nest and lit scented candles filled the air with the warm smell of frankincense. Three white sofas were arranged around a low silver table that was piled high with books. In the centre of the coffee table was a golden sculpture of a goddess doing a yogic pose. And on each of the walls to the right and left hung strange portraits of women with two faces on the same head.

'Those pictures remind me of Miss Hunroe and her two-faced spinster friends,' Micky observed.

'Yes,' Black replied. 'But the ladies in these pictures seem ugly on the outside but are beautiful people underneath – so it's the reverse. They are Picassos, by the way.' Then he took off his wet coat and shoes.

A woman in a black uniform came in with a tray of delicate chocolates that she put on the table and some velvet slippers that she gave to Black. She took his coat and shoes.

'Glad you're back, Mr Black,' she said. 'I was starting to worry.' She smiled at Leonard and at AH2. 'Nice to meet you.'

'Kookaburra sitting in an old gum tree,' Black said mysteriously.

'Oh good. Very glad to hear that,' the woman said.

'And thanks for the chocolates, Dot. Just what we need. Yum, those are the toffee fondant ones, aren't they.' Black picked up the silver tray and offered one to Molly.

'Yes, Mr Black. And that nice baker from Harrows dropped off some of those extra special croissants he makes. So you'll be happy at breakfast tomorrow.'

'Oh, well done, Dot. You are an angel. Looks like there'll be a few of us for supper. Is it possible to have lobster?'

'Rightio, sir.' Dot began to go. 'By the way, Lily is a bit, erm, well, let's say hot under the collar.' With that she went out.

At the same time the double doors on the left of the

room opened. There stood Lily Black in a black lace dress.

'Dad?' she said through gritted teeth. 'Is that you?'

'Kookaburra sitting in an old gum tree,' said Black. 'That's our code word,' he explained. 'Just in case someone has morphed into me.'

'Who are these weird guys?' Lily asked, staring rudely at the two strangers in the room. 'He looks like he thinks he's James Bond and he looks like he thinks he's a reggae singer.'

'Cool down, Lily,' said Black. 'These, believe it or not, are the twins you saw. Meet Molly,' he gestured to AH2, 'and Micky, who at the moment is Leonard.'

Lily didn't step forward to shake hands. Instead she scowled at Petula.

'We don't know how to change back to ourselves,' Molly started to explain. 'But luckily your dad said he'd teach us. In fact, we're a bit desperate. We left our bodies yesterday and we're feeling a bit . . .'

'Discombobulated,' Micky suggested.

'Don't some people find meegoing impossible?' Lily commented, with a malicious glint in her eye. 'It's not easy, you know,' she said coldly to AH2 and Leonard. 'So don't get your hopes up.'

Chapter Fifteen

'Lily, Lily, please. If you can't be helpful or nice, just go to your room.' Black sat down on one of the white sofas and invited Molly and Micky to sit on another. 'Molly, Micky make yourselves comfortable.'

Lily slumped down into a brown leather chair in the corner of the room and sulkily folded her arms. 'Morphing, morphing, morphing,' she muttered, kicking the bottom of the chair with her heels. 'And saving the world. All day long, it's all you ever do.'

'All right,' Black started, ignoring Lily, 'so, meegoing is something you get the knack for.'

'If you're lucky,' Lily interrupted.

'Lily!' After a very stern look at his daughter, Black continued. 'Just because you can't morph, don't be jealous!'

'Thanks!' Lily replied furiously. 'Maybe if you'd take some time to teach me, I'd be able to.'

Black went on. 'So, it requires a knack, a skill. But, contrary to what Lily is suggesting, I'm sure you'll both get the hang of it immediately.'

Lily smiled to herself as though she knew otherwise. Outside the skies lit up as another bout of lightning and thunder began. Petula dived under a cushion.

'Did you take a copy of the morphing lessons?' Molly asked. 'If we could read them, maybe it would be easier.'

Black shook his head. 'I'm afraid I didn't do that. Too risky. If it fell into the wrong hands, all sorts of people would be able to morph. There would be chaos.'

'You mean *I* might find the lessons and learn,' Lily grumbled. 'And you wouldn't want *me* learning any of that stuff, would you? Meanie,' she added under her breath.

Black ignored her. She leaned back and began to turn the light switch off and on and off and on so that the metal wasps' nest lampshade glowed brightly, then dimmed, over and over.

'So, back to you. How to do it,' Black elaborated, trying not to notice what Lily was doing. 'All you need is to quieten your minds. You have to hold quite a few thoughts in your mind at once. Are you ready to do that?'

'Ready to juggle a hundred thoughts if that's what's needed,' Molly said.

'Good. Well, I suppose the way back to your selves

is a bit like a recipe with different ingredients. Get all the ingredients together and then put them on the heat. I'll tell you what the heat is in a minute. The first thing to realize is this. If you think about it, you haven't lost your intellectual being. Both of you are in control of your minds. Even though you look like two men, you can actually remember everything of your own lives as Molly and Micky, can't you?'

'At the moment they can,' Lily piped up like a poison-spitting jack-in-the-box.

'That's it, Lily. You've been warned. Go.'

Grumpily, Lily slid off her chair and went to another room, slamming the door behind her.

'Sorry about that,' Black apologized. 'Now, where was I? Yes, so you have your *mental* selves. What you are missing are your *physical* selves. So, to get back to your bodies, you have to imagine them. What they look like and what they feel like when you're inside them.'

Black coughed and shut his eyes. His voice became like a hypnotic teacher.

'You must think of the time your *own* bodies, your Molly and Micky bodies, last felt physical pain. For me, for instance, it was when I nearly twisted my ankle running across St James's Park after you two when you were ravens. Next I want you to remember the last time your own body felt something *good*. Both of these things can be tricky. Recalling physical memories from your muscles isn't as easy as drumming up memories connected to emotional feelings or memories to do with images. Now think hard.'

Both Molly and Micky cast their minds back to when they had last been in their own bodies.

'I had a cut on my finger right along the side of my nail,' said Micky with delight, as though he'd just got a line of numbers in a bingo game.

Molly wished she had something as obvious as that to recall. 'Um,' she muttered.

'Did you hurt yourself in the air vents inside the casino?' Micky asked.

'No.'

'That morning?'

'Yes!' Molly said, equally joyfully. 'I stubbed my toe on the bed's leg.'

'Brilliant,' Black agreed. 'And can you both actually remember the pain?'

Molly and Micky shut their eyes and concentrated hard. They both nodded.

'I think so,' Molly said.

'Excellent,' Black went on. 'Now, think of a *good* physical memory.'

'Do you remember how nice it felt to stretch our legs after we got out of Miss Hunroe's car?' Micky asked Molly.

'Yes,' Molly replied. 'I really remember that. OK. So what's the next step?'

'The next step is perhaps easier,' said Black. 'Each of you must picture your real self, as if looking in a mirror at yourself. Really see yourself and your refection. Can you do that? Well, once you've got all these ingredients together – the good feeling, the painful one, the picture of yourselves, sort of layer them so that they are *all* present at once. Then rise up so that you are looking at your reflection from above. Lastly, do all this whilst you are staring at a space on the floor where you want to be. What you must do now is sort of push your imagined reflection, with the feeling of pain and pleasure, *into* this space where you want to be.'

'That sounds really complicated and really *impossible*,' gulped Micky. 'It's a kind of teleportation.'

'Yes, it is.'

Molly grimaced.

And so they began.

'I suggest,' Black said, 'that you look in these mirrors.' He gestured to the walls of mirror beside him. 'Stare at yourselves intensely. Stare straight into your eyeballs – and keep staring. If you don't take your eyes away, you'll find that the face of the man that you are now inside will drop away and you can *imagine* whatever face you like. Imagine your *own* face and go from there.'

'I know this,' Molly exclaimed. 'Ages ago I used to stare in the mirror and watch my face change.'

'There ya go.' Black rubbed his hands together. 'Are you ready?'

'Sounds difficult,' Micky mumbled.

As Molly glued her eyes to the sharp blue eyes in

the mirror, she was suddenly overcome with a longing to get back to herself. She loved being herself, Molly Moon. Odd-looking Molly Moon with close-set green eyes and a potatoey nose. Molly Moon with blotchy, skinny legs and sweaty hands. Molly didn't care what she looked like. She just wanted to be in her own body again.

She'd been a ladybird, a pigeon, an elderly lady, a beautiful young woman, a rat, a dog, a blackbird, the Queen, a raven, a schoolboy, a crazy red-headed Chinese tourist and, finally, a pilot obsessed with aliens. She'd been male and female, young and old, furry, winged, fat, thin, fit, unfit. And not one of those bodies felt quite as good as her own. Each body had felt like a piece of clothing that didn't suit her. Molly wanted her own imperfect but perfect-for-her body back.

So, as if nothing in the world mattered as much, Molly stared hard into the mirror, into AH2's eyes and tried to see her real self. She imagined herself in jeans and a T-shirt. She imagined her scruffy hair and as many of her other features as she could. And soon AH2's reflection began to disappear from the mirror, to be replaced by a faint and then a very definite imagined image of her self. Molly saw her own face crystallize and then her torso come into focus. Next came her arms and hands and her legs and feet.

Simultaneously, Molly tried to remember both the wonderful feeling of stretching out her own muscles and limbs, as well as the feeling of how it had hurt stubbing her toe. Molly had all the ingredients. Now came the most difficult part. Molly found a space on the floor. With all the intent that she could muster, she planted the phantom version of herself into that space. Her eyes throbbed as she stared. It was as though they were getting bigger and bigger, and suddenly as though they were becoming hollow. Something was happening now and Molly had no control over it. As though she had blown a crack in the wall of a dam, she now felt herself shooting, like spraying floodwater out through the crack – out of AH2's eyes, into the space on the floor. Her being gushed out of him.

And then she felt herself turn upside down, as though she was diving. Below her, she saw the crown of her own head – her own Molly Moon head. In she dived. Her own body greeted her like a long-lost friend. And then Molly came up for air and took a breath.

Molly was well and truly back.

'What the—?' AH2 began. He staggered to the other sofa and collapsed.

'Whoa! Man!' Leonard gasped, sitting down.

Sensing a change of energy in the room, Petula pulled her head out from behind her cushion. At once, she saw that Molly and Micky were back. Delighted, she jumped on to the floor and ran over to Molly, barking.

Molly bent down and gave Petula a huge hug. Then she turned to see what had happened to Micky. There on the chair sat Leonard, looking dazed and confused, and a metre away from him stood Micky, except it wasn't Micky as she knew him. His face and body were as furry as a brown bear's.

'Uuuaaargh!' he yelped, leaping about and pointing at his hairy arms and stomach. 'This isn't me!'

'Oh, um. Right,' Black said. 'Calm down and don't worry. This sort of thing is completely normal. Let's see. I wonder what you did wrong. You just got your skin wrong really. So do it again, but next time imagine your usual skin.'

So Micky had another go. This time it worked.

'You did it!' Black exclaimed, clapping his hands with delight.

'But I haven't got any clothes on!' Micky replied, frowning down at his bare legs. He quickly grabbed Petula's cushion.

'You didn't imagine them, that's why,' Molly laughed. And then she couldn't stop laughing. 'Oh, Micky, you're so funny!' Molly was so relieved that she lay on her back laughing until her ribs hurt. As she rolled around, Dot entered the room and handed Micky his old clothes, freshly laundered and nicely folded.

'I think these are yours? I came across them yesterday evening in the casino office. And,' she said, passing Molly her charm necklace, 'I think this is probably yours.'

'Oh, thank you!' Molly beamed. She fingered the animals on the chain. A pug, an elephant and two blackbirds. She put it on, and smiled.

'Congratulations, you two,' said Black. That really

209

was an achievement. To get it right first time is not normal.' He smiled, but then a bolt of lightning flashed outside the apartment window and his expression changed. 'You are, thank goodness, safely back in your selves, Molly and Micky . . .' His voice trailed off and he glanced up at the dark clouds. Rain was now dashing heavily on the window. He gazed back into the room, his eyes falling distractedly on AH2. 'But unfortunately Hunroe has the book. And I'm afraid that the whole world is probably now the most unsafe it has ever been.' Black's voice trembled slightly. He looked out of the window again. 'And you two may think that you've seen terrible danger, but I'm afraid that in days to come things are going to be worse.'

'W-what do you mean?' Molly stuttered, her stomach tightening. 'This doesn't sound good, Mr Black. How are things going to get worse?'

Black crossed his arms. 'That book held more than just lessons about the advanced hypnotic arts.' He shook his head worriedly. 'It held half of a very important key.'

'A key to what?' Micky asked.

Black put his hands to his temples and began to massage them, worriedly. 'A key that is, I'm afraid, *the* key to the *weather.*'

'The weather?'

'Yes.' Black sighed. Outside the hotel window the trees swayed. A strong wind now accompanied the storm. Black shook his head again. 'I can't believe this

210

is happening. I hoped it wouldn't. But it is happening. I'm afraid Miss Hunroe and her friends may soon have the power to control the weather all over the world! And, by the looks of it –' he pointed to the thrashing branches of the tree outside – 'the trouble has already started.'

Leonard stood up. 'I'm v-very sorry,' he stammered, his eyes wide and nervous, 'but I kinda t'ink I better be gettin' out of here.' He touched AH2's shoulder, as if testing whether he was real or not. 'It's all gettin' a bit too weird.' He eyed Molly and Micky. 'I t'ink I need to see a doctor!' With that, he backed himself towards the flat door and in the next second had opened it, and was gone.

Chapter Sixteen

Outside the French window, yet another flash of lightning lit up the hotel's winter garden. Hail began pelting down, ricocheting off the mossy paving stones and hitting the statue of the winged cupid in the centre of the pond like ice bullets.

'This is only the beginning of it,' Black declared, sinking his hands into his trouser pockets and gazing up at the sky. A twig struck the window.

'I don't believe it,' said AH2, staring at Molly. 'You're not an alien! You're a hypnotist. I saw. I saw you when you took my head over.'

Black threw a glance back at AH2. 'Is he safe, Molly?'

Molly considered AH2. He was a fanatical person, but he was also very clever. If things were about to get more dangerous, he might be just the person to have on their side. After all, he had been in Molly's head, so he understood things. And she had been in his head and trusted him.

'He's good,' she said. 'Brainy too. His name is Malcolm Tixley.' She nodded at their new friend. 'You might be able to help us, Malcolm,' she said. Then she turned to Black. 'So, Mr Black, you'd better lay it out for us.'

As if addressing the clouds that hid the sun, Black began. '*Hypnotism. Volume Two.* Where shall I start? Let me give you its story first. It was written and made by your great-great-grandfather, Dr Logan. It was kept in the library at Briersville Park. Logan died. And the book stayed in the family for years. Secretly. Then it was stolen. Stolen by a family of hypnotists called the Speals.'

'Speal said it had been stolen from *them*!' Micky exclaimed, moving closer to the fire to keep warm.

'Well,' continued Black, 'the Speals kept the book for a while. They were responsible for the terrible storms in England in 1953. Then the book was rescued back by the Logans. Again it stayed in Briersville, this time safely hidden. But, next, a bad Logan cropped up – your uncle Cornelius. I knew him at school. That's where I come into the story. Miss Hunroe knew Cornelius as well, you see. We were all at school together – a long time ago.'

'Ah! *That* must have been why Cornelius was so excited when Miss Hunroe arrived at Briersville that night,' Molly said to Micky.

Black nodded. 'When his father died, Cornelius got the run of Briersville Park. I heard of his inheritance and guessed that he would have found the book. I knew it would be a disaster for either him or Hunroe to have access to the book. So . . .' Black stopped and looked awkwardly at the twins. 'So I stole it.'

'You stole it?'

'Well, I had to.' Black paused and fiddled with a button on his shirtsleeve. 'I had it for years, and no one guessed that it was me who had stolen it. So it was safe. In the fabulously secure casino building of my brother's. Lily said you saw the book. Well, then you must have seen the three flat coloured stones in the corners of its front cover.'

'And we saw the fourth stone,' Molly said, popping a chocolate into her mouth. 'Speal had it. It was blue. She treated it like some sort of super precious thing. Mmm. Toffee.'

'Ah, so that is where it has been all these years. Well, Miss Speal is right. That blue stone is very precious. And that's why the book is extra-precious. The stones on its cover are the key. Each one of those stones can help to change the weather on its own. If I was holding a stone now, for instance, I could change the weather near here. But all four stones together can make mammoth-scale, world-wide weather changes happen, but to do this the holder of the stones has to be in a very special place.'

'Where?'

'And you think that is where Miss Hunroe is going

214

right now?' Micky guessed, opening a smart, leather-covered atlas that lay on the table.

'I am sure of it.'

Black played with the heavy sashes that tied back the curtains as he spoke. 'I think that Miss Speal has been manipulating the weather with the piece of blue stone for a long time. We've had monsoon-like down-pours in London lately, and do you remember that mini cyclone that went over Primrose Hill?' As he spoke, a massive blade of lightning jagged across the dark sky. 'Now Hunroe has the whole book and so all the weather stones. She can do enormous good, or enormous evil. She has the power to cause typhoons, hurricanes, high seas, tidal waves, tsunamis and droughts. She could drown millions in an afternoon. If she decides that the rain should stop, then crops die and millions of people have nothing to eat. She could cause millions of people to die slowly, of starvation.'

Black sounded so serious that Petula whimpered and hid her nose in the crook of Molly's arm.

'Wow, just think of the good things you could do with the weather stones,' Micky interjected. 'You could make it rain where there were droughts. You could make a jungle grow in the Sahara Desert! These stones sound fabulous, Mr Black.'

'Don't they? But remember, there is a flip side to the power of the stones. They can be used for enormous good, or enormous evil.'

'And you don't have a set of time crystals?' Molly

asked him, eyeing his vast collection of pendulums. 'Because, if you did, well, I could easily sort this all out.'

Black shook his head. 'Sadly, I've never had my own.'

'Hmmm.' Molly sighed, thinking how simple everything would be if she could use her time-stopping or time-travelling skills.

'I wonder whether Hunroe knows how to use your crystals,' Black said. 'I don't think she does or she would have used them by now.'

'Maybe then,' Molly mulled, 'we should just call the police and have her arrested. Then I might get my crystals back. And then we could sort everything out.'

'She'll be long gone from the museum by now,' Black said knowingly.

'How are you so sure that Hunroe wants to do bad things with the weather?' Micky said. 'I mean I know she's not exactly a cuddly doll, but maybe she's simply hoarding the book and the stones like an evil squirrel might.'

'I know Miss Hunroe,' Black said. 'Believe me, she is as twisted as a person can be. She looks wonderful, like a superstar beauty, but underneath she is as rotten as a gangrenous wound. Underneath she hates everyone. She's a misanthrope.'

'A misanthrope?' Molly asked.

'A misanthrope,' said Micky, 'is someone who hates other people.'

'Yes,' agreed Black. 'And Hunroe is that sort of person. When she hates, she really hates. I remember once at school we had a lecturer come to talk to us about the world's population, about how there were too many people on the planet. And I always remember Hunroe in that class. She must have been about ten. She said, 'Why don't governments just poison the water supplies of the major cities?' She wasn't joking, though the lecturer thought she was. With the book in her hands, the world is in serious danger.'

'Let's go back a bit,' Malcolm interrupted. 'All this stuff about the stones on the book's cover – *how* do they actually change the weather?'

Just then, Dot opened the door and came in with a tray of cups and a tall silver pot. On a plate was a pile of buttered crumpets.

'Hot chocolate and crumpets. You all look like you need it. Don't mind me,' she said.

'Ooh, thanks!' said both Molly and Micky, helping themselves.

'That is just what the doctor ordered,' said Black as Dot handed out linen napkins. 'Hmm. Yes, where were we? Well, the book's stones, once taken from their places on the book's cover, can be rubbed and, as I said, the weather *where they are* changes. Each stone represents one of the elements. The blue stone represents water; the orange, fire and heat; the grey, wind; and the green and brown stone is earth. Each one of these stones affects the weather, but used in any old place like this the effects are haphazard. For *controlled* weather changing – to change weather in different countries thousands of miles away, there is a special place where these weather stones have to be taken. And this is where Miss Hunroe will be heading. In the chapter of the book called "The Logan Stones",' Black continued, 'where weather manipulation is explained, Dr Logan refers to this place. Dr Logan found the Logan Stones, obviously, for they bear his name. They are great rocking stones, huge things. One is orange, one grey, one blue, one green.'

'Like the smaller stones on the book's cover?'

'Exactly. Logan describes in the book how the miniature pieces of stone dripped off the big Logan Stones. Apparently the giant stones are hard as diamond. Little pieces cannot be chipped off them. But *he* managed to cause the rocks to "drip" to produce the little stones for him. I have no idea how. *But* what I do know is this. In the hypnotism book he states that if you stand in the very centre of the force field that the four big Logan Stones make, with the four smaller stones in your hand, and if you rub the stones with your fingers, using your imagination, and going into a hypnotic trance to think up the weather that you would like to see in the world, that new weather will *happen*.'

'It sounds out of this world,' Molly said. 'Amazing that our great-great-grandfather found this place a hundred years ago. It sounds like it's from the future.'

'Yes, or like some ancient place from the beginning of time,' Black remarked.

'Well, what are we waiting for?' Micky asked with a mouth full of crumpet. 'Why don't we just go there?'

Black looked beaten. 'The book doesn't hold exact directions,' he said. 'It simply has a clue in it. A riddle – one which I've never succeeded in cracking.'

'A riddle?'

'Yes. In the back of the book there is a line that says, *Where there is a quill there is a way. Muse o' life, and you will find.* "Muse" means "think" in old English. "Muse o'" means "muse on". In other words, "*Muse o' life, and you will find*" means "Think about life and you will find the answer". It could be anywhere.'

'No,' said Micky, wiping his mouth. 'It couldn't be anywhere. That riddle must mean something extremely specific.'

'Yes, well, you're probably right,' Black admitted. The hopelessness that he felt was evident in his voice.

'And lucky for you, Mr Black,' said Micky, 'I happen to have a fondness for riddles.'

'He does,' Molly agreed, stroking Petula. 'Micky's really into crosswords and word puzzles.'

Black gave a half-hearted smile.

'In fact,' Micky went on, 'half of the riddle is obvious to me already.'

'What half?' Black asked, perking up.

'The second part.'

'What, *Muse o' life, and you will find* . . . What does it mean to you?'

'Well,' Micky went on, 'I think you've got the "o'"' wrong. You think it means "muse o' life", as in muse *on* life, as in think about life. But I think the "o'" means "of" and it says "muse *of* life" and I think "muse" is short for "museum".'

Micky bit his lip and smiled. And his smile was infectious.

'What museums are there?' he asked.

'Art museums,' Molly suggested. 'Science museums, history museums . . . And . . .'

'And?'

'And natural history museums!'

'Yes. They have the history of the planet, of animals and minerals and of humans, don't they? A natural history museum is a museum of life, isn't it? Yes, I think, "muse o' life", Mr Black, might be the same thing as "museum of life". I wonder, is it one big coincidence that Miss Hunroe and her horrid cronies hang out in the Natural History Museum?'

'You're a genius!' Molly exclaimed. Quickly she cast her mind back to Miss Hunroe's library. She remembered the painting that hung above the fireplace. She had thought it of a strange uprooted, pointed, poplar-like tree. 'The picture!' she said. 'The picture over the library fireplace! It wasn't of a *tree* – it was of a feather quill! What was the first line of the clue, Mr Black?'

'*Where there is a quill there is a way.*'

'Your turn to be a genius,' Micky said. The twins looked at each other. This was turning into a treasure hunt. And both knew that venturing back to the museum and sneaking about in Hunroe's rooms was a job that would be best done by them alone.

'Hopefully,' Micky said, 'Hunroe and her friends are already miles away from London on their way to these Logan Stones.'

Molly nodded. 'The rooms in the museum will be empty. I don't expect they will have left the book behind, but hopefully the next clue to where the Stones are will be there.' She sighed. 'Only a few days ago I was wishing my life was more exciting and adventurous.'

'You have to be careful what you wish for,' Micky said.

Molly gave Petula a squeeze. Outside a rumble of thunder boomed out of the now charcoal sky, making the windows of the hotel rattle.

Chapter Seventeen

'**D**o you really think Petula needs to come?'
Black asked.

It was properly dark now. Micky, Molly and Petula
were sitting in the back seat of Black's old Mercedes,
which was parked at the corner of the Natural History
Museum, near its second entrance. Malcolm Tixley
was in the passenger seat beside Black. His eyes followed the journey of the half-bent wipers as they swept
left and right at the sloshings of water that pelted down
on the windscreen.

'Petula's good luck,' Molly explained. 'She's like a
mascot. In fact, she has often helped me. She's been all
over the world with me, forward *and* backward in time
too. She's part of the team, isn't she, Micky?'

'Absolutely,' Micky replied. 'Wow, it's wet out there.'
A rumble of thunder rolled through the sky as if in
agreement.

Black turned his engine off. 'Here are a couple of

torches for you. You may need them. We'll wait for you here.' He consulted his watch. 'Remember, if you're not back by midnight, I'm coming in.'

Molly read the luminescent clock on the dashboard. It was ten fifteen. 'We'll be fine,' she said, far more confidently than she felt. 'Don't worry about us. Anyway, Malcolm, your red box can still track me, right?'

'Yes,' said Malcolm, pulling the gadget out of his pocket and switching it on. It bleeped reassuringly.

'Good. And, you never know, we may find my time-stopping crystals and time-travelling gems are in there somewhere. Then, wow, everything would be really cool. Ready, Micky?'

Standing in the rain outside, Micky rang the bell. Water seeped under the elasticated wristband of Molly's anorak. She held Petula tight.

A light came on inside the building and the night watchman, an elderly, whiskered man in a blue uniform, came through the inner safety door of the museum and peered out through the football-sized peephole of the main door. He couldn't see much as the glass was so wet, but it was clear that the two people outside were children. He knew how dangerous the London streets could be at night so he reached behind him to lock the safety catch of the inner door, and then he reached for the bolt of the main door.

'Hello, are you two all right?' he asked. 'It's raining cats and dogs out there.'

The little girl came forward.

'We're lost,' she said in a wobbly voice. 'We're lost. We ran away from home, see, and now we're lost.'

'Run away from home? Lost? Dear me!' The night watchman glanced out at the empty, black, glistening street that bounced with rainwater. Then he looked at the two straggly, sodden children and their black pug. They were harmless.

'Come on in then,' he said kindly, beckoning them inside.

'I'm very sorry,' said Molly as the old man led them through the second door into the museum, towards his office. 'And thank you very much.'

'What on earth are a nice couple of kids like you doin' runnin' away from home?' the watchman asked. 'That's what I want to know.'

Molly considered the man. Hunroe would have definitely hypnotized him, she thought. Hypnotized him not to be hypnotized by anyone else. Hunroe would have locked her hypnotism in with a password. But, if Molly *found out the password*, then she could override Miss Hunroe's hypnotism. So, using the skill that no one else knew she had, she opened a thought bubble over the man's head and she asked him, 'What is the password that Miss Hunroe used to lock in your hypnotism?'

The old man frowned. 'I'm sorry? I don't think I understand your question, dear. Come into the office, and have a hot chocolate or a cup of tea or something.

We'll sort everything out there.' But as he spoke a picture of an apple appeared above his head.

Molly switched her eyes on. As the hypnotic lasers of her pupils beamed into the old man's, she said, 'I unlock your previous hypnotism with the word "apple" and now, I'm sorry, I mean you are a very nice old man and all that, but until I set you free you are now completely and utterly under my power.'

Like a creature born to obey her, the old man stood obediently in front of Molly.

'How did you know the password?' Micky asked incredulously.

Molly shrugged casually.

'No, that's weird, Molly, how did you know?'

'Intuition,' Molly fibbed.

Micky held her gaze and tilted his head, as though he found this difficult to believe. 'Really?' he said.

Minutes later, Molly, Micky and Petula were being led by the hypnotized night watchman through the museum in a passage lined with stuffed birds. Ahead, in the musty gloom of the main hall of the museum, they could see the massive skeletal legs of the diplodocus.

'We'll see you later then,' Molly whispered to the old man. 'Wait by the side door to let us out.'

The watchman nodded and smiled. 'Right – you – are,' he whispered back in a halting tone.

Molly and Micky paused and surveyed the dark, cathedral-proportioned space with its grand staircase

225

that split into two, curving round to join the first-floor balcony. Petula sniffed the air and tried to read its swarms of smells. The overriding odour was floor polish. Under this were the smells of ancient bones, old fur and that afternoon's visitors' footsteps which had brought in scents from the street. And Petula could detect that onions and garlic had been fried a few hours before and a croissant had been eaten upstairs. The scent of lavender blossom flickered through the hall as though someone wearing it had recently walked by.

Sensing that the coast was clear now, though, Petula tapped Molly on her leg with her paw, nodded and stepped forward.

'Petula seems to think it's all right. Glad we brought her.' Molly put her hand under Micky's elbow and they both crept forward. Cautious as timid mice, they slipped through the shadows and climbed the staircase. They moved quietly along the upper balcony until they were finally up at the door to the botanical library.

Turning the doorknob, they went through. They began tiptoeing down the dark archive room, past its shelves of books and towering filing cabinets, to the column of drawers at the end that hid the secret entrance to Miss Hunroe's lair. Molly pushed the filing cabinet, and the secret door opened and they went through it.

Petula wondered what the twins were looking for. She supposed it was the book. If it was a bottle of lavender perfume, they were heading in the right direction, for the scent was drifting through the cracks along the edges of the door in front of them like heat escaping from an igloo.

Molly gripped the filing-cabinet handle and got ready to push. 'Here goes,' she said.

The door nudged open, revealing another dark room, this time, the library. Nothing had changed. The layout of the furniture was the same. The three sofas stood in a horseshoe configuration with the book-laden coffee table between them. There was the tall window with the stained-glass patterns on it.

Micky tapped Molly on the shoulder. 'Look,' he whispered, 'there's the feathery tree picture. And it's not a feathery tree, is it? You were right, Molly – it's a quill.' He turned his torch on.

Molly joined her brother beside the fireplace. '*Where there's a quill there's a way,*' she said. 'Do you think there's something behind it?' She reached up to lift the old picture from the wall. Micky helped her as they hauled it down. As they did, they saw that the wall where it had been was plain, without writing on it, or a safe embedded in it.

'It's heavy!' Molly whispered.

'Do you think there's something *inside* it?' Micky suggested.

'Crumbs. Bet there is,' Molly agreed.

The twins turned the picture over and by the light

of Micky's torch they saw that the frame's wooden back was taped down. Quickly, they stripped the tape off, and peeled the wood away from the frame, revealing the back of the quill drawing.

'Nothing here,' Micky decided disappointedly. The dark sky outside seemed to growl as though warning the children to behave themselves. Micky pulled the paper out. It was simply a drawing. Nothing more. 'Maybe it's got secret writing on it.' He shone his torch through different parts of the parchment to see whether any watermarked writing was hidden there whilst Molly picked at the frame itself.

'Perhaps something's hidden inside the wood,' she said. 'Shall we break it and see? I'll take the glass out first. I mean I know it's not good smashing things up and all that, but this is an exception.'

Petula watched with interest as Molly put her sneakered foot on the picture frame and broke it in half. Outside a distant crack of lightning seemed to echo the splintering noise.

Molly studied the wood. 'It's solid. Not hollow. Nothing in it.' She sat heavily on the sofa. 'It was only a hunch, wasn't it? I mean there are quills and feathers everywhere. Maybe we should be looking down in the stuffed-bird rooms.'

Micky sat down beside her and glanced up at the hundreds and hundreds of books. 'Why would there be a quill picture though? It must be to show that this room is special. There's something in here, there *must* be.'

Minutes later Molly and Micky were up on the balcony level of the room, rifling through the library's shelves for a box that might hold Molly's crystals or a book that might contain a good clue as to where the Logan Stones were. The books were organized alphabetically. Molly and Micky ran their torches along their spines, reading their titles.

'*The Andes*,' Micky read. '*Ancient Civilization, Annihilation of the World's Population and Other Extreme Ways Forward.*' Micky shook his head in revulsion. 'That sounds like a Hunroe sort of book, but not the next one. *Apple Picking, The Aztecs, Botany of the Amazon.*' Micky frowned while he thought.

'Damn!' Molly despaired. 'This is hopeless. The clue might be in a map or in a poem or it might be deep in a maths book written in a code in numbers!'

Micky turned round leaned over the ledge of the balcony and surveyed the mess of the picture frame below. They'd never be able to cover their tracks now, for the frame was unfixable.

At that moment a huge flash of lightning exploded in the sky. Petula froze with fear. And, as though some sort of giant thirty-metre-tall paparazzi photographer had his camera directed at them from outside the window and had detonated its flash, white light blasted in through the window. It flooded the room and something *extraordinary* happened.

Passing through the window's stained glass where the strange shapes were, and using the etched lines there, the light and shadows formed a *picture* and some *words* on the white wall where the picture of the quill had been.

The shadow picture was on the wall for only a second, but it was enough.

'WOW!' Micky gasped.

Chapter Eighteen

Molly and Micky stared at the wall in amazement. Every time a flash of lightning lit up the sky, the light of it shone through the stained-glass windowpane, past the etched lines there, and threw up defined shadows on the wall above the fireplace.

Quickly, they ran down the balcony's spiral staircase and waited for another burst of light.

'Come on, come *on*,' Micky urged. 'Don't let the storm stop now.'

Rain slapped against the window and thunder rumbled.

'Here we go,' said Molly. And then there was an enormous crack, as though two monster marbles were smashing into each other in the air above the museum. Petula hid under a sofa. The sky filled with white light. Again and again white light lit up the earth and Molly and Micky were able to read the wall.

'It's a map!' Micky declared, 'with a sort of picture

code. But the question is . . . Is that shape a country or a city or a village or a *small* area of land?'

'And what do the pictures inside the shape mean?' Molly agreed. 'The first thing looks like a cloud. Then, are those trees? Is that supposed to be a wood? Put the two things together and you get cloud trees or cloud wood. That doesn't make sense.'

'Cloud *Forest* does, though,' Micky interjected. 'There are places called cloud forests very high up in mountainous places where the trees are covered with cloud.'

'Where?'

'South America, I think. But we could find out for sure.'

'And those four tear-shaped things are definitely the Logan Stones,' Molly said. 'Then there's . . .' Molly waited for a flash of lightning to light up the wall again. When it did, she pointed to a shape. 'There's that. It looks like a spring – like a metal spring. Then there's the word "COCA" with that squiggly line after it. Coca. That must be a place.'

'No, it's not a place,' Micky said authoritatively. 'It's a river. The Coca River. I know it's a river. I remember reading about it when I was six and thinking how it was a river made of chocolate, of cocoa. And that spring shape is exactly that. A spring – you know, as in the origin of a river. A spring. That whole thing means: the spring of the Coca River.

Molly gasped. 'Where is the Coca River, Micky?'

Micky frowned. 'Let me think. What are the countries in South America. Um . . .' He paused and thought hard. Then he stared up at the wall as though for inspiration. Some lightning flashed into the room again, lighting up the wall. 'I've got it,' he practically shouted. 'That shape there is the shape of Ecuador. I know it is. This makes sense. Those books in the bookcase upstairs. Quite a lot of them were about South America, weren't they?'

Molly nodded. 'The Andes. The Aztecs. Weren't the Aztecs the people who used to live in South America?'

Micky nodded. I think we've nailed it, Moll. Come on. Let's go up there and see whether there's anything else that can help us.'

Quickly, the twins hurried back up the staircase to the bookshelves and found an atlas. They turned its pages to find the index, and searched for the word 'Coca'. There was only one entry.

'The Coca River!' Molly read.

Micky flicked back through the atlas's pages whilst Molly held the torch. 'Page thirty-three 2C.' His fingers found the page.

'This is extreme,' Micky announced. 'It's in northwest Ecuador.' He pointed to the map to an area that was coloured in grey. 'See all that? That area is the Andes Mountains. And see that? That's a volcano. Look, there's the Coca River. This is where it starts. And you can bet that it's all cloud forests in the high

233

mountains there. So, that's where the Logan Stones are! In a cloud forest place high in the Andes Mountains, near the spring of the Coca River.'

'Crikey,' Molly said. She looked outside at the terrible weather. '*How* are we going to get *there*?' The light outside again broke the darkness and showed the strange coded map on the wall.

'It's amazing,' said Micky. 'Somehow Hunroe worked out that the clue to the Logan Stones was here. Then she must have found all of this,' he pointed to the wall, 'and got so excited that she made the Natural History Museum her headquarters.'

'And our great-great-grandfather, Dr Logan,' Molly added, 'must have hidden the clue there in the window glass in the first place.'

Just then, Petula began to growl. She smelt chocolate biscuits and the lavender smell was getting stronger. She poked her nose out from under the sofa and began to sniff. There was a noise from beyond the library door. Someone was making their way along the central aisle of the filing-cabinet room. They were carrying an umbrella or a walking stick, for their footsteps were accompanied by the tap tap tapping of something else that hit the floor as they walked.

'Quick!' Micky hissed.

'Petula!' Molly whispered.

Molly and Micky scurried down the balcony stairs and whipped across the downstairs room to the door. If they could slip behind it, they could just sneak out as soon as whoever it was out there entered. But there wasn't time. The door opened. The light came on. They ducked behind the sofa.

The room was suddenly lit with the warm glow of its orange lights. Molly stared at Micky and put her hand on Petula. In only a matter of seconds, the person would see the smashed picture frame. They listened to the person putting something down on the far table. They breathed heavily as they moved.

'Miss Suzette?' Micky mouthed the name to Molly and puffed his cheeks out. 'Fat!'

Molly smelt lavender in the air and nodded. She hoped so. Miss Suzette was small enough to handle. Molly imagined Miss Suzette eyeing the room and discovering the mess, then seeing the disturbed book-case upstairs. She hoped Miss Suzette would climb the balcony stairs to inspect. Once she was up there, they could escape. But as she was imagining this a horrible thing happened.

Miss Suzette's large, fat face peered over the top of the sofa.

'YOUUUUUUUUUUUUUUUUUUUUUUU!' she bellowed.

Like birds set to flight, Molly and Micky moved up and away. Dodging Miss Suzette's pink-fingernailed grasp, and the swishing of her mother-of-pearl walking stick, they ran.

'Come on, Petula,' Molly cried as she dashed over the broken frame, the wood crunching under her feet.

Micky jumped on the coffee table, smashing a flower-filled porcelain vase and slipping on a pile of magazines. He hurdled the other sofa. It was Petula who got stuck. Miss Suzette reached out and seized her round the waist. She lifted Petula up, tipping her at a very uncomfortable angle, pinching her skin with her pincer-like grip.

With a furious bark, Petula sank her teeth through the old woman's lacy dress sleeves and into her forearm.

Miss Suzette shrieked like a banshee. 'Aaaah, you ghastly dog!' and dropped her.

Petula leaped on to the sofa and ran along it to the other end, where Molly caught her. Micky picked up Miss Suzette's sopping wet raincoat, bunched it into a ball and threw it at her so that it hit her in the face like a slop of wet seaweed.

'Ha!' Micky laughed. Miss Suzette tottered backwards and fell in a heap on the floor, her petticoats puffing up to reveal huge doily-like knickerbockers. 'Hope that makes you think twice before you hurt an animal again!'

And, not wanting to hang around any longer in case Miss Suzette decided to morph into any of them, Molly, Micky and Petula were away. They sped through the archive room and raced to the upstairs passageway. They skidded over the polished floors, Petula's claws skittering as they went. They leaped down the main stairs. And then they sprinted along the stuffed-bird corridor that connected the museum to its other side.

'Hope there aren't any more of Hunroe's friends here,' Molly said, panting and breathless, eyeing a stuffed owl.

The twins and Petula arrived at the side entrance. Behind them they could hear the far-off echoing sound of Miss Suzette's clipped footsteps as she puffed her way down the museum stairs after them.

Molly paused by the night watchman, who stood like a soldier awaiting orders.

'Thank you!' she said. 'After we're gone you will no longer remember any of Miss Hunroe's hypnotic instructions to you. No one will *ever* be able to hypnotize you again. And you will forget us, but only once you've stopped Miss Suzette, the woman who's chasing us, from leaving the building. Thanks.' Molly turned to leave then paused. 'And I seal all of this in with the password . . .'

'Frilly knickerbockers?' Micky suggested.

'Yes, with the password, "frilly knickerbockers".'

With that Molly, Micky and Petula burst out of the building into the wet night. Rain drenched them so that they climbed into Black's car, dripping.

'Got what we need?' Black asked.

As the car screeched away, Molly looked back at the museum's side door.

Through the football-sized porthole there, she could just make out the puffy figure of Miss Suzette and the night watchman blocking her path. He had her wrists in his hands and was shaking his head solemnly whilst she was struggling and shouting as though a demon possessed her.

Chapter Nineteen

'Had a nice little trip did you?' Lily had finally emerged from her bedroom and stood on its threshold with her arms crossed. She was wearing a red silk dressing gown and red furry slippers. Her pyjamas had pictures of roses on them. Her eyes darted angrily to the rattling French windows, and the balcony outside, where rain smacked down hard.

'Oh, Lily, we did ask if you wanted to come too, so please stop being grumpy,' said Black. 'Come and hear what Molly and Micky found out.' He gestured to the sofa.

'Come on,' Molly said.

Lily shrugged and came over.

Whilst Molly told Lily everything that had happened, Malcolm fiddled with the TV controls. Finally he got a signal and a serious-faced presenter appeared, standing in a studio in front of a large weather map of Europe. The screen flickered and her voice crackled.

'Our satellite pictures show heavy storms over the North Sea,' she said. 'And what looks alarmingly like the beginnings of a *tornado* has been detected in Northern Europe, near the southern coast of Sweden. It's anyone's guess how this tornado will grow and where it will move, as the winds are proving unpredictable, but the National Weather Agency's advice to everyone tonight is stay at home and batten down the hatches. Don't make trips out unless they are *absolutely necessary*. And keep watching news and weather reports to see how this storm and tornado are progressing.' The woman gave a stern nod and the cameras switched to another newsperson, a dark-haired man in a suit, and his guest, an elderly man with white hair and a bushy beard.

'It's crazy out there, Professor Cramling. In all your years working at Cambridge University you say you've never seen anything like this?' asked the anchor man.

'No. Never.'

'And how do you explain it?'

Professor Cramling scratched his hairy chin. 'I can only assume,' he postured, 'that this weather is the unexpected result of global warming. People expected weather to change – but not this suddenly. Every weather professional that I have spoken to is concerned, alarmed, confused.'

Malcolm flicked channels to look at the global weather and news reports. Lots of other countries were having strange, often fatally dangerous weather too.

One channel showed a weather map of the world. It showed that Canada, America, Europe and Russia were having snowstorms and blizzards and Asian countries were having typhoons. Other countries were suffering from severe wet-weather conditions similar to London.

'But look!' Micky pointed to the world map on the TV. 'Ecuador and other South American countries don't seem to have been affected at all!'

'All flights from British airports have been delayed,' a newsreader reported.

'Not good news,' said Malcolm, watching the bird's-eye TV footage of miles and miles of traffic stuck in a jam on the motorways to the airports. The massive queue looked like an electrical river, as the thousands of cars in it beamed out their red rear lights into the dark night.

'So what do you think?' Micky asked Lily. Lily narrowed her eyes and then softened, pleased that someone valued her opinion. She knelt down on the floor next to Micky.

'You see,' Micky went on, 'we've got to get here.' He pointed to the atlas page that showed northern Ecuador. 'To the top of that squiggly blue line. That's the Coca River.'

'And it's definitely the place where the weather can be changed? Where the Logan Stones are?' Lily asked.

'Hope so,' Micky said, making a face. 'Because we're

going a long way away for a mistake if we're not right.'

'It all seems a bit vague to me,' Lily sniffed.

Black, who'd been tapping away at his computer, now leaned back in his chair. 'The source of the Coca River,' he announced, 'is unknown. But the first signs of it are high, high up in the Andes, way above the cloud forest. At least they give GPS coordinates for this. So we can go there.' Black squinted at his computer. 'We have to fly to a city called Quito in Ecuador,' he concluded. 'And then drive from there up into the mountains.'

'Or we could get a helicopter,' Molly suggested. 'That would be quicker.'

Lily suddenly frowned at her father. 'You're not thinking of going, are you, Dad?'

Black turned. His face blushed slightly as though he had done something naughty. 'Well, I had thought, erm, I ought . . .'

Lily Black's face now turned red as a temper rose up in her. 'There is no way you are going,' she said, with a fimness that was a bit scary. 'You know what the doctor said. You mustn't fly. Your heart can't take it. You will have a heart attack.'

'What?' Micky asked.

'Dad is absolutely not allowed to go on planes,' Lily explained. 'If he does, he might have another heart attack.'

Black swivelled round, his face now crestfallen.

'Lily's right, I'm afraid,' he said. 'Molly and Micky, I would love to come, but the condition of my heart just won't allow it. Firstly, the flight wouldn't be good for me and, secondly, my doctor has given me strict instructions that I must not go to areas of high altitude. High altitudes are dangerous for people with weak hearts, you see.'

Molly shrugged. 'OK. We're used to doing things on our own. But it would be good if Malcolm would come. Will you come, Malcolm?' Malcolm nodded. 'Thanks,' Molly said, relieved. 'Anyway, Mr Black, we'll need someone here. Someone who knows what's going on.'

'We'll need walking boots and clothes for a steamy climate,' said Micky, his appetite whetted for the trip. 'And detailed maps of the area. Actually, who knows what it'll be like in the cloud forest? We'll need matches, water-purifying tablets, food rations, bug repellent, penknives, torches, a few necessary medicines. How about tents and sleeping bags and mosquito nets?'

'Well, your plans are already over,' said Lily, hoisting herself up on to the back of the sofa and pointing at the muted TV. 'The airports are closed.'

As she spoke, thunder rumbled overhead. Petula jumped off the sofa and buried her face under Molly's leg.

'You're right,' Molly said.

'Hell' Micky cursed. 'If we can't get out to Ecuador, we're skewered. This is the end.'

'Mr Black,' said Molly, 'couldn't we hypnotize people at the airport and then hypnotize a pilot?'

'We co . . . uld,' Black mulled, 'though it would be quite something to hypnotize a pilot to do this. It will be dangerous flying, you see. The pilot should really be fully alert. And, as you know, some people, when hypnotized, are not fully alert.'

'You wouldn't have to hypnotize me to do it,' Malcolm piped up. Everyone turned to look at Malcolm Tixley. They stared at him as though he had just announced that he'd laid an egg. 'Come on, Molly,' he said, 'you've been in my head. I'm an air force pilot.'

'Of course you are!' Molly exclaimed. 'But . . . but what about a plane? Can you get us one?'

Malcolm thought. 'I know the man to hypnotize to get a plane authorized. I can arrange to meet him at Northolt Airbase tonight.'

'Will it be safe to take off?' Lily asked. 'I mean, the weather's *realty* bad.'

'Oh, I've flown in hundred of storms before,' Malcolm reassured them. 'We just need to get up above the cloud as quickly as possible. Then it will be plain sailing.'

'Aeroplane sailing?' Molly said with a smile.

'You got it.'

Miss Hunroe was perched elegantly on a green baize stool in a clearing in a rainforest. A wall of rock was the backdrop to where she sat. A thin stream of mountain water gurgled from a crack in the rock there. It filled up a small pool and then drained deep into the earth beneath.

All about were luscious, broad-leaved trees, with vines climbing through them. Bushes and long-stalked ferns covered the ground nearby.

Two, huge, teardrop-shaped rocks flanked her. One was a fiery red and orange colour and the other blue, though not merely one blue. This stone was turquoise and azure, and sparkling blue flashed from deep within it. Two more granite 'eggs', one of these made up of complicated grey tones with flecks of fluffy or whispy white in it and another a cacophony of greens, were in the clearing too, completing the circle of Logan Stones.

Miss Oakkton, stout as a stuffed cabbage, sat on a low box between the blue stone and the grey stone. Miss Teriyaki sat cross-legged on a brightly woven rug on the ground between the grey stone and the green stone. Miss Speal was on a rough, makeshift wooden bench between the green stone and the red one.

In the middle of the ring of Logan Stones was an ancient termite mound the size of a giant toy wigwam, with turrets and twisting towers like a mad sand castle. A mist of low cloud hung in the air above and draped the trees like a silken veil. It filtered the sun's rays, so that the space where the ghastly women sat was filled with warm, green sunlight.

Miss Hunroe wore a smart khaki-coloured suit and a gauze scarf over her head. Batting flies from her face with a white-gloved hand, she suddenly slapped her neck.

'Blasted bugs! Why is it they always want to eat me?'

Miss Oakkton, cloaked in green, squatting on her box and puffing away at her tortoiseshell pipe, said, 'Zay don't seem to like ze smoke of my pipe. Vould you like to borrow it?'

'Certainly not,' Miss Hunroe retorted, curling her rosebud lips. 'I don't like your smoke either.'

Miss Teriyaki dug in her pink silk bag and produced a small white canister. 'Repellent?'

Miss Hunroe shook her head. 'I'm already doused in it. Any more and I'll be highly flammable.'

The four women were still in silent concentration for a moment. 'It's not as easy as it seemed it might be,' Miss Hunroe commented. She pulled her coin out from her pocket and began flipping it along her fingers.

'No, but ve vill get ze hang of it,' Miss Oakkton replied optimistically. Miss Hunroe sighed happily. Miss Oakkton chuckled like an old turkey. 'And is everyvun over ze altitude sickness?'

'Yes,' 'Yes,' 'Oh yes,' the women lied.

'Good. So everything is going as planned. And almost all of us are doing so well,' Miss Hunroe said mysteriously. Immediately the group was set on edge. 'Miss Teriyaki . . .'

Miss Teriyaki looked up with a terrified look on her face, expecting a terrible scolding.

246

Miss Hunroe quelled her fears. 'I admired the way you intercepted Black's bag and made off with it.'

'Thank you so much, Miss Hunroe,' Miss Teriyaki said, as though she'd just been given a prize. 'I'm glad you noticed.' She smiled smugly at the other women.

'And, Miss Speal,' Miss Hunroe continued, 'the cake you made today was splendid.'

Breathing out a huge sigh of relief, Miss Speal started tittering nervously and idiotically.

'But that's enough hysteria,' Miss Hunroe added sternly. Miss Speal was quiet.

Miss Hunroe went on: 'Miss Oakkton and Miss Teriyaki . . .' The two women's eyes widened as they awaited Miss Hunroe's words. 'You have been marvellous hunters! Miss Teriyaki, I am glad your leg is better and I am impressed by your use of the poison-arrow pipe and, Miss Oakkton, you throw knives with the accuracy of a circus performer! Without you two, we wouldn't have had fresh meat. Thank you!'

The two women in question nodded their heads as they accepted their praise and sniffed at the other woman in the circle.

'Miss Speal!'

Miss Speal sat up like a child who has just been caught smashing a window. 'Yes!'

'Well done, Miss Speal, for the lessons you have given me on weather morphing. Your personal experience, having owned that blue stone for so long, has been invaluable. But . . .'

'Yes, Miss Hunroe?' Miss Speal replied in a timid, spooky half-whisper.

'*But*, I am afraid, Miss Speal, there is a problem.'

All eyes turned on Miss Speal, who sat on her bench looking as though a pack of tigers surrounded her. Miss Hunroe glanced at the cloudy sky, as though in despair, and then moved her gaze to the thin woman. In a tight, quiet voice she began.

'Everything was so nice, Miss Speal. So tell me this. Why, why oh why, did *you* go and spoil it? What did you think you were *doing* to that bird when you cooked it? Giving it a trip to hell and back?' Miss Speal was speechless. Miss Hunroe went on. 'You ruined it. It was disgusting – burned to a cinder and baked to a dry mess.'

'But, Miss Hunroe,' Miss Speal whined in self-defence. 'I followed the recipe exactly . . .'

'Nonsense!' Miss Hunroe interrupted. 'It was quite the most disgusting meal I have ever eaten. When I think of all the trouble that Miss Oakkton and Miss Teriyaki went to to get it!'

Miss Speal sank into her bench as six hard eyes bore into her. She bowed her head and shook it from side to side.

'Forgive me. I will take more care next time, Miss Hunroe, I promise. I promise. I promise.'

Chapter Twenty

Molly, Micky, Petula, Lily and Malcolm sat in Black's Mercedes as he drove it to Northolt Airbase. There was very little traffic on the roads.

'These puddles are dangerous,' said Black as the car's wheels cut through one, spraying the pavement and dousing the underside of the car. 'They're more like little ponds.'

'I think we're travelling too light,' Micky complained. 'Malcolm, are you sure we'll be able to find places to stay? I mean we're heading for the Andes Mountains and for the jungle. I feel like we should have more than just our normal clothes and an anorak.'

'Think of it as an adventure, Micky,' Malcolm replied. 'I agree it would be nice to have properly packed suitcases with changes of underwear and socks but there just wasn't time. Besides we can get everything there. We can use jeeps and guides and eco lodges.'

'Eco lodges?'

'They're like tiny hotels usually, with huts for rooms, that don't damage the jungle and the environment. They use solar power and collect their own water from the mountain rainfall. They compost their rubbish and have their own sewage systems.'

'With sawdust loos?' Molly suggested.

'That sort of thing,' Malcolm agreed. 'Anyway – they are properly set up with snake-venom antidotes, medicine and food and water. We really don't need anything. The waterproofs you have on now are fine for this expedition. T-shirts, sweatshirts and trainers are good.'

Molly felt comforted by Malcolm's military background. He had been on lots of expeditions and he knew how to make shelters, collect drinking water from dew, forage from the wild and hunt. So, even if worst did come to worst, they'd survive. He spoke Spanish too, so there wouldn't be a language barrier in Quito, the large town they would be flying into.

From Quito, the plan was to get a helicopter to the small, high-altitude village near the start of the Coca River. Then they could begin their search for the spring and the Logan Stones – and Miss Hunroe and her horrible friends.

'Have you got any matches in the car?' Micky asked Black. 'Probably do, since you like the odd cigar.'

Black nodded and reached into the glove compartment as he drove. Finding a packet, he chucked them over his shoulder to Micky, who stuffed them into his anorak pocket.

'Thanks.'

'So you don't trust me?' Malcolm smiled. He loved a challenge and he loved to work in a team. Discovering that Molly was not an alien had been a disappointment at first. But he had taken on this new mission with zeal. He was a good man, and understood the prospect for the world if Miss Hunroe and her evil friends weren't stopped. Full of gusto and determination, he was now fully focused on his new job.

Molly and Micky on the other hand were very nervous. Rain pounded on the roof above them. The car's wipers were battling with the weight of water that sluiced down the windscreen. And every crash of thunder gnawed at their confidence in the plan. But neither voiced their worry, for this trip was necessary and un-avoidable now. Petula kept her head under Molly's arm, where she could pretend the lightning wasn't real. She didn't feel safe, though, for she sensed and smelt the nerves in the car, and the uneasiness was infectious.

Lily sat between Molly and Micky, uncharacteristi-cally quiet, zipping and unzipping her padded anorak and patting her trousers. She and Black had had a big argument before they'd left the hotel, because she had wanted to go on the trip.

'Don't be daft, Lily,' her father had told her. It's far too dangerous for you. And you don't like flying, even in good weather!'

After an hour of driving, Black pulled into the car park of Northolt Airbase. Moments later, Malcolm was inside the building with Molly at his side. He had called his superior, AH1, who, fascinated to meet an alien at last, was ready and waiting. Molly did the rest. AH1 was quickly hypnotized and he procured them a silver RAF plane. He efficiently obtained permissions for the plane to take off and for Malcolm to fly it.

Within half an hour, Molly, Micky, Petula and Malcolm found themselves on board.

Molly and Micky were in its doorway, waving down to Black, who stood, umbrella over him, on the runway tarmac. Lily wasn't with him. Furious that she had been banned from the trip, she had huffed a goodbye and stayed in the car.

'Good luck!' Black shouted, and gave them a big thumbs-up sign.

As if in answer to their apprehensive prayers, the skies had quietened and the rain had died down so that now it was merely spitting outside. Malcolm sat in the cockpit, with a dashboard of electronic screens and bright symbols in front of him. It was quite beautiful, Molly thought, getting a first-class view of it from her front seat. Micky sat beside her with Petula on his lap. They watched with fascination as Malcolm made fastidious safety checks, clicking switches and pressing buttons.

Behind Molly and Micky, the rest of the plane was airy and spacious. It was an aircraft equipped to carry thirty soldiers sitting along its sides. Their equipment, rucksacks and parachutes would normally have been firmly strapped on to the high racks in the top curves of the plane's torso. But today there were only a few parachutes hanging at the stern of the plane. They were like ripe fruit, ready to pop open.

Halfway along the aircraft was a galley that Malcolm had organized to be quickly stocked with some meals and lots of drink. 'Everyone should drink lots of water on a long-haul plane trip,' Malcolm had said. Molly was already sipping at a glass of concentrated orange squash. Micky had cracked open a can of the fizzy drink Qube. The plane had been kitted out too with duvets and roll-out mattresses, so even though it would be a ten-hour flight Molly, Micky and Petula could sleep for most of it.

It was only Malcolm who had to remain awake. Molly felt sorry for him. She could see why he had made himself a Thermos of coffee. And she admired how he had changed into official pilot mode. He wore earphones now and was talking to ground control about the weather ahead, and about the flight path they were to take.

'OK, *crew!*' Malcolm's voice came over the intercom. '*You'll be pleased to hear that the weather has calmed down enough for take-off. The runway is all clear, so buckle up. We're heading out.*'

The aircraft began to taxi towards the main runway. Once on it, Malcolm drew the throttle back and at once the plane picked up speed. In five seconds, the aircraft had accelerated sufficiently to lift. Malcolm pulled the steering controls towards him and with a tilt they were up in the air. Molly looked out of the side window and watched the land and the glittering yellow, orange and white lights of Northolt drop away behind them. The plane shuddered as its powerful engines pushed it upwards. Its insides shook and rattled. Then they came to the first tower of rain-filled cloud. The plane bumped its way up through it, like a motorboat setting out over high waves. Bump, bump, the plane bounced on the thermals of air that crowded the sky. But Molly wasn't too worried. She knew that the bumps were a bit like the uneven ground a jeep has to drive over when it is off-roading. She knew the aircraft was built to fly up through bumpy air.

'I once read about pilots who had to fly war planes in *terrible* weather,' Micky shouted, trying to make his voice heard over the noisy engines. 'And land on *tiny* aircraft carriers in open seas.'

The plane tilted to the right as it turned.

'Are you OK with flying?' Micky asked Molly.

'Yes,' she shouted back. 'There's more chance of me winning a twenty million pound lottery than this plane crashing. If ever I get nervous when I'm in a plane, I just imagine filling in a lottery card. I always get that I-couldn't-possibly-win feeling, and, in the same way that I know I'm not going to win the lottery, I know I'm not going to crash either.'

Petula hopped over into Molly's lap and Molly hugged her. 'Don't worry, Petula, it'll be fine.'

This part *was* fine, Molly thought. She just hoped the weather didn't turn bad on the journey. Because this plane *had* to make it. If it didn't, the world's weather would be turned upside down and inside out. Millions would probably die. As the plane walloped its way up through the clouds, Molly hung on to this thought. And the idea that she, Micky, Petula and Malcolm were on a mission to save millions gave her strength and courage.

Finally the plane levelled out, and Malcolm came over the intercom again. His voice was crackling and hard to hear.

'Folks, we're now cruising at fifteen thousand metres. The storm is below us and so won't bother us at all. Relax. Get some sleep. I'll wake you an hour before we arrive at Quito.'

Molly looked at her watch. It was two a.m. She was exhausted. If she fell asleep now, Malcolm would wake them in about nine hours, an hour before they landed. This would be eleven in the morning the next day London time, but of course, because Quito was five hours behind London, it would be six in the morning there.

Molly and Micky undid their belts and, finding their balance as the plane moved, went to the back to sort out their beds. Petula shook herself awake and began to sniff the air.

Oddly, as they approached the back of the aircraft, she began to smell popcorn. Before she could give a warning bark, Molly gasped. For there, crouching behind the duvets and pillows, looking pale as a glass of milk, was Lily Black.

'Lily!' Molly exclaimed. 'What are *you* doing here?'

Lily got up and nervously glanced towards Malcolm in the cockpit, who hadn't seen her yet.

'I want to come!' she said, determinedly. 'I *know* I can help. And I want to show my dad that I'm not just a useless baby. I am seven and a quarter you know. And I *am* brave.'

'Jeepers!' said Micky.

'Please,' Lily went on. '*Please* let me come.'

'How did you get on board?' Molly asked, amazed.

'Sneaked on when you were checking your equipment, just before the plane stairs were taken away.'

Molly tilted her head. 'Pretty good, Lily,' she said.

Lily bit her lip and nodded. 'So can I stay?' she asked.

'Your dad will be off his head with worry looking for you,' Micky said.

'Are you going to tell Malcolm to take me back?'

Molly shook her head. 'We can't go back now, because we may not be able to land or take off again if we do.' She gave Micky a look of resignation. 'So, Lily, it looks like you're part of the team.'

'Welcome on board,' Micky said.

Malcolm radioed to ground control to inform Theobald Black that his missing daughter was on the plane to Quito.

Molly, Micky and Lily laid out their beds on the aircraft's humming floor. And with Petula snuggled close to them all, they fell asleep.

Miss Hunroe settled down to sleep in her wooden forest hut. Special incense to ward off mosquitoes burned in a small hearth, so that the air was heavy and perfumed. The door was open to the jungle so that she could see out into the night. The afternoon cloud had lifted, and the sky was a magical canopy above, an inky blackness studded with stars. Owls hooted and nocturnal animals called to each other. Insects sawed the pure mountain air with their song.

Miss Hunroe leaned back on a pile of pillows and patted her silk-enrobed knees. She liked the sound of nature. How wonderful it would be when the world was rid of people, when many more places would resound with only the sound of nature. Sometime soon she would completely master weather control and she alone would be able to cause chaos just where it was needed. People were ruining the planet with their noise and their filth. Cities were spreading like cancers. The governments of the world were useless at sorting it out. They were lucky that she and her organization were taking matters into their own hands. A handful of typhoons and tidal waves, a score of hurricanes and tsunamis, some droughts and floods and it would be done.

Miss Hunroe sneered at how many horrid little people lived on the Earth. Six and a half *billion* people were crowded on to the planet, she thought. If, by using the weather stones, a few billion could be wiped off, then that was a result! Miss Hunroe could have trillions of acres of it all to herself! Swathes of magnificent countryside! Of course, she'd have to make sure that certain places weren't disturbed. It wouldn't do to wipe out all the airports, for instance, because Miss Hunroe wanted to be able to continue travelling to her favourite places, and her jets would need somewhere to land. And she wanted certain cities to be left unscathed. Beautiful cultured cities like Venice, Rome, Florence, Prague, St Petersburg, London, Madrid and Paris.

It crossed her mind that she'd given Paris to one of her minions. Well, she had a right to change her mind. She'd give them a grotty town in northern France instead. Paris would be *hers*. She would keep her favourite cities in tip-top condition, with wonderful hotels for her to stay in, fabulous restaurants for her to eat at and every one of her chosen cities would have lots of expensive shops for her to shop in. And she did so adore her trips to museums and galleries!

Just then the satellite telephone rang, shattering her reverie. She lifted the receiver. On the other end someone gabbled down the line. It was Miss Suzette.

'Why didn't you call before?' Miss Hunroe enquired angrily, her voice low and furious. She listened for a reply. It seemed Miss Suzette was equally cross with Miss Hunroe.

'How dare you be so impertinent?' Miss Hunroe spat. 'I was up the mountain, out of touch. No, the satellite phone only works at base camp. But what I want to know, Miss Suzette, is *how* did they get in? You were supposed to be on guard.'

Miss Suzette babbled her defence.

'But,' Miss Hunroe said, 'the night watchman was hypnotized not to let anyone past. And the command was locked in with a password.'

Miss Hunroe frowned as Miss Suzette replied.

'And you can't hypnotize him at all?'

There was another pause as Miss Suzette spoke.

'Well, the obvious thing to do is get rid of him. You should have already done it. A little accident on the stairs will do.' There was another pause. 'Well, if he's calling the police, you had better get out of there right now.'

Miss Hunroe picked up her coin from the bedside table and began flipping it through her fingers. 'Yes, Suzette, I'm still here. I'm just thinking. It's extraordinary to me that those Moon brats found the picture. Do you think they know where the Logan Stones are?'

Miss Suzette answered and Miss Hunroe pursed her lips.

'We will have to assume a worst-case scenario. There are only two ways here – by sea or by air. If they are already halfway here, I shall just put a small storm up. High winds and a little cyclone are all that we need. Highly irritating! The skies were so beautifully clear and I was enjoying the view. Besides, I was about to go to sleep. Now I will have to make my way back up the mountain to the Stones and *it is all your fault*. I am more than a little disappointed in you, Miss Suzette, for letting this happen. You will, I am afraid, be punished. Goodbye.'

Miss Hunroe put down the phone and swung her legs out of bed. She walked out to her balcony and surveyed the dense jungle surrounding the camp. When she turned, Miss Speal, grey and spooky as a ghost, was standing at her side.

'Urrgh,' Miss Hunroe gasped.

'Miss Hunroe, Miss Hunroe,' Miss Speal whispered, 'I had a feeling. It woke me. I can feel the Moon children. They are approaching. They are far away, but approaching.'

Miss Hunroe nodded, and shrugged. 'A bit late, Miss Speal. I know.' Then she scowled up at the moon. 'Interfering Moons. Let's arrange some surprises for you.'

Chapter Twenty-one

Molly was having a wonderful dream – that she was riding a big white albatross as it dipped and dived though curling flowers of cloud. In her dream Micky was sitting behind her. He tapped her shoulder.

'Molly, wake up!'

Molly opened her eyes and squinted at her brother while she gathered her senses. The plane lurched as it bumped into a heavy gust of air.

'Where are we? What time is it?' she asked. She turned to see Lily sitting on one of the plane's side chairs, wide-eyed and terrified, with her belt done up. The plane bumped again. This time, Molly was knocked backwards and Petula skidded across the aircraft floor. Malcolm's voice came over the loudspeaker.

'*We are passing through some turbulence,*' he said. '*Everyone put your be—*' His announcement was cut short as the plane went into another heavy column of cumulus cloud. '*Put your belts on,*' he repeated. '*And *don't worry – this is routine stuff. We just need to navigate around and over these thermals.'*

Molly smiled at Micky. Turbulence never worried her. The plane was so far above the ground that there was plenty of space to go up and down. The winds would never flip the plane. It was far too heavy.

Outside there was a white flash. Lily screamed. 'What was that?' she shouted.

'Just a bit of lightning,' Micky reassured her. He and Molly sat down and did their belts up too. Molly held Petula tight. Then in the next moment there was an enormous bang. The whole plane jolted. It was as though the aircraft was a tiny insect that some space giant had flicked with a giant finger. Petula let out a howl.

'Aaaaaaah! We're going to die!' Lily wailed.

'It's all right, Lily,' Molly said. 'These planes are built to fly in storms.' But as she spoke she saw Micky's face and the alarm there. She shot a look over at Malcolm. His hands were now firmly on the plane's controls.

'That was just some lightning hitting us, folks,' he informed everyone, his voice crackling on the loud-speaker. *'This plane has a lightning conductor on the front and back. So that was lightning zapping through the plane. Regular stuff.'*

As he spoke, the plane took a sharp turn upwards. The engine let out a kick of jet power and the aircraft thrust itself upwards, but as it did there was another terrifying bang. Petula head butted Molly and tried to hide under her sweatshirt.

Molly smiled nervously at Micky, then there was another bang. This time, the engine in the back of the plane began to make a strange, grinding noise. Still the plane went higher and, after a few minutes of noisy ascent, to everyone's relief it levelled out. The back of the plane was still rattling, but otherwise everything seemed calm.

'Phew!' Molly exclaimed.

Malcolm came over the speaker again. '*Micky, I need you up here.*'

Micky immediately unclipped his belt buckle and went to the cockpit. Molly, slightly annoyed that Malcolm was making this a boys' thing, unclipped her belt too and joined them. She caught the end of Malcolm's sentence.

'. . . bail out'

'What's going on?' Molly asked, shouting over the whining noise of the engine. Malcolm stared out through the windscreen at the dark night. The wipers fought against the rain.

'What's wrong?'

Beyond his right hand Molly noticed some flashing words on the control panel.

ENGINE DAMAGE the scary red letters declared.

'What –?' Molly asked. As if in reply, the very engine responded. From the back of the plane a loud KERCHUNK reverberated through the aircraft.

'Can you fly her?' Micky asked, looking at the dials and the warnings on the control panel.

'I'm not sure,' Malcolm replied uncertainly. 'I've never come across this type of damage before. The plane is losing fuel. It seems the tanks were damaged. The fuel's seeping out and air is getting in. That rattling noise you can hear is air in the engine.'

'That doesn't sound good,' Micky said, grimacing. 'Where are we? How far is Quito?'

Malcolm pointed to a screen that showed coordinates and the land layout below. 'We're close. We are flying over the Andes. In fact the area we intended to get a helicopter to is probably almost directly below us now. But there's a storm down there and, anyway, no sizeable airfield on which to land. But . . .'

'What?' Molly and Micky asked together. Malcolm shook his head.

'I'm not sure the engine will take the strain of flying much further. The fuel tanks might . . .' Malcolm hardly dared tell his passengers the truth of the situation, but he had to. 'The fuel tanks might blow,' he finished.

'What, like *blow up*?' Molly blurted.

'We'll have to risk it and fly somewhere else,' said Micky, 'where the skies are calmer and where it is possible to land.'

Malcolm paused and scanned his weather monitor. 'The weather conditions are bad almost everywhere,' he replied. 'That's the problem. Although that place there to the east seems clear.' He pointed at his electronic map. But as he did the rattling noise in the engine

264

became louder, turning into a grinding whine, and then the plane tilted sideways.

Malcolm grabbed the steering controls. Gritting his teeth, he pulled the aircraft to a stable position again.

A red buzzer began bleeping and an alarm bell sounded.

'I correct myself!' Malcolm said, switching to emergency mode. 'We will now *definitely* have to eject.' He put his headphones on and spoke into the mouthpiece attached to them. His voice filled the plane. '*It is now imperative that everyone listens to me carefully. I haven't got long to explain this.*'

Molly glanced to the rear part of the plane at the parachutes that had looked so innocent before. Now the parachutes were lifesavers. Molly looked at Micky and, nodding, they both rushed to the back of the plane for their equipment. They picked up their helmets, and shoved one towards Lily.

'This is your chance to prove yourself,' Molly said to her. 'Put this on.'

As Lily undid her belt, Malcolm's words crackled through the cabin.

'*Harness yourselves to parachutes. Equip yourself now and become familiar with the oxygen masks. They will have to be used at this height.*' The plane lurched again, this time to the left. Malcolm paused while he corrected the plane's level, and then went on: '*Each parachute's strap holds an altimeter that has a light on it. This is very important – it tells you how high you are in the air. The parachute's ripcord – the cord that opens your parachute, is on the top right-hand side of the packed parachute. Locate it now. And this is also very important. This cord must not be pulled until you are at six thousand metres above ground. The parachute should open automatically anyway. But, I repeat, do not open your chute manually until you are at six thousand metres or below. When your parachute opens, find your coordinate compass. This should be attached to the left strap of your parachute. The coordinates for the spring of the Coca River are 0, 08.00 south, and 78, 10.49 west. I repeat: 0, 08.00 south, and 78, 10.49 west. Steer the parachute using the toggles that you will find hanging down from the nylon parachute rigging above you.'*

Everyone stood still for a moment as they absorbed the terrifying instructions that Malcolm had just given. The plane gave another lurch.

'*What are you waiting for?*' Malcolm shouted. 'Go! Go! Go!'

Now Molly, Micky and Lily rushed. They helped each other to put on their anoraks, their parachutes and their helmets. The plane dipped sideways again.

Molly fumbled with her harness, her fingers unco-ordinated by fear. She couldn't believe this was actually happening. Her stomach, full of upset nerves, leaped about more than the plane and then the aircraft tilted suddenly so that she fell over. Micky kept his balance. He already had his parachute on and was now studying his helmet with its oxygen-mask paraphernalia.

'This is the oxygen,' he shouted to Lily and Molly, pointing to a silver canister that was attached to his mask. 'And this is the switch to turn it on. The mask covers your eyes and nose, like a snorkling mask. You'll be able to breathe normally when it's on.'

The plane whined and Lily shrieked. Micky helped to fasten her helmet and put his hands firmly on her shoulders.

'Lily, you have to be brave,' he said sternly. 'You are your own worst enemy if you panic. Calm down. These parachutes work. But *do not* pull the cord until six thousand metres. They will open on their own, but in case they don't *you* will have to pull the cord.'

'Then what?' Lily screeched. '*We're going to die!*'

'Lily, listen to me. You're tough enough to do this. We'll jump out together. We'll breathe with the help of the masks. I'm going to help you put your mask on now and turn your oxygen on in a minute. I will stay close to you, OK? But when the time comes to open our parachutes, we will all move apart *or our para-chutes will tangle*. When your parachute opens, you'll see two nice little toggles above your ears. One on each side. You can steer the parachute with these. Left toggle to go left. Right to go right.'

'You're crazy! You're crazy!' Lily screamed at him. 'I AM NOT GOING TO JUMP OUT OF THIS PLANE!'

'You are, Lily. If you jump, you will live. Take a

deep breath. Everything is going to be all right.'

As Micky helped Lily, Molly unclipped some equipment for Malcolm and took it to him. Then she grappled with the problem of Petula. How should she carry her? Molly found a strong nylon shoulder bag and strapped it on to herself. With her hands trembling, she put the shaking Petula inside before putting her oxygen mask on. Then she detached a spare oxygen canister and mask from one of the other helmets that hung on the aircraft rack. Molly pushed the small silver canister in the bag with Petula and switched it on. The mask was big for Petula, but if she pushed her face into the front of it, she got the oxygen that was gushing from the canister into it. Molly strapped and tightened the mask about her pet's face.

'Breathe, Petula,' Molly said, and Petula, her eyes shining with confusion and fear, panted. Molly felt like crying. But there was no time for tears now. Molly put a scarf and a jumper around Petula to keep her warm, then, double-checking that the whole bag was strapped properly on to her, she tightened its drawstring and held it close. Then she put on the gloves that came with her kit. Now Molly stood ready. She could feel Petula's heart beating through the bag and Petula could feel Molly's heartbeat too.

Molly leaned forward. 'I love you, Petula,' she said. 'Whatever happens, remember that.' Then Molly took a deep breath and tried to find some sort of calm in herself. She tried to think logically. She'd often watched sky dives on TV and it occurred to her that people all over the world jumped out of planes every day of the year for *fun*. Bolstered by this thought, Molly steeled her nerves.

'I can do this. I can do this. I can do this,' she said to herself. She watched Malcolm putting his parachute on whilst flying the ailing plane at the same time.

'I can do this. I can do this. I can do this.' Molly let her mantra wash through her.

Micky walked towards her, steadying himself on the walls of the plane. Lily clung on to him like a limpet. They were ready to jump.

'I can't believe this!' Micky shouted over the moaning of the engines. He sounded confident, but his eyes betrayed how terrified he was.

Then Malcolm's voice came over the speaker again.

'*I am going to open the parachute door at the tail of the plane. When I say "Go!", you go. I will be following right behind you.*'

Molly nodded. She couldn't believe this was happening. Her fear came back again in thick, fast breaths. She, Micky and Lily linked arms and moved to the tail of the aircraft. And then, with a rumble and a screech, the bottom of the plane began to open. The noise of the engines and the wind outside was now deafening. What was more, the children felt themselves being pulled towards the ever-widening opening.

Molly's hands were sweating profusely as apprehension tore through her body. Petula curled up into a ball in her bag, pressing her nose into her mask. She felt Molly's terror and was full of dread herself. She shut her eyes tight and tried to think of meadows and long grass, of streams and flowers. How she longed to be at home in her safe basket.

'Oh no,' Molly whispered, her heart pounding. 'This is *bad*.'

'Get a grip, Molly,' Micky shouted over the raging noise. 'Remember, people do this for fun!'

'Not in storms!' Molly yelled back as the tug of the cold air outside became so strong that she could hardly stop herself being pulled into it. But then she smiled. For she was touched that Micky had had the same thought as her. 'You're right, though, Micky.'

'Look!' Micky shouted. 'There are compasses on your straps. See – the numbers on it change as you move. Just kind of steer your parachute towards 0, 08.00 south, and 78, 10.49 west.' He linked his arm through Molly's and Lily's and together they resisted the pull of the wind outside.

Molly nodded and bit her teeth together hard as she forced bravery to overtake her natural instinct, which was to cry. She looked at Lily, who had gone all quiet and limp, and wondered whether she stood any chance at all of reading her compass. Molly held Lily's arm firmly and Micky's too. The threesome made a ring.

'*Ready?*' Malcolm's voice grated loudly over the plane's intercom. '*Holding hands. All together. Remember to let go of each other before your parachutes open at six thousand metres. Keep your legs together when you land. Now GO! GO! GO!'*

Molly put a thumb up at him, and in the next moment the bottom of the plane clunked fully open. It gaped wide, showing nothing but chilling blackness. At the same time, the air outside sucked like a massive, noisy, death-wishing vacuum cleaner so that everyone began slipping towards the dark void.

'One! Two! Three! JUMP!' Molly cried, and as though in a dream, and as if simply jumping into an inky pool, everyone leaped at once.

Chapter Twenty-two

Molly's body hit the air. Freezing cold, it smacked her face. For a moment, Molly wasn't sure whether she was dead or alive. She felt tiny – as though she was the size of a speck of dust tumbling in a gale-force wind. She was falling and spinning – flipping like a coin that had been tossed by some crazed devil.

'HEADS YOU LOSE, TAILS YOU DIE!' These words screamed through her head as though the icy wind was shouting at her. 'HEADS YOU DIE, TAILS YOU DIE!' Molly felt that Miss Hunroe was the fiend who had tossed her.

And then Molly remembered to *breathe*. With a deep breath from her oxygen mask, she tried to take control. But it was so cold and she was so dizzy that she could hardly think. She realized with horror that she could no longer feel Lily linked through her left arm but that Micky, with his arm through her harness, was still attached.

For a brief second Molly opened her eyes to see whether Lily was still holding Micky's arm. Micky's face, grimacing with fear, flashed in the moonlight, but there was no Lily beside him. And it was too difficult to make out anything else, so Molly didn't know where Lily was at all. Nor did she know whether Petula was still breathing or not.

Molly and Micky were alone, careering down through the icy air together. The out-of-control spin that they were in was horrible. Molly fought through her brain's utter confusion. With a huge effort, she pushed herself through the torrent of rushing air to swing her left arm towards Micky. Her helmet crashed into his. Terrified, they clung together, and continued to fall.

The crescent moon shone down on them. The twins held on to each other as they had done eleven and a half years earlier – before they'd been born. They dropped as one like a spinning black ball, down, down, down, through the sub-zero night sky. The moonlight reflected off them, spot-lighting them as they plummeted. It was bitterly cold and their bodies were numb. Molly's face burned, her eyes hurt and her stomach had swollen from the high air pressure. And she felt sick from the turning and falling.

Then she remembered watching a programme about skydivers and she remembered what to do.

'WE'VE GOT TO STRAIGHTEN OUT!' she shouted to Micky.

'WHAAAAT?' he yelled back with his eyes shut.

'STRAIGHTEN OOOOUUUUT. STAAAAR SHAPES.'

'STAR SHAPES?'

'YESS.'

To show what she meant, Molly pushed away from him and threw her legs out. This levelled them a little but still they flipped.

'DO IT!' Molly screamed.

As Micky straightened his legs, he stretched his arms out too. Molly and he were joined where their hands held each other's harnesses. Their legs flailed behind them like the forked tails of strange, high-altitude birds.

'BETTER!' Micky hollered. And it was. Without the mad spin, they could think properly. Both braved the sharp air and opened their eyes. Molly looked once again for Lily and now for Malcolm, but they were nowhere to be seen. She wished she could check on Petula.

Micky glanced at his altometer. Thirteen thousand metres!' he cried.

Both knew what this meant. Both looked down. Like a terrible beast that was waking up to the twins' imminent arrival, the clouds below them roared and flashed. Lightning showed Molly and Micky what was to come – a diabolical dark mass of air, full of electrical storm. And in the next moment, they were in it.

At once hail hit them. Freezing cold, hard, icy lumps

the size of conkers smashed in their faces and pum-
melled their bodies. But neither Molly nor Micky let
go of each other to shield their faces. Seconds felt like
minutes, but still they clung bravely to each other.

Eventually the hail turned to icy rain. Now Molly
and Micky felt like flies inside a massive cold shower.
Then, with a sudden rip and a tug that felt as though
a giant was poking them, their parachutes began to
open.

Both Molly and Micky opened their eyes.

'GOOD LUCK!' Molly shouted.

'KEEP YOUR EYE ON THE COORDINATES!'
Micky shouted back. And then, heeding Malcolm's
warning, with a push the twins separated.

Molly's parachute unfurled and she felt the weight
of her body supported by the canopy above. As soon
as she was able, Molly put her cold, half-numb hand
inside her bag to check Petula. Petula's oxygen mask
was still fixed to her. This was a comfort, but not enough
to make Molly feel better. She was now alone with
Petula in the unrelenting rain. She wondered if the
parachute had opened too early. Maybe, for it would
have been better to drop like a stone as fast as possible
though the tumultuous storm. Instead they were going
to have to parachute slowly down through it.

Molly did up Petula's bag safely and began to observe
the horrific weather below. Thunder rolled around her
deafeningly and lightning coursed through the heavy
air. She caught a glimpse of Micky hanging like a

barnacle from the bottom of his jellyfish-shaped parachute. Molly thought she saw another parachute behind him too, but wasn't sure whether she was simply imagining it.

Whipping her face, the wind now gripped Molly's parachute with a vengeance. Its gusts were so violent it could rip the silk of the canopy apart. Molly looked down as another blast of thunder and lightning thrashed the sky. Beneath her dangling legs was a dreadful swirl of black tunnelling cloud, like some hellish plughole. It was, Molly realized, some sort of tornado. Molly hugged Petula close. 'I'M SORRY, PETULA!' she yelled. Molly wished she could climb into the bag and snuggle up with Petula. But she couldn't, so she did the next best thing. She silently asked her pet, *What are you thinking?*

Like a magical screen, a thought bubble popped up over the nylon bag. In it were images, not of the storm, but of fields and flowers and blue skies and of places that Petula loved. There were the llama-filled meadows of Briersville Park and pictures of Micky and Rocky. They were all looking happy. And then Molly saw images of herself laughing and throwing sticks for Petula to fetch.

This was exactly what she should be thinking about now, Molly realized, the slapping rain hurting her ears. For these moments in the air might be the very last moments of their lives. Molly's eyes filled with tears as she saw the people in her life whom she loved. She thought of Rocky and wondered whether she would ever see him again. She remembered how she'd been dreading lessons and wishing for some adventure the last time she'd been with him. How she would love to be doing maths homework now.

Then her mind turned to all the people she hadn't seen for a long time. Not Rocky and Ojas, Lucy, Primo and Forest, but people from her past, the other orphanage children who were now in Los Angeles. She thought about Mrs Trinklebury, the kind, old lady who had, years before, found Molly in a box on a doorstep and saved her. She wished a giant Moons Marshmallow box would suddenly appear and scoop her and Petula out of the sky. Molly shut her eyes and held Petula close to her. And she wished. As her parachute was buffeted and she was swung violently underneath it like a human pendulum, she wished. She wished and wished with all her heart that everything would be all right.

And then the rain began to subside. Moonlight slipped through a crack in the clouds and Molly saw that the storm was above her now and that the worst of it was over.

She glanced down. There was one very bright spot on the land below. But Molly had no idea how far below her that bright spot was. Nor could she imagine why one spot was so bright when all the rest of the land was so dark. Then Molly realized. The plane they had been in must have nosedived. And the brightness below was fire – fire from its explosive crash. She hoped Malcolm hadn't gone down with the plane. She glanced at the altimeter on her harness.

3,000M, it read. Molly didn't know how long it would take for her parachute to drop through three thousand metres of air, but she suspected it wouldn't be long. So, reaching for the coordinate compass on her harness's left strap, she clicked its tiny light on and tried to work out in which direction she should be heading. The compass indicated that south-west and the spring of the Coca River was straight in front of her. She assumed that she was going in almost the right direction. She reached for the toggles on her parachute. They were, as Micky had said they would be, above her ears, hanging down from the parachute's canopy strings. Molly pulled on the left-hand toggle to try to start moving westwards.

Above her, the canopy sagged a little as she redirected it, and the parachute turned. Molly checked the compass. Its arrow flickered and altered. The altimeter now read 2,000M. Molly hoped the wind was strong enough to get her to where she wanted to go, but not so fast that it would push her past the spring of the Coca River.

Lightning lit the sky again and now Molly saw the land below, a vast, inhospitable jungle. With every flash of light, she searched the skies for the others. They must be out there somewhere, she thought, but she couldn't see them. Trying not to think about how alone she and Petula were, Molly concentrated on steering herself down.

The closer she got to the ground, the faster she seemed to be coming down, and the warmer the air felt. The rainforest was huge and mighty and packed full of trees. Molly really didn't want to land *in* one. Glad for the lightning now, she looked for a clearing. Spotting one, Molly turned her parachute so that the rain was hitting her in the face and she shot towards it. Then she loosened the fastenings on Petula's bag and took off her pet's mask. She took off her own too and breathed in the clean, warm air.

'Hold tight, Petula, this is going to be over soon!' she shouted.

Molly held her legs together as Malcolm had instructed, and she made them as bendy as she could, not knowing what sort of surface she was going to encounter.

Closer, closer the land came. Rushing up at her. And then there was impact. And with the impact came *coldness*.

It took Molly a few seconds to realize why everything was suddenly so cold. She had landed in *water* – in fast-flowing water. Wet and cold as she was from the icy air thousands of metres above, she hardly felt it. A panic gripped her. What kind of water had she fallen into? she wondered. Desperately, she tried to keep her head above the torrential stream. And then she began to worry about Petula who, she realized, must be half drowning in her bag. As the river tossed and threw her about, Molly did her best to lift up Petula, still in her bag, to make sure that she didn't drown.

The water knocked Molly and Petula, then carried them and submerged them, like some dreadful sprite that was playing with them. Molly swallowed mouthfuls of mountain water. It shot up her nose, stinging her sinuses. It crashed over her as its rapids splashed above her head. She and Petula were washed downstream like two bottle tops that had fallen into a rain-filled gutter.

A few miles away, Miss Hunroe cracked open a bottle of champagne. With a POP the cork flew out of the bottle's neck and shot up into a tree, sending a parrot squawking.

'Good shot!' Miss Oakkton cried, clapping. She, Miss Teriyaki and Miss Speal, all in their nightclothes, raised their glasses.

'Well done,' Miss Speal congratulated Miss Hunroe, her voice greasy and deferential. 'Your weather manipulation skills are now fully honed.'

'Yes, Miss Hunroe, those storms you conjured up tonight were perfectly directed,' Miss Teriyaki, in a flowery kimono, agreed.

'Far better to have zose Moon kids six feet under,' added Miss Oakkton, glugging back her champagne.

'They are tiny particles in the air, not under the ground,' Miss Teriyaki corrected her. 'That explosion will have blasted them into billions of bits.'

'It vas a manner of speech,' Miss Oakkton informed

Miss Teriyaki, irritated. '"Six feet under" means dead and buried.'

'Well, it was a *beautiful* sight to see that plane drop from the sky and to watch its explosion, wasn't it?' Miss Hunroe said dreamily. 'Now there is nothing to stop us! What a relief!'

Chapter Twenty-three

Everything was still now. Petula came to her senses. She was soaking wet and half drowned and the nylon bag about her was cold and clammy, but she wasn't in water any more. She was still reeling from the ordeal of hurtling down through the storm clouds with Molly. And the river had nearly killed her. It had mercilessly rolled her and Molly in its rapids. But then, like a careless small child throwing a toy aside, it had flung them on to its banks. Petula could feel that Molly was underneath the bag. She poked her head through its opening and struggled out.

The moon shone down and Petula saw that the cold water of the river was still lapping about Molly's legs. The rest of Molly's body was lodged on the muddy bank. Her head was supported by a hard, flat rock and Petula could smell Molly's blood.

Molly had cut the back of her head. Petula clamped her teeth round a good chunk of Molly's jacket and, using all her strength, she began to tug. Molly's body shifted a centimetre or two, which was enough to give Petula encouragement.

Fifteen minutes later, Molly was fully out of the water. The air was warm but Petula could feel with her nose that Molly was very, very cold. Being cold and wet all night could kill Molly, thought Petula, if a wild animal didn't come and *eat* her first. The smell of Molly's blood would alert all sorts of creatures. Right at this moment, animals would be sniffing the air and detecting that something had been wounded. Petula's only option was to get another human to help – though whether any people lived in this dense, dark forest was uncertain. Still, Petula had no choice but to hope, and so she began to howl.

Birds in their nests were woken; paca pigs and armadillos, jaguars and bears stirred in their sleep. Rodents, owls and other nocturnal creatures pricked up their ears and smelt the air.

Petula howled so long her throat hurt but still she howled more. Though each howl cut like a knife, she kept on until she was hoarse and could only whimper.

There was a rustling in the bushes behind. The beam of a weak torch cut through the dark and the light of it fell on Petula. She scrunched her eyes up and saw that a tall, thin figure had emerged from the undergrowth. It was man. He wore earth-covered brown linen shorts, a waterproof anorak and heavy walking boots. He smelt to Petula of cloves, parsley, leaves, campfire smoke, and paper and ink and dog. Clicking his tongue to Petula, he crouched down over Molly and lay his palm on her forehead. He listened to her breathing, checked her body and unclipped her harness so that she was no longer attached to the parachute. Then, swiftly, he lifted Molly up. Raising her on to his shoulders, so that she hung either side of his neck like a human scarf, he clicked his tongue again to Petula and set off into the forest.

Petula followed blindly. She'd never been so pleased to see anyone. The man was like an angel. Any second now, Petula thought, wings would sprout from his back.

Ignoring her body's exhaustion, Petula trotted after the man along the jungle paths. His booted feet pounded the forest paths as he walked determinedly on. Around her, the thick, muggy air seethed with insect buzz and the chatter of small animals. And, far away, thunder clattered and rumbled as though it was saying goodbye.

Petula panted heavily. Her heart began to pound, and then her head began to swim. She looked up. It seemed that great pale wings *had* grown from the man's back. 'Goodbye, goodbye,' the thunder rumbled. And now Petula wondered whether in fact she was dead.

The angel was going to fly away with Molly, Petula thought. Desperately, she squeezed out a weak rusty, bark.

'Raewerrgh! Don't leave me!' Then she tipped as her legs gave way and she fell to the ground.

Then Petula felt strong arms scoop her up. And she too blacked out.

Chapter Twenty-four

The man arrived at a small cluster of thatched wooden huts built on stilts. A large scruffy brown dog rushed out of one to greet him.

'Good boy, Canis,' the man said.

Canis sniffed at Petula and Molly, and keenly followed the man to the largest hut. There was a veranda outside its entrance. The man placed Molly and Petula on a daybed. Molly's bloody head immediately stained the pillow. He fetched a towel and a blanket. Then he removed Molly's sodden trainers and her wet outer clothes, dried her and covered her with a blanket. He towelled Petula down and put her by Molly's side with the towel on her too. All the while the brown dog sat by his side, watching his every move.

A warm fire burned in the veranda's hearth. The man added kindling to it. Then he washed his hands under a tap that was beneath a rain tank beside the hut and he came back to Molly to tend her wound. He set up an oil lamp to inspect and clean the cut under Molly's hair. He pasted some ointment on to it and with a few green leaves layered on top of that he bandaged Molly's head up.

'Must have had something to do with that explosion,' the man muttered. 'Expect the noise was a plane crashing.' The dog Canis tilted his head to one side, and woofed. 'But we should be quiet now,' the man said. 'Let them warm up and rest.'

Molly slept. She sank deeper and deeper into her unconscious mind, like a fish that normally swims on the surface of the sea diving down to depths it never thought possible. Like colourful deep-sea corals, powerful images passed by Molly's closed eyes, and, like ocean-dwelling monster fish, frightening pictures appeared too. Kaleidoscopic and vivid, the feelings in the dreams were equally intense. She was in a copse of trees full of birdsong and woodpeckers that rattatatted on bark. And then rattatatts became louder, becoming harsh and booming until the forest was full of the clamour of scary, hard noise. And then all the birds died and the stream became a torrent of rushing water that swept the forest animals away to their deaths. Behind, the meadow of flowers shrivelled under a scorching sun, the fields became a desert and in no time at all the river dried up to a dusty, stone-filled ditch. Molly found herself calling for help as she walked along the ghostly riverbed, but no one answered. Then Miss Hunroe's face emerged from behind a cloud and she laughed like

287

a crazed devil before turning into a massive black insect that flew down from the sky and bit Molly on the back of the head.

Early-morning light and shade mottled the hut's floor and, like gentle fingers, it stroked Molly's eyelids. Molly stirred. Her head hurt. She felt something warm on her leg and reached down to stroke Petula. Then with a rush everything came back to her. The plane! The parachute jump! The others! Where were they?

Molly opened her eyes. Her limbs were stiff and sluggish; she felt like she'd been asleep for days.

Now inside a hut Molly gazed out through its door and saw outside. In a clearing, she saw a man in khaki shorts and a whitish shirt crouched on his heels, stirring something in a campfire pot. Beside him sat a brown dog with velvety ears. The dog raised its head to look at her. Molly tried to sit up but she grew dizzy, and too tired to do anything more she fell back to sleep.

A day later Molly woke up properly. The man was beside her. Molly stared at him, not fully understanding where she was. She looked at the man's matted, shoulder-length hair and the feather earring in his right ear. His eyes were green and his face was very tanned, so that when he smiled, his teeth seemed especially white. His nose was straight and his cheeks were ruddy. He wore a red and orange bead necklace that sat above his collarbones, shorts and a white shirt with a print of leaves on it.

'How you feeling?' he asked gently, with an accent that sounded French.

Molly slowly sat up, leaning her shoulders heavily against the wall of the hut, and she reached to the back of her head to touch it. It had a big bandage on it. She wondered how badly she had hurt herself and for how long she had been unconscious. Petula nuzzled at her leg. She felt her face. Her eyes were puffy and her forehead and cheekbones bruised. Molly remembered the huge hailstones that had smashed into her in the sky. Then she swallowed hard. She was horribly thirsty.

'Have a drink,' the man said, offering a cup to her.

The water tasted deliciously sweet and pure. Molly took small sips at first. Then she gulped the whole cup down, and chased it with another. Dazed as she was, Molly found herself wondering whether the water was from the spring of the Coca River. Her body, like a parched plant, soaked up the fluid. It cleared her head. Suddenly Molly felt ravenous.

'Um, I'm sorry' she said to the man, 'I know you've saved my life and everything, and you want to know things, but I'm really hun—' Before Molly had finished her sentence, the man passed her a plate of food.

'It looks a little strange,' he said, 'but it tastes great. You'll see.'

Molly began to eat. It was delicious – some sort of vegetable mixed with onions, herbs and garlic. But her mouth had forgotten how to chew and her stomach had shrunk to the size of a ping pong ball. After only a couple of mouthfuls she felt full.

Molly wiped her mouth. 'Thank you,' she said, her brain now ticking properly. 'Where am I? Are the others here too?'

'You're the only one I've found,' the man said.

Molly shook her head in horror. Then she studied the man's face. 'And – and who are you?'

'My name's Bas.' The man smiled. 'Basile is my real name but people call me Bas. Basile is like your English word, basil. You know basil leaves, they're green and taste really nice with tomatoes. Kinda funny name to have, I suppose. I'm a botanist – I study plants. It's like my parents knew I would like plants. And as you can see we are right in the middle of a place with a lot of green stuff.'

Molly reached down and stroked Petula. She could feel her strength coming back by the minute. She looked up at Bas gratefully.

'Thank you for finding me. I could have died.'

'Certainly could have. You were lucky that I was out that night tracking a wild pig. You are also fortunate that I know a lot about the medicinal properties of rainforest plants. I was able to mix an ointment that was perfect for fixing your wound.'

'Was it bad?' Molly asked, reaching up to the lump on the back of her head.

'Pretty bad. You kinda split it and bumped it. You've

been concussed for a few days. Knocked out. Have you got a headache?'

'No.' Molly suddenly felt sick with fear. *She* was alive because she had been lucky. What about the others? 'Do you think the others are dead?'

Bas tilted his head. 'We can look for them,' he said. 'The best thing is to stay optimistic and you mustn't worry.' He paused and changed the subject. 'You've probably acclimatized to the mountain air while you've been asleep. It's really high up here where we are – less oxygen in the air. Takes a bit of getting used to. Are you feeling OK?'

Molly nodded. She wondered how long he had lived in the Ecuadorian jungle.

'How come you're here?' she asked.

'Oh, I'm writing a book. It's been taking me years to research – three years and four months so far, to be precise. It's all about the precious herbs and plants in the cloud forest and how they can help cure people. It's all about not letting the forest be chopped down. Because if we lose the trees and the unique plants and fungi here, we lose the wisdom of the place. There are amazing cures for human illnesses in this jungle.' Petula gave a little growl. 'OK, and for dog illnesses too. How about cat illnesses?' Bas studied Petula's face. 'Can't imagine you care so much about cats.'

Molly laughed.

'So I'm here,' Bas continued. 'Eating what grows here and kinda getting away from it all. Hardly talk to anyone. My radio, you know, the type to communicate with people, is broken. Every so often I take a trip on my motorbike to the town thirty miles away. I stock up with supplies of stuff that I can't grow, like chocolate. And coffee and matches and pasta. Stuff like that. I'm pretty self-sufficient. I have a little windmill that creates electricity, and some solar panels too that harvest energy from the sun. I collect rainwater ... There's a lot of water up here. And I grow things. Got a big vegetable patch. Just have to watch the naughty critters who come to nibble at it. Grow everything from garlic to soya – I'm a vegetarian, see, so need some protein.'

Bas pointed to Petula. 'Your dog seems to like the soya too. Anyway, corn, salad, potatoes, tomatoes, pumpkins. Everything grows here. So fertile. And I keep chickens for their eggs. Got a natural loo, full of saw-dust. I sprinkle bacteria on it and it all just rots away in an amazing way. It doesn't even smell. And I got Canis here. Oh, where is he? Anyway, got my dog. And all the company of the forest, with its birds and mon-keys, and I've got a good library so lots to read, and occasionally I watch a movie on my computer. Got about fifty movies.'

Molly realized that Bas had been hit by a torrent of verbal diarrhoea. He obviously hadn't spoken to anyone for months. Then her mind changed gear.

'Erm, Bas,' Molly said. 'My friends – I know you said not to worry but ... Do you think they're all right?'

Bas looked Molly in the eye. 'How many of you were there?'

'Four. Malcolm the pilot, and my brother, Micky, and a girl called Lily. We were trying to get to the Logan Stones. We've got to sort a big problem out.' Molly tried to swing her legs out of bed. Her head swam.

'You can't move today,' Bas said. 'But you can tell me your story. And maybe by tomorrow you will feel better enough to start searching for your friends. They may have been lucky,' he added kindly. 'There is lots to eat in the forest. I heard the plane come down. We can search for them. The dogs can help. But for now see whether you can eat some more. And tell me about about your problem. Maybe I can help.'

And so Molly ate a little more and told Bas everything.

The more she talked, the more anxious she grew about her friends and Micky, and the more worried she became about Miss Hunroe's plan. Molly might be the only person left in the world who could try to stop Miss Hunroe. The weight of her responsibility sank in as Molly told Bas her story. The lush and peaceful forest rippled with birdsong, as though refusing to believe that anything bad was happening. But Bas's face dropped as he listened.

'You probably think I'm delirious or something,' Molly concluded. 'I mean hypnotism, morphing and all that must sound pretty far-fetched. Like I've gone funny in the head since being knocked out.'

'Well, I'm not sure,' said Bas. 'I mean you could hypnotize me to prove it, or even morph into me! But you might relapse and knock yourself out again with the effort.' Molly was too tired to read Bas's mind to see whether he believed her. He went on talking. 'No, the best thing seems to me that tomorrow we oughta go to my viewing crane. I've got this crane that's high up in the canopy that I normally use for inspecting plants and stuff. The views from it are expansive to say the least. You never know what we might see from up there. And as far as the Logan Stones go, I know where they are.'

'You do?' Molly gulped as she spoke. She hadn't expected this. Bas's revelation had tripped off his tongue so lightly.

'Sure. They are quite a way from here. But I can show you.'

Chapter Twenty-five

Molly got stronger. She ate and ate, little bits here and there, and by the end of the day she polished off a whole bowl of Bas's sweet-potato soup in one sitting. By the evening Molly was walking about his encampment admiring his vegetable garden. It was a fantastic mountain allotment fenced in with rabbit-proof wire mesh. Bas had a book called *The Vegetable A to Z*, and it seemed that he grew everything in it. From artichokes to zucchinis. Molly tried to feel optimistic, but she couldn't help being dreadfully anxious. She sat on a rock and stared at a bean plant. And, as though her body could no longer take being strong, as though it could no longer contain the relief of being alive mixed with worry for the others, she cried.

Petula was worried too, but in another way she had never felt happier, because as she'd spun down through the sky in the storm she had realized she wanted to *live*. Life was wonderful – full of *life*. Sucking a stone and sitting comfortably here on a warm rock, watching Molly as she walked through the vegetable garden, Petula breathed in the air to see what lovely things the cloud forest had to offer. Petula smelt a monkey nearby and then she detected the scent of the scruffy mountain dog.

A mongrel with wolf-like features and scruffy, tufty brown hair. This was the closest he'd come to her. It was as if he wanted to introduce himself for he looked straight at her, and sniffed at the air. Then he approached.

'Good evening,' he said politely, sitting down beside her. 'I've been waiting for an opportunity to introduce myself. My name is Canis. I don't think I've ever seen your breed before.'

Petula was impressed. Most dogs couldn't help having a close sniff before they introduced themselves. This dog had manners.

'I'm a pug,' she explained. 'I come from a long way away. My name is Petula. It's great to meet you – I haven't spoken to another dog for days.'

'That makes two of us!' Canis replied.

He was one of the messiest-faced dogs Petula had ever met, but his eyes were wise and gentle.

'In fact,' he went on, 'the last dog I spoke to was in the village down the mountain, and that was weeks ago. I met a couple of wild dogs a few months back, but usually they're on a different mountainside. Occasionally I hear them howl at night.'

Molly heard the sound of a generator whirring mechanical noise into the evening air. It was coming from a hut nearby. Leaving the dogs to it, she knocked on the door.

'Come in!'

The door creaked as it swung open. The main room was small and very full. Its walls were lined with books and the tables were laden with microscopes of varying sizes, pads of writing and white sheets of paper with drawings on them. Bas was working on a drawing now, under a bright light. The wind-powered generator provided the electricity for this light and Bas obviously only turned it on when he really needed it.

'You're very good at drawing,' Molly observed. 'I would never dare to do it in ink straight away like that. I'd smudge it or make a mistake. Anyway I can't draw anywhere near as brilliantly as that.'

'Well, you have other talents,' Bas said. 'This bobbly plant with its dangling fronds is from a tree called "dragon's blood". This variety grows in the cloud forest. Under its bark is a resin that is blood red. It is good for healing wounds. I used it on your head wound. You'd be amazed how many amazing plant medicines there are up here. It's like nature's pharmacy. That's one good reason why we should stop chopping the forest down, just in case there is a cure for some disease in the forest.'

Bas shook his head. 'There are amazing orchids up here too. So pretty. I like the insects too and sometimes draw them just for fun.' He pointed to one wall, which was covered with drawings of insects. 'My favourite one is that insect that looks like a leaf.'

There were photographs too of monkeys and birds and spiders.

'Did you take these?' asked Molly.

'Yes,' Bas said, concentrating on the stem of his dragon's blood plant. 'That little monkey is a capuchin monkey. Call him Cappuccino. See the way his black hair looks like a skullcap on the top of his head? And the way he's all fluffy with that white part there? Well, he looks a bit like a nice frothy cup of coffee, doesn't he? Cappuccino suits him.' Molly looked at the small brown monkey with the furry white chest and face. 'He's eating a tomato I gave him. Sweet, isn't he? He's round here a lot. Mind you, he's not always sweet. He's a very good judge of people. Anyway, I've been thinking. I reckon you're strong enough to make the journey to the Logan Stones. On the way, we can look for your friends. Chances are if they've got the coordinates they'll be heading in that direction too. Now, want to draw a picture? It might relax you. Take your mind off your troubles.'

Molly sat down. Bas passed her a pencil and a rubber. 'Fancy drawing a twig? Twigs are good. I love twigs. Don't hurry it. You've got the whole evening. The more you practise the better you will get, for sure.' A scratching noise outside attracted his attention. 'Or look,' he said, pointing to a tree outside, 'there's Cappuccino. You could draw him. He will move a bit, but it might be fun to try.'

Molly looked at the monkey and then she had an idea. 'I know you don't believe me about hypnotizing and morphing, Bas,' she said. 'Want to see me hypnotize Cappuccino and then morph into him?'

Bas's eyebrows lifted as though he'd just seen an apple talk. 'Well . . .' He smiled uncertainly. 'If you like . . .'

'Hmmm.' Molly nodded. 'I can still tell you don't believe me, so come on.'

They went outside. There was Cappuccino the monkey sitting in a tall bush, eating a flower. Bas sat down on a wooden bench to watch whilst Molly walked slowly towards the wild creature.

'Hello,' she said, trying to catch his eye. The monkey stared into the distance to the left, as though looking at Molly was not a good idea. For a moment he glanced at her, but then he turned away again. 'Come on,' Molly coaxed. 'All you have to do is say hello.'

Monkeys are very inquisitive creatures. Cappuccino was no exception. And so he couldn't keep up his shy act for long. He lifted his head and peered at Molly.

Molly already had her green eyes switched on, so when his small black pupils met hers a current of hypnotism, like invisible glue, stuck the monkey to Molly. At once Cappuccino was under her power. He had lost his own will. And suddenly, as far as he could see, this girl was as wonderful as any monkey he'd ever known. He was ready to follow her to the ends of the forest. The girl clicked her fingers at him, and, dropping the flower, he sprang from the branches to be by her side.

She leaned this way and that – Cappuccino copied her. She turned round and wiggled her bottom. Cappuccino imitated her strange dance as well as he could.

'Extraordinary!' the man in the flowery shirt was saying.

'And now,' the queen-of-the-monkeys girl was saying, 'watch closely. I am going to morph into Cappuccino. Give me a complicated task, and when I am Cappuccino he will do it.'

'Um, um, OK,' the man said. 'When you are him, go inside, fetch the teapot, put a tea bag in it and bring it back.'

'Got it,' the girl was saying. Then Cappuccino felt her staring at him again. And the next thing he knew it was as if the girl outside was rushing into his head. And now he found himself moving – running inside the hut, where he'd never been before, into a room with tables and pans and plates. He found himself picking up a strange-shaped pot the shape of a pear, with a stick-like part to it. He saw his own furry hands opening a wooden box and finding a little sack, like a white spider's egg nest. He was putting the sack into the pear pot. Then he was opening a door to a box on the wall and taking out a smaller box. In this were fruit-smelling food things. He put three on a flat, white, round rock thing and then he was bounding outside.

Cappuccino gave the teapot and the plate of biscuits to Bas.

'Amazing!' Bas shook his head in wonder and squinted into the monkey's eyes to see whether he could see Molly there. Molly stuck out her tongue at him.

Molly knew she had shown Bas enough. But before she left Cappuccino's head she wanted to leave some instructions with him. She realized that Cappuccino might be very helpful to her if she ever encountered Miss Hunroe.

And so Molly thought some very specific instructions to her new furry friend, and then she set him free from her hypnotism. Remembering everything that Black had taught her about meegoing, Molly poured herself out of Cappuccino into herself. She gave herself clean cotton shorts and a cool, loose linen shirt. And she fixed her head.

'Wow!' Bas gulped, nearly falling off his stool as Molly materialized. 'Wow! Your clothes are different. Your head is . . .' Bas sprang up and rushed over to Molly. He hardly dared touch her as the way she had popped up out of nowhere was so eerie. Then he examined her head. 'And your head and your bruised face are . . . completely better!'

301

'Believe me now?'

'Yes I do. Unless I'm going mad.'

Cappuccino shook his fur. He nodded at the girl before hopping off to the trees. He would sit in the trees. Sit there and wait for the girl. And when she went anywhere, he thought, he would follow her.

Chapter Twenty-six

The birds of the forest had been up for hours. And so had Miss Speal and Miss Teriyaki. They stood a little distance away from each other, Miss Speal in a long, grey cotton dress that smelt of mothballs with a white apron on top and Miss Teriyaki in a short-sleeved, white laboratory overall. They were in a cooking area outside the hut that served as a kitchen for them in the jungle. Miss Speal was at a gas cooker stirring a pot of something meaty with a chopping board nearby laden with cloves of garlic and pots of dried chilli and spices whilst Miss Teriyaki was at a counter beating a batter. Miss Teriyaki's face and arms were covered with mosquito bites that had swollen into hard, itchy lumps.

'I've tried morphing into forest birds, then meegoing back into myself, but these bites are always still on my skin. They're driving me crazy,' she complained, adding cocoa to her cake mix.

'You're already crazy!' Miss Speal observed cuttingly.

'Some of those lumps seem to be going septic. Most unattractive.'

'Your stew looks most unattractive,' Miss Teriyaki hissed. 'Hope you're not trying to poison us again. That bird was difficult to shoot so don't waste it.'

Miss Speal gave Miss Teriyaki a hard look. 'Oh, I see! Miss Goody Goody! It won't be long before you're in trouble again.' Then she added sweetly, 'I have some marvellous anti-itch cream in my spongebag beside my bed. I can't leave this meat right now,' she hummed with a sigh, 'wouldn't want it to *burn*! But if you want to use the cream you're welcome to it. It really soothes bites.'

'Really?' Miss Teriyaki put her whisk down. 'That's exactly what I need. I can't think why I didn't bring any myself from London.' With that, she wiped her hands on a cloth and walked away round the side of the kitchen where the water tank and the washing pots were, off towards the main living quarters a little way away.

'You didn't think of bringing it because you're a pleased-with-yourself idiot,' Miss Speal declared under her breath as Miss Teriyaki disappeared from view. Then, checking all about to see that no one was watching her, and with a malicious look on her face, Miss Speal pulled a glass pot out of her apron. *Extra Hot Chennai Spice*, its label read. She walked over to Miss Teriyaki's cake mix, unscrewed the pot's lid and tipped a good quantity of the brown powder into the batter. Then she gave the mixture a stir.

'That should liven things up a bit,' she said, smiling.

Miss Hunroe was sitting outside her hut at a table where she had eaten her breakfast. She wore a smart Ecuadorian trilby and a green cape to match it, with lightweight safari trousers and a crisp shirt. Her gold coin was in her pocket. She stroked it fondly and she smiled across at Miss Speal, who sat opposite her, looking nervous. On the table between them, beside a pot of coffee and a plate with a half-eaten croissant, was a radio.

'Coffee or tea, Miss Speal?' Miss Hunroe asked.

Miss Speal shook her head. Miss Hunroe poured herself a black coffee.

'So you say you can sense the Moon girl?'

'Y-yes, yes, I think so,' Miss Speal stuttered. 'The feelings were weak to start with but they are getting stronger.'

'And the boy?'

Miss Speal shut her eyes. Then she shook her head. 'No, I don't feel him.'

Miss Hunroe eyed Miss Speal coolly. 'And you're not just imagining it to try to get in my good books? I seem to remember that sometimes your "feelings" can be a little misguided.'

'Oh no, no, no, Miss Hunroe.'

'Hmmm. Well we'll see.'

Miss Speal nodded. 'So what are we going to do

today, Miss Hunroe? I've cooked a delicious fowl stew for lunch. You – you won't be disappointed, I promise you.'

Ignoring her, Miss Hunroe leaned forward and switched the radio on.

The radio crackled. An American voice became audible. '*Yes, it is terrible,*' the voice was saying. '*The cyclone has caused complete chaos. People have had to leave their homes and stay the night in shelters. Train services are down, traffic has been disrupted. Ordinary folk can't go about their business. But emergency services are doing the best they can and the army is working flat out to help fix things.*'

Miss Hunroe turned the volume down. 'Miami,' she said. 'The little cyclone we gave them yesterday obviously worked. Hope it's wiped those horrid theme parks out. What an eyesore those rollercoasters are!'

Miss Speal agreed, nodding and twitching at the same time. 'Hee hee hee.'

'Hmmm. Miss Speal?'

'Yes!'

'I want to talk to you about the blue stone.'

Miss Speal's smile dropped. 'What about it?' she asked, starting to wring her hands.

'I want you to give it to me for safe keeping,' Miss Hunroe said, looking her straight in the eye.

Miss Speal shook her head. 'Don't make me, Miss Hunroe. I can't. I need it, you see.'

'Don't be ridiculous.'

'I do. It's become a part of me . . .'

'You may keep it for today. But tonight I want to find it in the gold box beside my bed. Do you understand?'

'Y-y-yes, Miss Hunroe.'

'And, Miss Speal?'

'Yes?'

'I don't want you wearing clothes that smell of mothballs any more. Is that clear?'

Half a mile away, Miss Teriyaki and Miss Oakkton crouched down low in the bushes. Both were in camouflage shirts and khaki shorts, though Miss Oakkton's were many sizes bigger than Miss Teriyaki's. On the ground beside them was a hessian bag. A dead rabbit's foot poked out of it. Miss Oakkton gripped the horn handle of a sharp steel knife whilst Miss Teriyaki held a bamboo pipe up to her lips. Four fat guinea pigs stood in the shade of a tree, nibbling at the grass on the other side of a clearing in front of them.

'I'll get ze orange one,' Miss Oakkton decided, quietly raising her knife and taking aim.

'I'll get the brown one then,' Miss Teriyaki said. Her nose wrinkled. Then she sniffed the air. 'Miss Oakkton, have you done a – a . . . hmmm . . . you know.'

'Sorry,' Miss Oakkton apologized. 'It vas zat bean soup Miss Speal served us last night. It's given me a bit of an upset tummy.' As she spoke, the eggy smell drifted over to where the guinea pigs were. All four of the creatures lifted their furry heads and sniffed at the air. Then the orange guinea pig gave a terrified squeak. The others joined in, and in a cacophony of squeals, they were gone.

'You slab of rotton sushi!' Miss Teriyaki hissed. 'Please control your – your bott next time, Miss Oakkton.'

Miss Oakkton lifted her head proudly. 'I sought it smelt rarzer good.'

At dawn, Molly woke to the sound of Petula's clawed paws clipping across the wooden floor. Molly drifted back to sleep. She woke a few hours later. The sun was still coming up. She drank some water and sat up to see Cappuccino sitting on her windowsill.

'Good morning, Cappuccino. How are you?' Molly asked.

The monkey nodded and then turned to look into the forest. He began to chatter.

'Sorry, I don't understand you,' she said, getting up out of bed. Then she went outside.

Bas was all already dressed, stirring a saucepan on an outdoor fire. A kettle sat beside it. 'Porridge?' he asked.

Just then Cappuccino began to shriek and jump up and down, pointing into the bushes.

Something was moving in the undergrowth behind Bas. The leaves swayed and rustled as if something was crouching there, ready to pounce.

'Bas!' Molly called. 'Watch out!'

Bas snatched a stick from the fire. Its end was smouldering. 'Where?'

Then, in answer, the thing in the bushes let out a cry. A human cry.

'Molly, it's me, Malcolm!'

Moments later, with Cappuccino watching on, Molly and Bas were helping Malcolm up the stairs to the hut. Malcolm's injuries looked worryingly bad. He had a nasty gash in his calf, and his ankle was swollen and raw and pink. His face was scratched as though someone had rubbed it with thorns.

'I landed in a huge spiky plant. That was after I hit a tree and tumbled through it,' Malcolm mumbled, as they lay him down on the veranda daybed.

'Bas'll sort you out,' Molly said. 'He knows exactly what plants can help you.' Her head spun as a thought occurred to her. 'Did you see the others?'

'No,' Malcolm croaked. 'I don't know where they are.'

Molly's heart sank.

'Bas can you fix this?' Malcolm gasped, with a look of desperation in his eyes. 'My calf looks like it's going gangrenous. I don't really want to have my leg chopped off.'

'Gangrenous? What's that?' Molly asked.

Bas wrinkled his nose as he inspected Malcolm's bloody wound. 'It's when an untreated infected wound goes bad,' he explained, 'because the swelling, which is very bad in Malcolm's ankle, has stopped the blood flow. So the white blood cells that normally fight the infection can't get there.'

'Can you help him?' Molly whispered.

'Luckily for you, Malcolm,' said Bas, licking his lips as though he was really excited, 'I have some special little friends that *can* help you. I began cultivating them yesterday as part of a little experiment.'

With that, Bas hurried off to his hut.

Molly took Malcolm's hand. 'How did you find me?'

'The tracking device . . . it's in my pocket. I've been crawling day and night. I knew I had to get to you. Had a feeling you'd have been lucky.' Malcolm smiled.

'I'm very glad to see you, Malcolm. You flew that plane brilliantly, by the way.'

Malcolm grinned. 'It was a bit hairy.' Then he frowned. 'I wonder what happened to the others.'

Molly shook her head. 'I don't know. I just don't know.'

The door of the hut swung open again. Armed with all sorts of medical supplies, Bas hurried back to them. As he passed the fire, he picked the kettle up off it. 'Perfect timing,' he said. 'Just boiled.'

Molly sat on a chair beside Bas and watched. First of all, he washed his hands under the rainwater tap, then he disinfected them with some medical alcohol that smelt sharp. Next, he set to work on Malcolm's leg. He took wads of cotton wool and, using first hot water and then the alcohol, he cleaned Malcolm's gash. Malcolm winced and bit his lip. Then, when the wound was clean, Bas lifted a shallow plastic pot out of his bag.

'What's that?' Malcolm asked worriedly.

Bas nodded.

'This is going to surprise you.'

He peeled back the lid of the pot. To Malcolm and Molly's horror, there in the pot was a mass of little white maggots.

'Maggots!' Malcolm gasped. 'They'll eat me alive!'

Molly's tongue stuck out as she felt sick.

'Don't be alarmed,' Bas assured them both. 'Maggots are *brilliant* with gangrene. You see, they like to eat rotten flesh. They don't eat good healthy flesh. So what we do is put them on your wound and the little fellows will eke out all the nasty gangrenous stuff and the bad bacteria and then, when their work is done, I will put them back in their pot to, erm, well, to digest!'

'You're joking,' Malcolm said, his eyes wide. 'They're revolting.'

'I'm one hundred per cent serious. These are your friends.'

At these words Molly found herself giggling. The idea of Malcolm having a party and all the little maggots being invited because they were his friends had occurred to her.

'Sorry,' she said, knowing that it wasn't very tactful to laugh. But still she kept laughing.

'Don't worry,' said Malcolm. 'You're just a bit

hysterical. It's because this is so odd. We're in the middle of the jungle and my leg looks like something out of a sci-fi film and Bas here who is like a wild man of the woods is about to put wriggling maggots on to me. It is quite funny, I suppose, in a macabre kind of a way.' He waved a finger at the maggots. 'Be good now, maggots!' he said, breathing out heavily.

'Whoa!' whispered Molly as Bas began to prod the wriggling maggots into Malcolm's wound. At once, like things that had been starved, the maggots began tugging at the rotten flesh there. 'Does it hurt?'

'Not at all,' Malcolm replied. 'Just got to get over my squeamishness. It's only the idea of it that's freaky.'

They all sat marvelling at the miracle maggots, until Malcolm croaked. 'I'm a bit hungry. Don't suppose you've got any food?'

As they had breakfast, they decided that while Malcolm rested Molly and Bas would go to the lookout tower and see if they could spot Micky and Lily. Bas brought Malcolm a pair of his clean underpants, shorts and a flower-patterned shirt. They left food by his side and water to drink and blankets to keep him warm if he got the shivers, as well as a book about cloud forest wildlife.

'I'll probably just sleep,' Malcolm yawned. 'By the way, have you got a radio?'

'A broken one. If you get a moment, you could see if you can fix it.'

'Sure thing.' But before Bas could explain where it was, Malcolm had shut his eyes and gone to sleep.

Molly whistled for Petula.

'She's off with Canis,' Bas said. 'Come on, Molly, let's go. Two down, two to go. We need to find your brother and Lily.'

Across the cloud forest, a few miles away, Micky and Lily were waking up. Their bed had been the hard ground of a shallow cave. They were bundled up warmly, under their green synthetic-silk parachutes. Unlike Molly, they had avoided the eye of the storm. Lily had lost her grip of Micky and Molly in the initial part of the fall, but then once her parachute had opened Micky had been swinging under his parachute just ahead. Seeing her in the moonlight, he'd steered close by and shouted instructions to her as they had parachuted down.

Unlike Malcolm and Molly, they'd had a good landing. Their parachutes had got tangled in the trees, but, miraculously, they had been deposited in a clearing. Micky had untangled the canopies, knowing that they would be useful. Lily had been most unhelpful. Shocked by the fall, she'd simply sat shivering under a tree. So it was Micky who'd braved the branches and rescued the bundles of material. While Lily sat with her knees pulled up to her chest, he'd hunted for shelter and found the cave. He'd laid the canopies out like sleeping bags. Then they'd sat close together and stared out at the dark night, listening to the creatures of the jungle. It had been dawn before they'd fallen asleep and an afternoon sun had been high in the sky when they'd woken.

For the rest of the day a hot sun shone down on the children's clothes, which Micky laid out on rocks to dry. Lily sat in her vest and underwear, huddled and scared, whilst Micky focused his mind. He knew that Lily and he might not meet another human for weeks and that it was essential he found a way for them to stay alive in the forest. He had read many adventure stories. In fact, he had read both fictional and factual accounts of survival stories set up mountains and out to sea, in deserts and the jungle. Even though it was scary to be in such strange terrain with no knowledge of what plants around them were poisonous or whether there were dangerous insects or snakes about, he found the whole business quite exciting.

Micky knew that he and Lily might have to eat grubs and insects, and the fruit on the trees. That afternoon he spent a lot of time foraging and digging.

'Why don't we just walk somewhere and get *help*?' Lily called out from her nest-like place under a tree.

'Walk where?' Micky replied. 'We don't know how big this forest is or if we *will* find help.' He pulled an orange tuber out of the ground and, brushing the soil off it, put it on a pile of other roots.

'I am *not* eating that rubbish.' Lily crossed her arms belligerently.

'You might have to,' Micky retorted. 'And, Lily, you

should try to drink as much as you can. It's in the leaves, look, there's tons of it everywhere. You may be getting altitude sickness. You see we're very high up.' He tapped the altometer. 'We are at about a thousand metres and that can make some people feel funny.'

'I don't feel funny. But you look funny.'

'Ha. Ha. Why don't you come and help me dig for potatoes?'

'No way. I'll get dirty,' she said, taking her clothes from the rocks. 'Dry clean only.'

Micky laughed. 'Dry clean only? Are they allowed to go through the washing machine of a whirlwind storm? Come on, Lily, get a grip. Come and help.'

But Lily shook her head and went to sit back under her tree.

That night, Micky lit a fire. He cooked the roots, and though they were black with char Lily, now starving hungry, helped him gobble them up. The smoke from the campfire kept the insects at bay. And as a modicum of comfort crept back into their lives both Micky and Lily felt a little bit better.

'Well done for remembering the matches,' Lily said, nodding towards the fire. She reached into her anorak pocket and passed Micky something small and silvery.

'Chocolate?'

'You're joking.'

'No, always carry it. Never know when you might need it.'

Micky took the chocolate gratefully and they both unwrapped it. 'Mmmm. Tastes a million times better here, doesn't it?'

'Yup,' Micky said. 'Thanks.'

'No, it's me who should say thanks,' said Lily. 'I'm really sorry. I'll try not to be so useless tomorrow.'

'Don't worry,' said Micky. 'It was the shock of the jump. Crazy, wasn't it?'

'Really frightening.' Lily shivered.

'I think we ought to start looking for the others tomorrow,' Lily said.

'Agreed,' Micky replied, rubbing his eyes and yawning.

'Do you think they're still alive?' Lily asked.

Micky shrugged. Inside, he had a strange feeling that Molly and Petula were all right since they seemed to have a habit of falling on their feet. 'If we use our compasses and follow the coordinates to the stones, I'm sure we'll find them. Now let's get some sleep. Yam for breakfast?'

Lily groaned. 'Again?' She closed her eyes. 'Chocolate croissant!' she murmured dreamily.

'Sausage roll,' Micky replied.

'Marmite sandwich,' Lily suggested.

'Victoria sponge cake.'

'Toasted cheese sandwich . . .'

Miss Speal sat on a little wooden stool in some bushes high above the camp. She liked this place because it was very private and yet it had a good view of every-thing that was happening in the clearing below. She pulled out her blue stone and then hugged it to her chest. 'Oh, my dear Stone. What shall I do without you?' She began to weep. 'I shall miss you.' Then she sat up. She'd heard a noise and voices.

'I vill put a nice hidden trap here,' Miss Oakkton was saying. 'Zen it's not too far to walk to check it.'

'And a pit would be good here,' Miss Teriyaki said, slapping away an insect.

Miss Speal jumped up in alarm. She tried to think whether she was doing anything that she might get into trouble for. She was doing nothing. That in itself could get her into Miss Hunroe's bad books. She quickly shoved her blue stone back into her pocket and, making haste, pushed past the bushes to take the shortcut back to the camp.

The blue stone lay on the ground by the wooden stool. It had not quite dropped into Miss Speal's pocket. The pocket's flap had obstructed its entry, and as the woman had hurried away the movement had tossed the stone out.

Chapter Twenty-seven

Petula trotted after Canis, who moved swiftly up the mountain paths. They had been walking since before dawn.

'How much further, Canis?' Petula called after him.

Hearing her panting, Canis stopped. 'We'll rest now,' he said. 'Look, there's a nice pool of water in the dip of that rock if you're thirsty.'

Petula lapped up the sweet cloud forest water and wiped her muzzle with a wet paw. 'We've been gone for hours,' she said. 'I wonder whether I should have woken Molly up to explain.'

'She never would have understood what you were saying,' Canis replied. 'Besides, these people are dangerous. Before you involve your mistress you must see whether they have anything to do with the crazy women you told me about.'

'How many of them did you say there were?' Petula

asked, scratching her neck where an insect had bitten her just under her collar.

'Two but I smelt more in the distance,' Canis replied. 'And there was definitely a hint of flowers about them. I smelt the scent of rose thorn and orange blossom. And blood. That's how I found them in the first place. I found a rabbit that they'd trapped,' he said, getting even more serious. 'It hung by its noosed legs from the branch of a tree.'

Petula shivered. 'Let's hope we don't step in one of those traps ourselves,' she said.

After a brief rest, they set off again up the mountain path.

Petula decided she would find out for sure whether this lead of Canis's was a good one and then she would report back to Molly before nightfall.

'Smell the barbecue?' Canis asked, sniffing the air with his wet nose. 'They must be having a meal.'

Petula could detect the whiff of cooked meat – curried cooked meat on the air. It made her mouth water. Trying to ignore this, she sniffed the wind more, searching for a hint of orange blossom and thorn and rose. She found it.

'It's them,' she gasped.

'Good work, eh?' Canis gave a short arf.

Petula nodded.

The dogs now trod stealthily through the under-growth, following their noses and reading the air. The smoke from a fire became stronger and stronger, mixed with the smell of baking and the stench of dead animals. And then, just like a car stopping unexpectedly at a dead end, Petula and Canis arrived at a rocky outcrop. It was obviously a place humans liked to be, for there was a wooden stool there and, what was more, the smell of mothballs from someone who had been there only shortly before hung in the air. They had been scared too for the odd smell of electric lemon lingered.

Down below was a clearing with eight huts. The two dogs surveyed the scene. From four of the huts wafted floral smells of perfume. Nearby was a hut with a water tank over it that Petula supposed must be the bathroom hut. And closer to the ledge that they were on were two more scruffy-looking huts. Outside these were outdoor cooking stoves and ovens and tables with large chopping boards and bowls on them. Tin basins for washing pans and plates lay on the ground. Nearby was a small water tank on wooden legs.

Much further to the left, segregated from the other huts by bushes, was a hut that was obviously used by hunters. Outside this one were colourful forest birds, green and red feathered parrots and cockatoos, hanging upside down in bunches. A rabbit skin was nailed on to a board, drying out in the sun.

Canis growled.

'I wonder where they are?' Petula pondered.

Just then Miss Speal came out of the kitchen hut with oven gloves on. She opened the oven door and pulled out a hot cake tin. Then she poked at the barbecue fire.

'She must be the cook,' said Canis. 'I wonder where the hunters are. Can you smell them?'

Petula sniffed. A mixed odour of sweat and whisky with an edge of blood was very dense in the air. Then she smelt the mothball smell very close to her on the ground. She put her nose down, and sniffed. The smell led her to a beautiful blue stone. Unable to resist it, Petula picked it up in her mouth and gave it a suck. It felt smooth and cool.

'Gives me the creeps,' Canis was saying. 'They don't smell of anything good.' As he spoke, a cloud began to thicken in the sky above.

Petula nodded. 'And is it my imagination,' she said, 'or is their scent getting stronger?' Her heart began to pound, and her fur bristled.

'You're right,' Canis agreed, looking alarmed. 'They're behind us. Getting closer. Quick! Run!' He put his head down and dashed into the bushes.

Petula followed Canis. It was a bad move.

Moments later a cord caught round Petula's back foot. This released a trap catch. The cord tightened and with a yank that practically pulled her limb off she was tugged off her paws and swung up into the air.

Petula nearly swallowed her new stone from the shock. Her world turned upside down. And then a horrible pain in her leg cut through her. The ground was now three metres below her; her body hung heavy and helpless from the hunter's noose. Canis barked up at her. Minutes later, Miss Oakkton and Miss Teriyaki arrived.

'I don't believe it!' said Miss Teriyaki. 'A wild pug! The Chinese were in South America long ago, so obviously the breed stayed here. How extraordinary!'

'I hate pugs,' Miss Oakkton replied, her huge face screwing up as she strained to look at Petula. 'Ugly sings. Can't tell ze back from ze front.'

At that moment Canis attacked. He bit Miss Oakkton's ankle as though it was a bone left over from a Sunday roast. With a scream of anger, she plunged her hunter's knife down. It struck Canis on the back. He skulked off, whimpering.

Desperate, he barked up to Petula. 'I'll come back with my master and your Molly.' And then he dived back into the undergrowth and was gone.

Miss Oakkton rubbed her leg and pointed after Canis, bellowing curses. Miss Teriyaki prodded Petula with her bamboo shooting stick.

'Ahhh,' she said admiringly. 'You know, Miss Oakkton, people *eat* dog in the East. It is a delicacy. I wonder whether pug tastes good.'

'Ha! Vell, I'll let zat be *your* delicacy, Miss Teriyaki!' said Miss Oakkton, spitting on the ground. 'I don't vant to eat anysing zat barks! *Disgusting.*'

Petula looked at the upside-down visions of the ghastly women. Miss Oakkton's body smelt of rotten eggs. She came closer and closer. Then, lifting up her knife mercilessly, she cut the trap rope. Petula dropped to the ground with a thud.

For a moment she lay still, winded and unable to breathe and frightened that she wouldn't ever be able to breathe again. Then she felt a stabbing pain in her ribs.

Miss Oakkton bundled her into a bag already full of dead rabbits and birds. And, half suffocated by fur and feather, Petula was carried down to the camp.

As though she were something as disposable as firewood, she was unloaded into a small, dark hut. Petula curled up into a ball and, spitting out her blue stone, fell unconscious for the second time that week.

Chapter Twenty-eight

Molly was very, very hot. The heat of the Ecuadorian sun had soaked through the clouds above, turning the forest into a steamy sauna. Bas walked at a fast pace along the tree-lined, branch-covered pathways, and it was exhausting keeping up with him. Cappuccino swung through the branches of trees behind them, stopping occasionally to pick fruit. The air was thin with less oxygen to breathe in it, and so Molly began to feel light-headed.

'Are you OK?' Bas asked. 'It is difficult to walk in the high altitude, because your body isn't used to it.'

Molly nodded. 'I'm fine.' She didn't want to hold up the trip and so she walked on without complaining. Her body grew damp with sweat and she was glad she was wearing cool clothes. She thought back to when she used to go to school and how she'd grumble about cross-country runs. This walk was ten times as hard yet she was doing it without complaining, doing it because she needed to. The back of her calves and the muscles in her thighs ached, but Molly gritted her teeth and kept going. The sun was starting to burn her skin. Yet she didn't care. She had to get to Bas's viewing tower. Every so often Bas would stop and they'd have a drink. He had brought with him a bag of energy-boosting dried fruit and while they rested they sat in silence, nibbling the fruit sticks. Cappuccino would sit in the trees a little way off with all his attention trained on Molly.

After a three-hour walk, Bas stopped.

'We're here.'

Ahead of them, camouflaged because it was painted green, Molly saw a metal structure. 'Hope you like heights,' Bas joked. And he led Molly to the crane's steps. They were set like a ladder into it.

Ten minutes later, Molly and Bas were up at the crane's top, standing in a box-like viewing platform. Cappuccino had nipped up ahead and was already chewing a flower he had found.

'Wow!' Molly said, cupping her eyes with her hand and looking out. 'The view is incredible from up here!' She could see for miles and miles over a sea of treetops. She saw far-off mountains that seemed to touch the highest clouds in the sky.

'That's a volcano,' Bas commented, pointing to a beautiful white mountain top in the distance. He had pulled out his binoculars and was scrutinizing the forest. His gaze mowed over the distant trees, swinging back and forth as he thoroughly checked for any signs of life. 'There's the plane,' he said.

Molly looked through the binoculars. Far away, she could see a gash in the jungle, and what looked like a charcoal grey whale parked there.

'We were lucky to get out,' Molly commented. She examined the forest for evidence of parachutes and the others. 'I wonder where they landed?' she sighed, and sadly put the binoculars down. 'Petula can sense where I am. Wish I could feel them. I'm so worried about them, Bas.'

'Cheer up,' said Bas. 'Listen, you never know, maybe Petula can feel Micky too. After all, you are twins. Maybe that's where she went this morning. Maybe she's already found him.'

He flapped open a silk flag. 'Let's hang this red warning flag up, and if they're up a tree they'll see it. Look at those monkeys,' he said, trying to change the subject. 'And those insects.' Then he pointed to the north-west. 'And there, Miss Molly, though you can't see them, are the stones you are interested in.'

'Really?' Molly gulped.

'Yes. See those far-off crags shaped like owls' heads?'

'Yes.'

'Well, the stones are under them. It's going to take us the rest of the day to get there. Are you ready?'

Molly gulped again. 'I am,' she said.

And so they started walking again, their paths

passing over pretty tree-covered humps of land that undulated up and down the sides of the mountain. The cover of foliage and leaves above was often so dense that only spots of the cloudy sky could be seen, and their path was patched with mottled light. It was like walking through a strange forest palace. Sounds were muffled, though every now and then bird call pierced the air. At other times the forest and mists cleared and wonderful views of the cloud forest stretched out green and leafy below and beyond. Walking uphill was strenuous, but walking downhill was hard too. Molly's knees felt like they were going to buckle and bend back on themselves. On and on they walked with Cappuccino hopping casually behind them.

Molly remembered what Forest, her hippy friend, had once said to her. 'There's an old Chinese saying. Wise man who climb mountain, climb one step at a time. He no look at top of mountain and see how far off it is. He enjoy each step.'

Molly decided to try to do this. Soon she found herself in a walking zone, as though her body was hypnotized to just keep taking steps.

'I will keep walking. I will keep walking,' Molly hummed to herself. 'One step at a time.'

The forest paths became thinner and overgrown. On and on they trudged. Hours passed. The light started to fade. And then Bas tapped Molly on the shoulder.

'This is it, Molly,' he whispered. 'There's the owl

mountain. See? Now you sit down and eat this.' He passed Molly a snack with some sort of soya curd in it. 'Cappuccino's here. Everything is just fine.'

Molly obeyed in an exhausted daze. She ate her food and watched as Bas set about making a shelter.

She knew that tomorrow she was going to need all the energy she could muster. So as soon as the shelter was ready Molly rolled out her sleeping bag and crept inside. A moment later, before the forest's daytime animals had returned to their nests, dens, lairs and burrows, Molly was fast asleep.

Less than a mile away, Miss Hunroe and her accomplices were finishing their dinner.

'Edible at least,' Miss Hunroe said to Miss Speal, flipping her gold coin through her elegant fingers. Miss Oakkton surreptitiously wiped her finger across the sauce on her plate, and then licked it, eyeing Miss Speal like a dog eyes an unwelcome guest.

Miss Teriyaki bobbed up to fetch her cake, and Miss Speal hurriedly collected up the plates, her head bowed. Miss Hunroe tossed her coin and inspected it when it landed in her palm.

'Goodness knows we had worked up an appetite . . .' Miss Hunroe went on, glaring at Miss Speal. 'You really are a Little Miss Butterfingers, aren't you, squealy Spealy?'

Everyone stared at Miss Speal who continued clearing the table with her head low.

Miss Oakkton clicked her tongue in agreement. 'Tttut, ttttutt.'

Then Miss Hunroe snapped. 'I cannot believe you were so *stupid*! You make me sick. Can't you feeeeeel where it is, Miss Speal?' she taunted. She sat still for a moment to compose herself. 'Think again. Where did you drop the blue stone, Miss Speal?'

'Erm,' Miss Speal spluttered. 'I'm . . . I'm not entirely sure. As I said, I think . . . I think it was up there.' She pointed to the ledge above the encampment.

'We *know* you think that,' Miss Hunroe hissed. 'Miss Oakkton and Miss Teriyaki have been crawling about up there *all afternoon*. Miss Speal, are you sure you are *telling the truth*?' Miss Hunroe pulled out a set of pan-pipes for the third time that evening and put them to her red lips. She blew gently and a gorgeous sound like a playful mountain wind blowing through the trees filled the air. The gaggle of women gazed adoringly at Miss Hunroe, and a dreamy look filled their eyes. Miss Speal stared at the panpipes, transfixed.

'Tell me again, Miss Speal,' Miss Hunroe cajoled. 'Did you really lose it, *or have you hidden it because you love it so much*?' Above them was a roll of thunder.

Miss Speal sighed. 'I have not hidden it – I lost it.' She began to weep. 'And I can sense that girl is near.'

Miss Hunroe blew suddenly into her instrument, making it shriek. 'The girl may be near, Miss Speal. But she is dead. No one could have survived that plane crash.' She looked disdainfully at the skinny pale woman. 'Imbecile.'

Miss Teriyaki stood holding out her chocolate cake. 'At least some things are dependable, Miss Hunroe,' she said wormingly.

Miss Hunroe smiled, watching as Miss Teriyaki cut her a large slice. 'You will never guess what we found today,' Miss Teriyaki went on, trying to change the subject. 'We found a—'

'Does this cake have coffee in it?' Miss Hunroe asked suddenly. 'You know I can't have caffeine at this time of night or I won't sleep.'

'Of course not,' Miss Teriyaki replied, passing her pudding plate. Miss Hunroe prodded her fork into her cake. Miss Teriyaki continued. 'It is a strange variety, but shows what an influence the Chinese had on Ecuador . . .'

'What *are* you talking about, Miss Teriyaki? Come on, spit it out.' Miss Hunroe raised her fork to her lips.

'Well, we found this—'

Miss Hunroe interrupted once more. 'Does it have alcohol in it, Miss Teriyaki? You know I can't abide alcohol in food.'

'Oh no! Just pure chocolate.'

Miss Hunroe put a forkful of chocolate cake into her mouth.

'We found this—'

'Ahhhh!' Miss Hunroe spat and coughed, and chocolate cake went splattering all over the table. She rose from her seat furiously. 'WHAT ARE YOU TRYING TO DO, MISS TERIYAKI? POISON ME?' Miss Hunroe picked up her plate and frisbeed it away from the table so that it flew through the air and clatterered into a tree. 'I've had ENOUGH of this foul cooking.' She glared at her assembled team. 'If there is ANY more of it, the chef responsible will GO and never, never . . .' Miss Hunroe's voice dropped a few decibels as her anger raged. 'NEVER COME BACK! Do I make myself clear?'

'Yes, Miss Hunroe,' the gathering whispered.

'Yes, Miss Hunroe,' Miss Teriyaki whimpered. She lifted her eyes dolefully. As she did, she caught the eye of Miss Speal. Miss Speal's small brown eyes seemed to be laughing as though what had just happened was the funniest thing in the world.

The next morning Molly was woken at dawn by a giant long-beaked toucan squawking in a tree near her shelter. It had started to rain. Above, the sky was grey and rumbling with thunder again. Cappuccino chattered at her from a nearby tree as if to say good morning. Bas was already up. When he saw Molly stir, he came over and put his blanket round her shoulders.

'You'll need your energy today,' he said. Then he went to his rucksack. Taking a large, leathery, bowl-shaped leaf he put something from his bag into it. He added some sort of juice from a bottle, and then came back with this forest bowl full of sticky, cold porridge. Molly ate her stodgy breakfast. Bas watched her like a teacher might watch a precious student. Molly knew that he believed everything she had told him about Miss Hunroe. It now seemed to her that, as though she was a prizefighter about to enter the ring, or a warrior on whose victory many people's lives depended, he was treating Molly with the utmost respect.

'I'm ready,' she said.

'Good.'

Bas led Molly to a clearing in the trees. Ahead and above them, magnificent in the morning light, were the owl-shaped crags. Molly's insides began quivering with nerves. She swallowed hard. She knew that soon she would be facing Miss Hunroe. Molly had no idea how many of the other horrible women were with her, or what the challenge ahead was. Her mind raced. She hoped Miss Hunroe was not expecting her. Molly felt like a person on some sort of twisted, dangerous TV challenge show, except of course this was real, and there was no getting away – no calling up the producer of the TV show and saying, 'Stop! I've had enough.'

'I hope I *can* sort this out,' she said to Bas. 'There's ... there's a good chance that I won't be able ...' Molly's voice trailed off as the immensity of the task ahead sank in.

'It's amazing that you're trying,' Bas said reassuringly. 'I think you are very brave.' He put his arm round her shoulder.

They headed directly for the crags. Bas led Molly down the slope towards a wall of bushes. He helped Molly climb a tree and they both peeped over the top.

'There they are,' he murmured.

As if transported from a dream and glistening in the rain, glowing red, grey, green and blue like alien objects, were the four vast weather rocks, the Logan Stones. They stood in a circle, huge, majestic and utterly beautiful.

'And the rock behind the stones,' Bas whispered, 'with the water gushing out of it – that's the spring of the Coca River. And that giant mud mound that looks like a sandcastle in the middle of the stones – that's a . . .' He fell silent.

What Molly saw next was like a vision from a nightmare. Miss Hunroe and Miss Oakkton stepped out from behind the mud mound and into view. They stood in the rain in the centre of the stones. Molly and Bas shrank back. Molly could hardly believe it. She had to pinch herself to make sure she was awake. To have come all this way, to be in the middle of the wilderness and to be actually looking at Miss Hunroe in a khaki jungle suit and Miss Oakkton in a tent-like robe was surreal. Both of them were soaked to the bone, their clothes and hair sopping wet. Neither held the hypnotism book. They simply stood beside the stones, staring at their hands.

'OOOOW!' Miss Oakkton suddenly boomed, and,

as fast as genies disappearing into a bottle, the two women both vanished, leaving two piles of clothes on the muddy ground.

The area was completely still. Molly scrutinized the space between the stones. She was *sure* that Miss Oakkton and Miss Hunroe had just morphed. How else could they have disappeared like that? Yet where had they gone? What had they turned into?

Molly readied herself. 'I'm going in,' she said. 'Don't worry, Bas. I'll be fine. Wait here, OK?'

Bas nodded. 'Good luck, Molly.'

Molly approached the stones cautiously. Her hands were sweating from fear.

Cappuccino swung himself up into a tall tree and sat on a branch to watch. Molly felt strange, her skin prickly. This wasn't from terror, she realized – this prickly feeling was from the energy of the four giant stones. As she moved into the area in the centre of them, she felt their power. The grey and blue stones both emanated a cold feeling whilst the reddy-orange stone gave off heat. The green stone made the hair on her arms stand on end. All the stones had a pull that tugged as though they were gigantic magnets and Molly was made of metal.

Molly's eyes darted nervously about. Perhaps Miss Hunroe and her posse knew that she was there. Perhaps they had morphed into birds and were watching her. Molly switched her whole self on to high alert, vigilant to every splashing raindrop and to every sound about her. Maybe the women had learned human-to-human morphing by now. If they had, they might try to morph into her. Molly steeled herself. She would *not* let them get into her mind. Then she had a horrid thought. What if they all tried to get into her mind at once? Molly shivered. She stepped gingerly past Miss Hunroe's and Miss Oakkton's discarded clothes and shoes, and around the sand-castle-like mound of earth.

Then Molly went over to the blue Logan Stone and gave it a gentle push. It ground against its stone base as it moved, rocking smoothly to and fro. Molly walked behind the stone. Did it hide a secret entrance? She gently pushed the giant stone again and then one by one prodded the others but they all seemed to be simply enormous rocks with curved bottoms on stone plat-forms.

Where had the women vanished? She stared at the ground to think. Above her the sky rumbled with thunder again. A yellow butterfly darted by, dodging the rain, and made Molly jump. Was that Miss Hunroe? Then she noticed a beetle scuttling across the mud by her feet. Was that Miss Oakkton? What if they had turned into venomous snakes or stinging scorpions or poisonous spiders? Maybe they were preparing to attack her! Molly's flesh crawled and she glanced from side to side, checking all about her for dangerous creatures.

It was then that she noticed an enormous ant-like insect trotting across the ground towards the mound of mud in front of her. And there was another.

The turreted mound was definitely a sort of anthill. Then Molly remembered the huge model insect in the museum in London and realized that this was a *termite* mound. As she studied the termites crowding into it, Molly considered how it must seem a massive kingdom for the termites that lived there.

'If you stand in the very centre of the ring of the stones, in the very centre of the forcefield that the four big Logan Stones make, with the four coloured stones in your hand, and if you rub the stones' . . . Theobald Black's words echoed distantly in her mind.

Molly saw instantly that the termites had built their mound exactly in the centre of the ring of stones, in the centre of the Logan Stones' forcefield.

Molly remembered how the women had been staring at their hands and how Miss Oakkton had yelped. Had they been staring down at termites so that they could morph into them? Had Miss Oakkton been bitten by one? Molly watched a small termite carry a piece of bark six times bigger than itself into the mound. She'd heard somewhere that ants and termites can carry ten to fifty times their body weight. Why, if Miss Hunroe and Miss Oakkton turned into termites, they could easily carry the small pieces of stone from the cover of the hypnotism book inside the mound! The sky gave a huge roll of thunder and then opened. Heavy rain poured down. Molly had to wipe her eyes in order to see. Had Miss Hunroe caused this weather? Had she seen Molly and switched this rain on? Molly wasn't sure *what* Miss Hunroe was doing. But the answer to *where* Miss Hunroe *was* now seemed glaringly obvious.

If Miss Hunroe and her horrid gang were now termites inside the mound, turning it into some kind of termite-built weather-changing chamber, and if Miss Hunroe had the coloured stones with her too, well, inside the termite mound was where Molly must go.

For a split second, Molly wondered if she should destroy the mound, but then thought better of it. Perhaps, if she did, all the bad weather Miss Hunroe had already caused might be set like that forever in the stones.

Molly didn't want to become a termite. The idea of becoming a termite, with big pincers and a poisonous bite, and then of coming face to face with other termites was terrifying. One termite paused near the entrance of the mound. It was carrying a large twig and struggling in the rain. Molly took a deep breath. Clearing her mind of all worries and negative thoughts, she began to concentrate.

Chapter Twenty-nine

'I'm not leaving here,' Lily declared stubbornly. She was sitting on a mossy rock with her shoes off beside a stream. 'I've got blisters and it's too wet. There's no point anyway. We've been walking for ages and we're just as lost as we were before. We're stuck in a stupid soaking wet forest on a mountain in the middle of nowhere. *And* I've got four mosquito bites from last night.'

Micky was halfway up a nearby tree. 'You remind me of what I used to be like,' he said. 'I used to grumble a lot. Hey, there's a good view from here.'

'Of what? Trees? Lovely.' Lily threw a stone hard so that it hit a rock and cracked in two.

'Actually, I can see a road.'

'Really!' Lily stood up.

'No, not really. But I might have.'

Just then a dog came out of the forest. Lily took one look at it and screamed. Frantically, she stepped deep into the stream right up to her waist. 'WOLF!' she yelled. 'MICKY! THERE'S A WOLF!'

Canis looked at the screaming girl. The fear smell coming off her was electric.

'RUUUUAARFF!' he barked, which meant, 'It's OK.'

The girl backed further into the water so that it was up to the chest. Then Canis smelt the boy. It was very strange. The boy had an odour distinctly like Petula's mistress. Canis followed his nose and squinted up into the tree. Now he could see the boy and was struck by how similar to the girl he looked. He was from the same litter, in fact he must be the girl's brother, whom Petula had spoken of. Canis smelt that the children were nervous of him and so he gave them a sign not to be scared. He wiped the air with his paw four times, and then lay on his back to show his tummy. All the while, he wagged his tail a lot.

'He's not a wolf,' Micky laughed. 'Lily, look, he's a pet!' Carefully, Micky came down from the tree and, gently, he approached the animal. He stroked Canis's tummy. Canis grinned up at him.

Gradually Lily waded out of the stream. Once both the children were close, Canis took the material of one of Micky's trouser legs in his jaws.

'What? What are you . . .' Micky started. Canis began to tug, trying to pull the boy towards him.

'I think he wants us to follow him,' Micky said. Then he exclaimed, 'Lily, if he's a pet, then that means he must belong to somebody! *They* can help us find the others!'

Lily nodded, and for the first time since they'd crash-landed in the forest, she grinned. 'What are we waiting for?' she said. 'Let's go!'

At that precise moment, three miles away, Molly was nothing. She had left her own body and was careering though the air towards the termite that she'd singled out near its earthy mound. And in the next second she was *becoming* it.

Molly's personality poured into the termite's un-suspecting black armoured body, and at once Molly felt, from top to toe, totally termite. The termite's character was more robotic than the other creatures she'd inhabited. Molly saw that all this insect ever thought was about was light, dark, work and rest, food, food, food, build, build, build, and its colony and the Queen. The importance of the colony was hard-wired into the termite's reasoning. The existence of other termites and the Queen was a huge part of this termite's sense of self. And the survival of the colony was the prime desire of each and every one of the termites in it.

Molly noticed how light the twig that the termite was carrying felt. If she were human, a piece of wood this much bigger than herself would feel like the weight of a piano. It would squash her flat. Yet this load felt as light as a schoolbag. Then a raindrop hit her. Its force knocked her sideways. Molly realized that she must get under cover.

The termite mound ahead was massive. The Logan

Stones about it seemed like mountains that touched the sky. Molly saw fellow termites trotting through the water and mud towards a low entrance in the side of the mound, their six legs working along the ground so that they moved incredibly fast. Carrying the lump of sweet-smelling wood in her pincers, Molly followed them. She fell in line and was soon brushing sides with other termites. Molly was scared by their alien-like heads but she was determined not to let alarm take hold of her because, if it did, the other termites would sense her fear and it would spread like wildfire through the colony.

The tunnel into the insect palace was dark but Molly soon found her black eyes adjusting. She followed the termite ahead of her, who was carrying a piece of bark, and found herself in yet another smooth-walled corridor. Ignoring the thought of how deep into the mound she must now be, she continued to tail the other termite. Other passages joined her tunnel and other busy termites bustled across Molly's path as they made their way to other parts of the labyrinthine mound, or walked past her in the opposite direction, heading outside.

It was rather like being in the passageways of an underground train station. The termites were as unfriendly as strangers in a city and as preoccupied as people on their way to work. Despite this, Molly sensed a thin, metallic buzz that rattled through the air. The termites were talking to each other. Molly took a right turn, a left turn, and an upward turn, all the time not

341

really knowing what her plan should be or where she should go to find Miss Hunroe.

Molly's guide dropped away to the right into a burrow with high ceilings where other bits of bark and rotting vegetable matter had been dumped. Molly dropped her load too but instead of following the other termite again, now she chose her own direction. She wasn't sure exactly what she was going to do but, oddly, she felt a pull. Just as the giant Logan Stones had done earlier, it was as if Molly was made of metal and there was a magnet drawing her towards it. It was pulling her deeper inside the termite mound. She hoped that the stones from the book of hypnotism were somehow responsible.

Soon the tunnel ended. It opened up into a large oval chamber. Four other tunnel entrances were dotted about the walls and a little weak light filtered through a hole in the side of the mound's roof. Molly could hear the rain hitting the shell of the mound. It sounded like a frenzy of drums.

Fewer termites scurried in and out of this area. Some were busy working at the walls, regurgitating something sticky from their mouths and smudging it on them. Beyond, in the depths of the chamber, termites were dropping sweet-smelling food in front of what looked like a ginormous, sluggish caterpillar. This monstrous creature was at least two hundred times the size of the termites. It lay as still as an obese person on a daybed, oozing a slime that smelt of wood and moss. Molly knew instinctively that this revolting-looking thing was the termite Queen.

Her eyes fell upon an area in front of the Queen where two big termites stood. Once more, Molly felt the strange magnetic pull. And, oddly, a rush of warmth. Just as the reddish-orange Logan Stone had radiated warmth, something was giving off heat here too. Molly moved closer.

Then she saw three of the stones from the cover of the hypnotism book. They were huge now because she was so small. The green stone, the grey stone and the red stone.

Molly was astounded. Now she knew for sure that the two monstrous termites beside the coloured stones were Miss Oakkton and Miss Hunroe. And this lowly termite cave was the very nerve centre of world weather control!

Molly realized she was staring. She snapped her gaze away and tried to find something ordinary and termite-like to do. Whatever happened, she must not let them know that she was in the room. So, joining the other termites who were mending the wall, Molly tried to do what they were doing too. She gave what felt like a heavy burp and a chunk of sticky spit came up into her mouth. Getting to grips with her mandibles, she prodded the stuff on to the wall and smoothed it out just as the other termites were doing. As she worked, Molly trained her hearing on the twittering ants around her.

'*Pat it pat it flat it mend it*,' said the termite beside her.

'*Great one, we adore you*,' a termite was saying to the Queen.

'*Great one, we are your servants*,' said another.

And, '*Feeeeeeeeeeed you. Feeeeeeeeeeed you*,' said a fourth.

Molly now caught the sound of the Hunroe termite. She was talking in an angry, electric buzz. 'I would like to put some cyclones up over the Pacific,' she was saying, 'but because of stupid Miss Speal losing the blue water stone I can't.'

'Sink zem up! You can do it, Miss Hunroe. Use ze grey stone instead,' came the unmistakable reply of the Oakkton termite.

Molly watched as Miss Hunroe lay her front four termite legs on the three flat stones in front of her. The coloured stones began to hum and throb and beam so that the whole chamber filled with red, grey and green light. Both the alien-faced termites with their huge pincers and antennae were lit up. The scene was like something out of a science fiction horror film. The termites beside Molly turned to look.

'*Disturbance for Queen!*' one of them protested.

'*O Queen, are you happy?*' another asked the big fat worm.

'*Comp-leeeeeeeeeeeeeet-ly*,' came the deep sonorous tones of the Queen. '*Laaaaarva-lee.*'

Miss Hunroe and Miss Oakkton didn't seem remotely bothered by the Queen or the other termites. Their attention was solely fixed upon the glowing weather-changing stones in front of them. Miss Hunroe squealed with delight and Miss Oakkton cackled with mirth as the chamber throbbed and glowed.

Molly wasn't sure what to do next. The termites had finished fixing the wall and were moving off. Molly couldn't think of a good reason why she should be in the chamber any longer. Reluctantly, her eyes settled on the oozing, bubbling slimy Queen. She could, she supposed, be a termite feeding the Queen. Slowly, Molly moved towards the smelly, sluggy creature.

Chapter Thirty

Micky and Lily followed the friendly, scruffy dog through the rain. They arrived at a bush-covered cliff ledge where there was a low wooden stool. Micky and Lily peered over low ferns to see what was down below. Immediately, they saw the collection of huts in the clearing. One hut had rabbit skins pegged on a board outside it.

'Wonder who lives here,' Micky whispered. As though in answer, they heard a dog barking. 'That sounds just like Petula!' Micky gasped. 'It's coming from that shed.' He stroked the mountain dog. 'Good boy.'

Lily began pushing through the sopping leaves ahead. 'How do we get down there?'

Micky grabbed her arm. 'I think Petula's locked up, Lily. We don't know who lives down there. It could be really dangerous. We're going to have to play this one carefully.'

Lily stared at him. 'Who's locked her up? Do you

think Molly is with her? Or Malcolm?'

'I don't know,' said Micky. 'Let's watch for a bit and see.'

And so Micky and Lily waited. Petula could obviously smell them, for she continued to bark. Their patience paid off. In five minutes Miss Teriyaki and Miss Speal, both holding glasses containing some sort of brown liquid, emerged unsteadily from one of the huts.

'Ooh, it's raining cats and dogs!' Miss Teriyaki exclaimed.

Then, ignoring the downpour, the two women went to the shed where Petula was locked up. Both were giggling.

'Miss Hunroe is going to be furious when she finds out that you found a pug and didn't tell her!' Miss Speal tittered. 'I mean, how could you think that the breed of pug was native to Ecuador?'

'I don't know!' Miss Teriyaki replied, hiccupping, and then laughed. 'What an idiot I am! What a twit! I'm going to get into so much trouble!' When she said this, both of the women fell about giggling.

'That's not funny!' Miss Speal exclaimed. 'She'll skin you alive! We know how nasty she can be!'

Micky watched them. 'Miss Speal and Miss Teriyaki. Drunk as skunks!' he whispered. Miss Teriyaki picked up her poison dart tube. 'I could always get rid of the dog now,' she said. 'Blow a dart and finish it off. This poison kills instantaneously, you know.'

'I could cook it and give Miss Hunroe dog pie for

supper!' At this suggestion the two ladies creased up with laughter.

'Ooooh, you are so funny, Miss Speal! I can't think why we haven't got on like this before.'

'Maybe Miss Oakkton's special rainforest brew has something to do with it,' Miss Speal replied, slurring her words. 'Come on, let's have some more.'

With that, they sauntered back to the hut.

The two children tried to think what to do next.

'I could morph into one of them,' Micky suggested.

'Or couldn't you hypnotize them?'

Micky pulled a face. 'I can't hypnotize.'

It was then that Lily noticed a bunch of keys on the table outside the hut.

'Look! Bet those are the padlock keys,' she whispered. 'I've got an idea.'

Canis watched the two humans and wondered what they were talking about. He could smell fear on both of them. Then he saw the girl beginning to edge forward.

Lily parted the ferns and, finding footholds below, climbed carefully down the slope. Once down at encampment level she quickly crossed the wet dirt ground behind the kitchen hut and quiet as a cunning fox she crept towards the women's cabin. The radio was on. The voice of a newsreader blasted out of the hut.

'*We are getting reports of strange cyclones in the northern Pacific. These are causing grave concerns that tidal waves will hit the west coast of America, costing millions of lives.'*

'*Oh*, not more weather!' Miss Teriyaki complained. 'Switch channels!' Ecuadorian pop music now blared out into the damp mountain air. 'Ooooh yeah!' Miss Teriyaki shouted. 'Move yer body!'

'What a dancer you are, Miss Teriyaki!' Miss Speal cried.

'I know! You should see me with my disco outfit on!'

Lily ignored them. She tiptoed past cautiously, dodging behind a bin and moving silently in the rain. The padlock keys twinkled in the dappled green light. Taking a deep breath, Lily ran quietly towards them. Swiftly she grabbed them from the table and darted behind the kitchen hut. As she did, Petula began barking again. Lily winced. If Petula made too much noise, the women would be out again. Lily had to act immediately. So as quickly as she could she stole across to Petula's shed.

'Shh, Petula! It's me, Lily, but you have to be quiet.' She matched a key to the padlock, put it in and turned it.

Light flooded into the hut and Petula bounded out and leaped up into Lily's arms.

'Good girl!' she whispered. She looked at the keys. She knew she ought to return them, because then the women would still think that Petula was locked up. And so, slipping behind the kitchen work table, she began making her way back to the disco hut.

But, as she approached, the hut door opened. Miss Speal stumbled out. And as she lurched forward she saw Lily.

'Ahhh!' she shrieked.

Lily turned. 'Petula!' she shouted. 'Follow me!' She began to scramble for the slope. But it was too late.

'It's a girl, Miss Teriyaki!' Miss Speal screamed, diving after Lily. 'Get her!' As she rushed forward, Miss Teriyaki came out of the hut. She was clasping her poison-arrow pipe. Lily glanced behind her and saw her putting it to her lips.

'Quick, Petula!' she urged.

She ran, but Miss Speal ran too, like a lean, thin muscly athlete. She tripped over a trailing root but this did not hold her up for long. She was now alarmingly close. Petula shot past Lily, barking encouragement as she went. And then Lily slipped; she trod on a shiny leaf and slipped down the slope. Miss Speal, her hand like some horrid killer vine, caught Lily's foot.

But, as she did, something else happened too. Miss Teriyaki blew her poison-arrow pipe. Drunk as she was, her weapon jolted sideways when she blew it, and the poison arrow intended for Lily hit Miss Speal's bony bottom. Miss Speal froze, her expression one of utter surprise, as though a monkey had just appeared in front of her dressed in a pink tutu. She winced and squealed: 'EEEEEHWEEER!' And then she went green.

Lily didn't stop to watch her keel over. She shook

her foot free and scrambled up the hill as fast as she could.

Micky watched Miss Speal fall. Like a bird shot down with perfect aim, she fell backwards, dead on the ground.

Miss Teriyaki saw what she had done and screamed. And then full of fury, for she blamed Lily entirely, *she* began to chase her. With her poison-arrow pipe clutched in her right hand, and spare arrows in the other, she leaped up the slope.

'Come on!' Lily cried. And she and Micky, Petula and Canis bolted.

They ran on blindly, trying to keep together as they went. Leaves and wet branches whipped their faces, bushes caught them and the vines tripped them up, but still they ran. And, behind, they heard Miss Teriyaki's war cries as she too sprinted through the undergrowth. She was like some horrific hunter, intent on the kill. Micky and Lily had no doubt that they were her prey. They waited to feel the sharp stab of one of her darts, followed by the rush of poison in their blood. Micky turned to check how close behind she was.

It was then he saw that Petula had stopped. Like a person standing on a road waiting for a car to run them over, she was standing waiting for Miss Teriyaki.

'Petula, come on!' Micky cried. But Petula didn't budge. She sat still and expectantly, her velvety ears pricked up.

The horrid form of Miss Teriyaki came bursting out

through the trees. Her face was pulled into ugly contortions and she was growling like a wild animal. But still Petula didn't move. And then, suddenly, Miss Teriyaki's face changed.

She began to smile inanely, and then she stopped running. She dropped her blowpipe and fell on her knees with her mouth hanging open.

Petula's hypnotic eyes stared up at hers, glowing and throbbing. The woman was completely at her mercy. Trapped in the cage of Petula's mesmerism.

'Stop, Lily!' Micky cried. 'Look!'

Micky went over, picked up Petula and hugged her. 'You are brilliant!' he said, brimming with admiration. He gave her soft fur a stroke. 'Still sucking stones, I see.'

'Do you think she's properly hypnotized?' Lily asked nervously, going up to the puppet-like version of Miss Teriyaki and prodding her.

'I think she is,' said Micky with a smile.

'Amazing,' barked Canis, sitting down by Petula's side. 'Did you do that?'

'Yes. I've done it before, but it was a risk. I didn't know it was going to work,' said Petula with a smile.

'You are a brave dog,' Canis said with a nod.

'What are we going to do with her?' asked Lily, slumping down beside Micky.

The forest calm had now returned. A parrot squawked from a nearby tree and a couple of monkeys went back to foraging for sweet tree orchids. There was a rustling noise in the bushes to the left. A few guinea pigs, an orange one, a black and white one and a brown one, came out from the cover and began to graze on the lush grass.

'Look, guinea pigs!'

'Yes, they have them up here,' said Micky. 'I think the forest people actually eat them.'

'Really? I used to have a smooth-haired guinea pig as a pet,' Lily reminisced. Then she looked over at Miss Teriyaki, who sat on her haunches in front of them. 'You don't suppose . . .'

'Are you thinking what I'm thinking?' Micky asked.

'I think I might be.'

'You do it,' Micky said.

And so Lily began. She looked hard into Miss Teriyaki's mean face. 'From now on, Miss Teriyaki, you will think you are a mountain guinea pig, and you will be happy being a mountain guinea pig . . .' The Japanese woman nodded. Then she got down on her hands and knees and squeaked a high-pitched squeak. 'And . . .' Lily continued, taking her task very seriously, 'you won't be lonely, because there are lots of other guinea pigs in the forest that you will make friends with. And I lock this instruction in with . . . with the word "Lily".'

Miss Teriyaki snuffled, then she wrinkled her nose and seeing the other guinea pigs, scuttled towards them on her hands and knees. They gave a 'YEEP!' and moved away.

'Oh, they'll get used to her,' Lily said.

'Amazing,' Canis said to Petula. 'Now, do you think you can find your friend Molly?' Petula lifted her head to sense where Molly was. Sucking on the smooth blue stone that felt so watery and cool in her mouth, she began to concentrate. Above her, there was a roll of thunder.

Chapter Thirty-one

Rain slapped down on the outside of the termite mound as though hundreds of tiny hands were patting it over and over and over. Molly moved closer to the squelchy Queen termite. Behind her, Miss Hunroe and Miss Oakkton toyed with the weather stones. Molly tried to work out what to do, but it was difficult to concentrate as to the left of her a large, red termite with enormous mandibles was clicking its pincers together and tutting.

'*You no inviteee to feeeeeed Queen,*' it niggled nastily. Molly tried to ignore the criticism but again the termite complained, '*You no feeder. You no foooood.*'

'I bringeeee Queen foodee later,' Molly said, hoping this would shut the insect up.

'*Later, laaaater?*' it screeched, alerting another termite.

'*Out! Out. No later foodee! YOU NO FEEDER!*' it insisted. The Queen said nothing, though bubbly noises squelched out from under her. Molly stood up on her back legs, hoping it would intimidate the nosey termites. Now more turned upon her.

'*You should knowee rulesees!*' the first nagged. '*OUT OUTEE NOWEEE!*'

With a push Molly fell backwards so that she toppled close to Miss Hunroe and the stones. Miss Hunroe and Miss Oakkton looked down at the fallen termite near them and their antennae twitched. They were at once suspicious.

Miss Oakkton stepped towards the stray termite and trapped one of Molly's legs in her pincers.

Miss Hunroe peered down at her. 'Who are you?' she asked, her big eyes bulging. Molly didn't answer. It was terrifying to have her legs trapped in Miss Oakkton's pincers. Desperately, she tried to think. She could morph *into* one of them, but both Miss Hunroe and Miss Oakkton were suspicious now, and she might get stuck inside one of them. Or perhaps they'd pre-empt her move and prevent her entering their bodies *at all*. That would be even worse. She'd be floating about in the air with no body to go into. She struggled to get out of Miss Oakkton's grip.

'Get off me!' Molly growled in pain.

'So it *is* you. What shall ve do vis you now, little Moon termite?' Miss Oakkton muttered darkly. 'Vot a strange place to die – in a termite cathedral!'

'You're so much larger than her, Miss Oakkton,' declared Miss Hunroe. 'Crush her!'

'Oh! Yah!' laughed Miss Oakkton. 'And zen zese uzzer termites vould eat you. Perhaps zey'd even feed you to zeir Queen!'

The Queen! Molly turned. So many termites were now attending to the Queen that Molly could barely see her. Miss Oakkton had given her a brilliant idea. Molly desperately looked for a pattern in the cracked mud floor and thought hard. She sank her mind deep into the idea of slimy sluggishness. And miraculously, seconds later, she had left her termite shell and morphed into the pulsating termite Queen.

At once Molly saw how totally in control the Queen was, and how all the termites served her completely. Molly looked at Miss Oakkton, who was still under the impression that the insect she was holding was Molly. Miss Oakkton was about to kill that termite, to squeeze the life out of it, and Molly felt entirely responsible for this. And so Molly the Queen whispered to her feeders: 'The large termite there is an *imposter*!'

In unison, the termites turned to look at Miss Oakkton. They stopped what they were doing. And, as though their brains were synchronized, they moved towards her. Before Miss Oakkton knew what was happening, the termites had walled her in.

The smaller termite that had once been Molly escaped from the termite scrum, scurrying out of the chamber in terror, whilst the termite that was Miss Oakkton . . . she was destroyed.

Molly the Queen termite shuddered, her multi-abdomined body wobbling like a jelly. It was then that she noticed that the termite that was Miss Hunroe had slipped away. And the stones were gone.

'*You all rightee, my Queenee?*' came a loyal termite's concerned question.

'*Yessee*,' Molly replied. '*Thank you. I want messageeee sent out to all the colony. Messageeee is this. The termite that took the coloured stones must be caught.*'

As she spoke the termites listened. '*Yesssee, Your Highnesssss*,' they said in unison, and immediately they left the chamber to spread the word.

With no time to lose, Molly morphed into a big black termite. And, back inside an armoured body, she darted down the tunnel after Miss Hunroe.

She hoped that once the Queen's wishes were known every one of her subjects would surround the termite that was Miss Hunroe. Miss Hunroe was likely to be heading for the exit – unless she'd hidden the coloured weather stones somewhere in the termite mound, and hidden herself too. Molly was going to have to take a guess. As she scurried along, a wave of termite whispers flowed beside her.

'*Find the termite with the stones*,' the whisper went. '*The Queen wants that termite caught.*'

And then Molly heard barking outside. It was muffled because of the denseness of the mud walls but Molly would recognize that bark anywhere. Petula! She was barking incessantly – a bark that meant there was trouble. Breaking into a run, Molly followed the sound of Petula's bark and pushed through the crowds of soldier termites that were entering the mound. She burst out into the open.

Above her, a massive Petula barked up at Miss Hunroe, who was so big that Molly could hardly see her face. Micky was there too, as well as Lily, and Bas and Canis. Cappuccino sat on a low rock surveying the scene. It was pouring with rain and the ground was so muddy and waterlogged that small rivulets flowed next to the termite mound and beside the Logan Stones. To Molly the termite these streams were like torrential rivers. She looked up at Miss Hunroe and wondered desperately whether it would be possible to morph into her.

All the while Petula and Canis barked and snapped at Miss Hunroe, who was brandishing a stick, and trying to hit anyone who came too close to her. The commotion of barking and shouting, along with the thunder, was deafening.

Then Molly saw Petula drop something on to the ground. It was the blue stone. Miss Hunroe saw it too. All at once, Molly understood that it had been her dear friend Petula who had been changing the nearby weather. *She'd* been causing this rain.

Miss Hunroe dived for and snatched the blue stone and then, like some insane person, began to scale the tall termite mound. Slipping as she gripped its wet surface, she made her way up to its top turret.

In a flash, Molly meegoed into her own body and surveyed the scene.

Miss Hunroe was sitting on the top of the colossal termite mound, holding the stones aloft.

'Get the stones!' Molly yelled.

'Molly!' Micky shouted through the rain. In the next moment, Miss Hunroe disappeared. All that was left of her was a pile of safari clothes and balanced on top were the four coloured weather-changing stones.

Wasting no time, Molly dived on to the termite mound and began climbing towards them. But in the time it takes to turn a page, Miss Hunroe was back. This time she was wearing a long red dress with flames embroidered up the side. A pattern of green leaves twisted round the side and its hem was blue like the sea. A scarf of grey chiffon framed her beautiful face.

'It's heaven!' she exclaimed, holding the four coloured stones up to the sky. 'Heaven, I have complete control!' She saw her audience's amazement. 'Yes, I look wonderful, don't I? This is called style. You didn't think I would wear an ordinary safari suit to become the Queen of the Weather, did you?' She began to laugh.

Molly raised her head and stared straight up at Miss Hunroe. 'Look me in the eyes, Miss Hunroe, if you dare.'

Miss Hunroe began to giggle like a crazy schoolgirl. 'I shall have to decline your offer, my dear,' she tittered. 'Instead, why don't you look down the barrel of my—'

The instant the word 'barrel' left her lips, Molly

knew what Miss Hunroe was about to pull from the silk of her dress. Micky realized too, and, thinking as one, the twins *both* morphed into Miss Hunroe.

As Molly arrived, she saw how twisted and cruel Miss Hunroe was. But she didn't have the time to dive into Miss Hunroe's memories and see *why* she was such a vindictive sociopath. Like a great friendly presence, Micky arrived and joined Molly. The battle was on.

Molly and Micky worked together. Using all their mental might, they wrestled with Miss Hunroe. They edged and shouldered her into a smaller and smaller place, taking the fury that they felt for the woman and turning it into strength. With two determined minds against one, Miss Hunroe didn't stand a chance.

Though she pushed and wriggled, she couldn't expand herself past the twins. In fact she was shrinking. Shrinking and shrivelling like a poisonous flower in the hot sun. Like a car in a metal crusher, she was being squashed. The button-sized thing that was her now was flattened to the size of a sunflower seed, and then was squeezed to the size of a poppy seed.

'NOOOOO!' she screamed, her voice now a tiny squeak.

And then, using the tiny amount of energy that she had left, Miss Hunroe did what might have been a clever thing. She somersaulted out of her own body, and into the form of the white-faced capuchin monkey that sat on a branch eating a piece of fruit.

With a pop, Miss Hunroe's body disappeared.

Molly and Micky were prepared. Simultaneously, they morphed into themselves and calmly watched Cappuccino. He was doing exactly what Molly had told him to. He pushed his shoulders up and down as he positively refused to let Miss Hunroe take over his body and mind.

'Did you hypnotize the monkey?' Micky guessed.

'Yes,' Molly replied, and grinned. 'Hello, Micky.'

Bas and Lily ventured out from their hiding places.

'Look,' Molly said. 'Miss Hunroe morphed into Cappuccino. He's got her completely under his thumb.'

'How long can he keep her in check?' Bas asked, watching as Cappuccino nibbled at the core of his forest fruit.

'I told him to keep her quiet until he's convinced that she's turning good.'

'Really? Do you trust Cappuccino to do that?'

'Yes,' Molly replied. 'You said he was a very good judge of character so I thought he should decide.'

'Wow,' Bas sighed, rubbing his head. 'This is just all too amazing.'

The rain had stopped and the sun was now out. Rays of light lit up Miss Hunroe's gold coin lying abandoned in the mud. Molly bent down, scooped it up, and put it in her pocket.

Lily put her arm round Molly. 'I'm so glad you're all right,' she said. 'I was worried about you.'

'I was worried about you too.' Molly gave Lily a

hug back, then picked up Petula.

Micky picked up the four stones.

A termite on the ground caught Molly's eye. It was carrying a piece of rotten bark. Molly watched it. It had no idea what drama had just unfolded.

'Hey!' Molly said to the termite. 'Telleee all your friendseees thank you!' But of course the termite had no idea what Molly had just said. It simply felt a wind from the giant moving thing above, and it moved on.

Chapter Thirty-two

'	I wish you were here,' Molly said. She was
	. . .		on the phone to Rocky, with fat head-
phones on her ears and a mike to her mouth, sitting in
a moving helicopter, hovering above the rainforest
canopy. 'And it's so lucky that Hunroe's hypnotism on
you wore off . . . It's been a bit hairy here. Actually,
that's an understatement. But it's over now and everyone's fine.'

She paused as Rocky spoke.

'Yup, we got the hypnotism book . . . No, couldn't
find the crystals . . . Maybe Miss Suzette has them. And
I can tell you, if I ever find them, I'm not letting Lucy
and Primo take them again. But I got Hunroe's coin.
It's quite cool.'

Molly took Miss Hunroe's coin out of her pocket
and fingered it before putting it away again. 'A
memento.'

Rocky asked something.

'Oh yes, the stones are all back on its front cover.' Molly patted the book. It was on her knee. 'I know, isn't it amazing! . . . Yeah, maggots . . . Malcolm says he's going to stay here with Bas for a bit. Says he wants to forget about aliens and get into ecology. The cloud forest is so beautiful, you see . . . Hey, why don't you come out?'

Molly paused. Below her the jungle was vast and green, rolling away on every side, and ahead in the western skies the sun was setting in red and pink. A pink blush spread through the white cumulus clouds there so that they floated like magic puffs of rose-tinted smoke.

Molly hugged Petula. Sometimes life felt too good to be true.

At Briersville Park, Todson was eating scrambled eggs at the kitchen table.

'Terrible, terrible,' he muttered to himself as he flipped through a newspaper full of horror stories about the recent floods and tornados all over the world. A rusty, old-fashioned bell on the wall above the cooker rang. 'Ah, front door. Wonder who that can be.'

Todson wiped his hands on a napkin, and made his way upstairs, taking his apron off on the way. Walking towards the front door, he straightened his tie. Then he peered through the hall window.

'Goodness me,' he gasped. Outside, was a grand long black car with a little flag set on its roof above its front windscreen. Checking his hands to see they were clean, Todson opened the door and found himself looking into the eyes of someone dressed rather like himself.

'Good morning,' Smuthers, the Queen's butler, said. 'Is Molly Moon in?'

Todson's eyes opened wide, as he saw the Queen herself, dressed in a country coat, talking to a Rasta on the steps below.

'I'm a-a-afraid she's not,' he stuttered. 'But her best friend, Rocky, is upstairs. I could call him down. Could he help? Please come in.'

'Thank you very much,' Smuthers said. Then, in a whisper, he added. 'You've got a bit of egg on your collar.'

'Ah, thank you.' Todson nodded with a wink. He removed the egg and stepped back to let the visitors in.

The Queen smiled graciously as she passed. 'Thank you so much.'

'T'ank you,' said her Jamaican companion.

'I was lucky, Leonard,' Todson caught the Queen saying to the man. 'I had Smuthers to talk to. Poor you! You must have thought you were losing your marbles. You know, no one else believed me. Thank goodness for Smuthers.' She paused as she looked at her surroundings. 'And thank goodness for the Moon children. I am so looking forward to meeting them.'

Leonard smiled. 'Yeah. Feel like I've known them for years.'

Dear Reader

In this book you will have seen something of what might happen if the world's weather went mad.

It struck me that you could help stop the world heating up and so help the weather stay stable. I know you might think you don't have the power to help. But you do have great power. Because your parents listen to you.

Maybe you can persuade the adults around you to:

* change to renewable energy so that they get their electricity from sun power, wind power and water power instead of smelly fuels
* drive less or drive an electric car
* recycle things more
* use less paper
* plant more trees
* grow more vegetables

And if you can't persuade them to do this, hypnotize them!

One day you will be looking after our fantastic planet. I hope your generation can get to grips with some of the problems previous generations have created. I'm sorry we've all been so careless about the mess we've made of the place. It was very short-sighted of everyone.

But I do believe that one day things will be better. We will have bigger rainforests, cleaner air and seas full of fish and whales once more. I hope that one day tigers and elephants and pandas will be living wild in great numbers again, and people will appreciate what a wonderful world we have.

Love from
Georgia Byng

Georgia Byng

MOLLY MOON'S

Incredible Book of Hypnotism

Orphan Molly Moon was found as a baby in a box marked 'Moon's Marshmallows'.

For ten terrible years she's lived under the sinister rule of Miss Adderstone in gloomy Hardwick House. But her life changes overnight when she finds a mysterious book on hypnotism and discovers an amazing talent – the power to make people do anything she wants them to!

Escaping from the orphanage, Molly heads to New York in search of fame and fortune. But her adventures lead her into the clutches of a dangerous enemy, who will stop at nothing to steal her hypnotic secret . . .

'It is hard to imagine a child who would not enjoy this original, funny and inventive book' *Eva Ibbotson*

Georgia Byng

MOLLY MOON

Stops the World

Molly Moon is an orphan with mind-blowing hypnotic powers. She can make anyone do anything she wants them to.

But when she's asked to investigate the sinister activities of an American billionaire, Molly finds herself up against a deadly opponent. Primo Cell is a master hypnotist who secretly controls the minds of Hollywood's biggest stars. And when Molly, Rocky and Petula the pug meet him at the Oscars, they make some astonishing discoveries.

Can Molly's mesmerizing eyes stop the most dangerous man in the world?

Georgia Byng

MOLLY MOON'S

Hypnotic Time-Travel Adventure

Brilliant hypnotist Molly Moon has just found herself in the wrong place at the wrong time . . .

Molly and her best friend, Rocky, are stranded in nineteenth-century India – whisked there by a time-travelling maharaja. He's even kidnapped four younger Mollys and petnapped Petula as part of a crazy plan to stop Molly ever learning her amazing hypnotic skills.

With not only her past but the future of the world at stake, Molly must outwit the mad maharaja and master the art of time travel before it is too late . . .

Georgia Byng

MOLLY MOON,

Micky Minus and the Mind Machine

She knows what you're thinking. No, really. SHE KNOWS WHAT YOU'RE THINKING.

Molly Moon, the girl with hypnotic eyes is about to make a stunning new discovery: she is a MIND-READER! But can her incredible talents help rescue her lost twin from the future? And will Molly be a match for the maniacal Princess Fang and her brain-scrambling mind machine?

A selected list of titles available from Macmillan Children's Books

The prices shown below are correct at the time of going to press. However, Macmillan Publishers reserves the right to show new retail prices on covers, which may differ from those previously advertised.

Georgia Byng

Molly Moon's Incredible Book of Hypnotism	978-0-330-39985-2	£5.99
Molly Moon Stops the World	978-0-330-41577-4	£5.99
Molly Moon's Hypnotic Time-Travel Adventure	978-0-330-43461-4	£5.99
Molly Moon, Micky Minus and the Mind Machine	978-0-330-43462-1	£5.99

All Pan Macmillan titles can be ordered from our website, www.panmacmillan.com, or from your local bookshop and are also available by post from:

Bookpost, PO Box 29, Douglas, Isle of Man IM99 1BQ

Credit cards accepted. For details:
Telephone: 01624 677237
Fax: 01624 670923
Email: bookshop@enterprise.net
www.bookpost.co.uk

Free postage and packing in the United Kingdom